THE SILENCE OF

LIGHTNING

Marie S. Crosswell

A NineStar Press Publication

www.ninestarpress.com

The Silence of Lightning

Printed in the USA

Print ISBN: 978-1-64890-118-8

First Edition, October, 2020

Also available in eBook, ISBN: 978-1-64890-117-1

WARNING:

This book contains sexually explicit content, which is only suitable for mature readers, racist language and behavior by minor characters; predatory stalking of a woman by a secondary character; outing of a major character; and cheating by a major character.

Former pro-rodeo champion Smith Rose and his cousins Cooper and Christa Boone live a quiet life together in the town of Cody, Wyoming—until the summer of 2015 shakes them to their foundations.

Stuck in an unhappy rut since his retirement from the rodeo five years prior, Smith is forced to reckon with his past, present, and future when his former friend and lover John Henry Walker shows up at Smith's bar. Meanwhile, the Boone sisters face a threat they never would've predicted when an out-of-town stranger begins to stalk Christa after meeting her at a party. While trying to support her sister and their cousin, Cooper secretly agonizes over her fears of their little family splitting apart and where that would leave her.

When Smith, Cooper, and Christa's problems converge in a dangerous confrontation, will the three of them survive?

Cody, Wyoming

SUMMER, 2015

The three of them sit sprawled in a booth: Smith, Cooper, and Christa. Their table's littered with beer bottles and the shucked off metal caps. Smith's got a cooler on the floor alongside his seat because this is his bar and he can do whatever the hell he wants. He opens each beer with the bottle opener on his key ring. His cousins got a pretty good buzz going on, the two of them pink-faced and smiling, leaning into each other. Smith is mellowed out, not drunk. He doesn't watch the saloon or Georgeanne filling in for him at the bar, just nurses his drink and considers his cousins.

"There is no way in hell I'm riding fifteen hundred miles on the back of a motorcycle," says Christa.

"Why not?" Cooper whines. "Labor Day weekend, it'll be beautiful. We won't see weather that good in between here and Austin until next spring, which is almost a year from now."

"I wouldn't go in the spring either. I'm not traveling that far on a bike. Period."

"You don't even have to worry about the bike. I'm the one handling it. All you have to do is hold on and enjoy the scenery."

"I wouldn't be enjoying anything, Cooper! I'd be terrified the whole way. What's fun about that?"

"I wouldn't even go fast!" Cooper says. "I'll cap it at five above the speed limit; I promise."

"Eighty miles an hour on a motorcycle is still enough to kill you!"

"Okay, first of all, it would be seventy half the time, and second of all, why don't you trust me? I'm not some reckless yahoo looking to cheat death taking a corner too fast, and even if I was, I would never gamble with your life."

Christa gives her sister an indulgent smile. "It's not about you. It's about all the things you can't control. My fear included."

Cooper sighs in defeat and blinks at Smith sitting across from her. "Will you go with me?"

Smith pauses. "Might follow in the truck."

Cooper rolls her eyes. "Forget it. I'll go on my own."

"You're not making that trip alone, Cooper," says Christa, sipping on her beer.

"Well, I wouldn't have to if you'd come with me."

Cooper's been restoring a 1966 Triumph Bonneville T120TT all year, tinkering with it in her spare time at the garage where she's an auto mechanic. She reckons she'll be finished with it by the time September rolls around, and she's been pestering her sister about a long road trip to Texas.

Christa ignores Cooper's pouting and gives Smith a pointed look. "You coming to the rodeo with us?"

"No, ma'am," he replies and draws on his beer. He's sitting in the interior corner on his side of the booth, and he's got his left arm stretched out along the top of the seatback behind him. He might be hiding a little, from the rest of the room.

"Smith. Come on."

"Every year, you two go out there, and every year, I don't. I figure that'll never change."

"Why can't you just suspend your boycott for one night and spend some time with us?"

"I'm spending time with you right now. I'll follow you anywhere, except the damn rodeo. Why don't you skip the rodeo and do something else with me? We could take the motorcycle course at the DMV and get licensed."

Christa makes a face at him. "Very funny."

"Well, we're going tomorrow night, with or without you," Cooper says to Smith. "And I'm betting whoever places first in bronc and bull riding won't come anywhere near your records, like I always do. Then I'll be proven right like I always am. At least half a dozen people will recognize me and Chris as your family, ask us how you're doing, and then recount some memory of your glory days we've both heard about a thousand times. We'll smile and nod and agree you were the best in the West, shake hands, and go home."

"Clearly, I'm not missing anything," says Smith, his face shaded under the brim of his cowboy hat.

"If you hate the rodeo so much, why did you decide to live in Cody?" Christa asks. "You could've gone back to Rawlins or Cheyenne. Left Wyoming altogether."

"Cody ain't a bad place to live." Smith flicks his eyes past his cousin and gives the saloon a once-over. "You two are here."

"We're here because of you," says Cooper.

Smith glances at her but doesn't respond, draining his beer bottle instead.

"Where's Smith Rose?" somebody calls out, loud enough for the whole room to hear.

Cooper and Christa peer over their shoulders at the young man standing a few paces from the door, bright-eyed and ruddy in his tan cowboy hat. He searches the saloon with his eyes before landing on the bartender, who lifts her chin toward the cousins' booth. The young man turns toward the booth and stares until he recognizes Smith's face in the shadows of his seat corner, then beelines for the booth with the keen enthusiasm of a puppy dog. He takes off his hat and clutches it in both hands, staring at Smith as if Cooper and Christa aren't there.

"Mr. Rose?" he says.

"Yeah," says Smith. "That's me."

The young man smiles. "I've wanted to meet you since I was ten years old, and now I don't know what to say."

He worries the brim of his hat in his hands and gawks like Smith is a big-name celebrity. The tips of his ears are pink.

"What's your name, kid?" Smith says to him, nonplussed.

"M-Michael Grant, sir."

"You're not a local, are you, Mr. Grant?"

"No, sir. I'm from Sheridan. I'm here to compete in the Nite Rodeo. It's my first year in Cody, and when I heard you were living here, I had to find you. I used to watch you compete on TV. Nationals and all. My family took me to see you live one time when I was a kid. I haven't ever seen any bronc rider as good as you, sir. It's an honor to meet you. A real honor."

Smith nods and says, "I appreciate that. If you're old enough to drink, go to the bar and order what you want on the house. Hell, if you're not, you could anyway. Pretty sure Georgeanne won't card you."

"Thank you, sir," Michael says, still clutching his hat in both hands. He's browned from spending the summer outside, darkened freckles dusting his face.

Smith drinks from his water glass, waiting for the young man to leave him alone, but Michael lingers, obviously wanting to say more. Cooper and Christa peer at him, and Smith waits for them to pick up the polite small talk on his behalf.

"Sir," Michael starts, rubbing both thumbs against the brim of his hat. "I was wondering—well, I wanted to ask if you would come out and watch my rounds. I'll be steer wrestling and bull riding the next few nights. It'd mean a lot to me if you came and maybe told me what you think."

Smith regards the kid and considers saying yes. He can feel his cousins staring at him from across the table. "Look," he says. "I understand this means something to you, and I know why you're asking. But I don't go to rodeos anymore. Haven't been to a single one since I retired. I'm not turning you down personally. I just won't set foot on rodeo grounds, no matter where they are. I'm sorry to disappoint you, but it is what it is."

The kid does his best not to let his face fall as he nods. "No, I understand. It's all right. I just wanted to ask you while I had the chance, but it's no big deal. What I really wanted was to meet you, and now I have. So, I guess I'll go and get that drink."

He puts his hat back on and finally looks at Christa and Cooper, nodding at them in acknowledgment. He looks back at Smith, pauses, then steps forward and holds out his hand.

Smith shakes with him. "Good luck out there," he says.

"Thank you, sir," says the kid. He turns and starts heading for the bar, but halfway there, Cooper raises her voice at him.

"Grant," she says.

He stops and faces her.

"How'd you like to see Smith ride that bull?"

She nods at the opposite side of the room where the saloon's mechanical bull stands in the middle of thick, blue tumbling mats. The kid follows her line of sight.

Smith starts to protest, but the kid's eyes light up.

Christa stands up on her seat, still holding her beer. "Who wants to see Smith ride the bull?" she yells.

The saloon roars.

Cooper grins at her cousin over the table.

Smith gives her a surly look, then slides out of the booth in resignation and stalks across the saloon floor.

The mechanical bull wasn't Smith's idea. His cousins convinced him a saloon in Cody, "Rodeo Capital of the World," should have a mechanical bull. At least two other bars in town have one, and what would people think if Smith Rose didn't have a bull in his? But he's never ridden it himself, on account of a decision he made right after he retired—a decision about never getting on the back of a bucking animal again, never having anything to do with the sport again.

Smith swings onto the bull with the smoothness of someone who's mounted these things a hundred times since he was twelve years old and full of rodeo dreams. The saloon goes quiet, except for the country music playing on the sound system. He glances at Big Bob, who's manning the operator box, and nods.

The mechanical bull starts to bob back and forth like a seesaw, slow enough that Smith doesn't have to make any real effort to stay on it. He could fall asleep if the machine kept this pace, buzzed on a six-pack and feeling like he's home again for the first time in five years. But pretty soon, the bull starts bucking a little faster, swiveling around in a half circle. It's not like the real thing, not even close, but all the same instincts and training committed to his muscle memory kick in, keeping him on the machine past second marks anybody without rodeo experience wouldn't make.

The bucking quickens, the bull rotates a full circle and a half. If he had to guess, he'd say Big Bob has the speed dial on six.

His cousins are hooting and hollering, their voices clear amongst the others.

"You ride that son of a bitch, Smith!" Cooper yells.

"Hold on, baby, hold on!" Christa says.

Smith grips the handle where the bull's right shoulder blade would be if it were a live animal, his left arm held out parallel to the floor for balance. He grips the machine tight between his legs, knees digging into the sides, but he's loose from the waist up, leaning with the bull. He follows the jerking like going with a current, his body an extension of the machine.

Some old twangy tune's playing on the fancy jukebox that cost Smith about three grand. The Flying Burrito Brothers.

The bull's bucking as hard as it can, as hard as the real thing could, swirling him fast enough to blur the saloon. But he's not dizzy. His heart's beating faster than it has since the last time he was on a live animal, his body flooded with adrenaline, and something rushes up his chest and through his throat from his gut, something like a river breaking through a dam. A smile. A smile he's too proud to let loose.

The mechanical bull finally throws him, and he lies sprawled on his back in one corner of the mat, blinking up at the ceiling as the whole saloon screams and beats the tabletops.

"Ladies and gentlemen!" Big Bob says into his microphone. "The new record holder for longest ride on the Bad Moon bull, one minute and forty-eight seconds. Our very own Smith Rose!"

Smith ducks his head at the applause and cheering, standing alongside the bull with his back toward his cousins in their booth. He used to do this on his feet in arenas, under the white lights, listening to the people in the stands. He'd pause as the handlers got a hold of the bull or the bronc and led it out. Those days and nights smelled like dirt, livestock, and animal shit. Here, it's just booze.

When Smith turns and looks up, the first thing he sees is a ghost of rodeos past.

A Black man stands with his fingers in the front pockets of his jeans, staring at Smith as if they're the only two people in the room. He's tall in his heeled cowboy boots but not as tall as Smith. He's wearing a shirt tucked into his jeans. A large, oval-shaped, silver belt buckle gleams at his waist, but despite the size, it isn't flashy. The man's hips are slightly canted to the right, and his dark eyes smolder. He doesn't appear any different than the last time Smith saw him, six years ago. Not any older and just as handsome.

Smith makes his way across the mat, stepping back onto solid floor next to the man. Standing face to face with him, Smith feels an uneasiness he knows is irrational; nobody could guess his history with this guy by seeing them together now. But he still wants to take his visitor outside.

"Looks like you still got it," the man says.

"What are you doing here?" says Smith, his voice low and his hands on his hips.

"Working, up in Montana."

"What are you doing in my saloon, in Wyoming?"

The man gives Smith a silent look. "Why don't you buy me a drink?" he says, then lopes over to the bar and takes a seat.

Smith glances at his cousins, who are watching him with curiosity from their booth. He goes behind the bar and relieves his stand-in bartender, trying his best not to give the visitor attention everybody else can see. He rolls his sleeves up to his elbows to show off his strong forearms.

"I think I'll start with a beer," his visitor says.

Smith reaches into the cooler underneath the bar and pulls out a Miller High Life. He pops off the bottle cap and slides the beer across the bar.

The visitor smiles. "All this time and you still know what I like."

Smith doesn't reply. He didn't know he remembered what John Henry drank until just now.

"How'd you find me?" Smith asks, bracing his hands against the edge of the bar top. He keeps his voice low.

"It's no big secret you live here," says John Henry, tipping the beer bottle against his lips. "People still talk about you in the circuit. Montana guys know you're here. Wyoming riders too. Some of them are from your county."

Smith doesn't reply. He never tried keeping himself and his whereabouts a secret, but he also never expected someone like John Henry Walker to track him down.

"I gotta say, Rose, when I pictured your retirement, it didn't look like this," John Henry says.

"Oh, yeah?" says Smith, feeling defensive. "What did it look like, then?"

John Henry shrugs. "I thought you'd have a wife and a couple babies by now. A little piece of land. A ranch, I guess."

"Someone tell you I don't have any of those things when they got done telling you where to find my bar?"

John Henry doesn't quite smile. "No. But are you going to tell me you do?"

Smith clenches his jaw, staring at the other man.

Cooper comes up to the bar, right along John Henry's left shoulder, and leans forward to give Smith a soft shove. "You all-around champion bastard!" she says, happier than he's seen her in weeks. "That's the Smith I know. You're not even rusty! You been riding the bull in secret?"

"Hell, no," says Smith.

"Look at that." She points to the chalkboard where Big Bob's already written Smith's name at the top of the bull rider list. "You outlasted the old number one by a minute and a half!"

"You better watch out, Rose," says John Henry, lifting his beer to his lips. "People are going to want to see you do it again."

Smith's face darkens. That's one reason why he's refused to ride the bull since he opened the Bad Moon Saloon four years ago.

"I'm sorry. Are you a friend of Smith's?" Cooper says to John Henry.

"Just someone he used to know in the rodeo. I'm up in Montana for the next few weeks. Got the Yellowstone PRCA in Billings and something smaller in Livingston, a couple other little things. John Henry Walker."

He reaches over the bar with his right hand to shake hers.

"Cooper Boone."

"Nice to meet you. You Rose's girl?"

"I'm his cousin."

John Henry smiles like he's in on a secret and sips his beer.

Christa comes up to the bar and slings her arm around Cooper, standing on drunk-jelly legs and three-inch bootheels. She gazes at Smith with a proud light in her eyes. "I will never ask you to go to the Nite Rodeo with us again. That was better than dragging you to Stampede Park could ever be."

"Well, at least something good's coming out of it," Smith replies.

A young, drunk man charges the bar a couple seats away from Christa and yells as he slaps the bar top. "God*damn*, that was some bull riding!" he tells Smith. "I'm gonna buy you a drink!"

"It's my saloon. Why don't you buy yourself a drink?"

"All right!" The man slams his empty beer mug on the bar.

Smith refills it, knowing he should throw the guy out instead, and sends him on his way.

"We're going home," Cooper tells him, her arm around her sister's back.

"You good to drive?" he says.

"I am. This one'll be asleep in the truck before we hit the first traffic light."

"I'm not that drunk," says Christa, but she does look ready to pass out.

"Call me and let me know you got there okay," Smith says to Cooper.

She nods, tells John Henry to keep Smith out of trouble, and leads her sister out of the saloon.

John Henry gives Smith another one of his looks.

"You almost done with the beer?" Smith asks him.

"Why are you so ornery about me being here?"

Smith pauses. He lowers his voice. "You know why."

A secret he left behind in his rodeo career, one the residents of Cody can't even imagine, a secret Smith has done everything in his power to keep buried as he moved on with his life, a secret John Henry knows all about. Smith isn't worried about the other man letting that secret slip—John Henry has as much reason to keep it as Smith does—but the last thing he needs is people asking questions, following a trail of somebodies that might lead to a guy who saw something once he wasn't supposed to see, a guy who remembers Smith and John Henry, a guy they never noticed.

John Henry drains his bottle and sets it on the bar as calm as Smith is tense. "We're just two men having a conversation. There's nothing wrong with that, is there?"

Smith gives the saloon a once-over. Nobody's watching him. He reaches under the bar for a clean shot glass, puts it in front of him, and fills it with whiskey. A few shots and he'll be drunk, but he doesn't see how else he's going to calm down as long as John Henry's there.

"Those are some good-looking cousins you got," John Henry tells him.

Smith glares and points at John Henry with his forefinger. "Don't you bring them into this."

John Henry lifts his hands in front of him. "I'm not bringing anyone into anything. Just paying a compliment."

"I don't want you talking about them to your Goddamn rodeo buddies. All right?"

"Smith," John Henry says as patient as he always was. "I didn't come to make trouble for you. I came to check in on an old friend because I thought you were. My friend. Maybe I remembered wrong." He gets up from his stool, reaches into his back pocket for his wallet, and leaves a five-dollar bill on the bar. "Thanks for the beer."

Smith watches him leave. John Henry doesn't peek back at him. As soon as he's gone, the knot in Smith's chest loosens.

*

Friday morning is like most others. Smith cooks himself breakfast in the firepit he dug next to his trailer and eats it sitting in the old beach chair he bought at the Goodwill. He could use the small kitchen in the trailer, but food always tastes better cooked over a fire. He likes to be outside as much as he can in the summer months anyhow. It's warm enough now he can sit out here all day without a jacket or gloves. He's wearing a shirt tucked into his jeans, and his favorite cowboy hat because the wind isn't too bad.

The dog sniffs at the ground, and he watches her, resting his arms on his knees with his coffee mug in his hands. A little warmth comes off the fire, the smell of it laced into the clean Wyoming air. He sips on his coffee, studying the mountains in the distance, and thinks about John Henry. Yellowstone isn't far beyond them, straight west.

When he retired from the rodeo, he bought twenty-five acres of land in Park County, ten miles west of Cody. A parcel of flat, green pastures and grassy fields surrounded by mountains, trees scattered throughout and a creek cutting through the western edge. He got the old trailer used because he needed a place to stay while he had a house built. Five years later, he's still in it.

His cousins tell him every winter he can't go on like this, not with the wind and snow and the cold that drags on for months. Sell the land or build on it, they tell him. He spends plenty of nights sleeping in his room in their house, between November and April—but that's more for them than himself. They've started asking him in the last year or two if he wants to move in, as if they suspect he's secretly wanted to all along but assumed they didn't want him as a permanent roommate. They keep reminding him he's already got a room, and he might as well stay if a trailer is the only alternative. He likes having his own bed in the Boone home, but he likes it out here on the land too. His cousins aren't the reason he hasn't started on a house.

Smith turns his head at the sound of a vehicle rolling toward his campsite on the dirt road. An old '72 F-250 XLT Camper Special, red-and-white, the paint faded and mud-flecked. Cooper's truck. He watches her until the truck stops, then looks away again and listens to her footsteps as she crosses the space between them. The dog gets up and meets her.

"Why aren't you at work?" Smith asks.

"Half-day," says Cooper, standing with her hands on her hips.

"You hungry?"

"I'm having lunch before I go in."

"There's coffee if you want it." Smith lifts his mug to his lips. "Inside."

"I'm good."

They're quiet for a beat.

"So did you feel like a drive or do you need something?" Smith says.

Cooper pauses. "When you woke up earlier, how did you feel?"

He blinks at her. "Fine."

"Not different? Not better?"

"No."

He stands up and takes his plate, fork, and mug back into the camper. He'd hoped his cousins would move on from his mechanical bull ride without any more comment, but it was naive of him.

Cooper comes up the camper steps but stays outside, leaning against the doorway on her forearm. She watches him as he rinses off his dishware in the sink. "I saw you, Smith. On that bull. You were happy. For a whole minute forty-eight, you were having a good time. You can't look me in the eye and deny it."

Smith doesn't reply. He turns off the faucet and dries his hands on the dish towel, then braces them on the counter edge and sighs. "What do you want from me, Coop?"

"I don't want things from you. I want things for you."

"It doesn't make a difference what I want for myself..."

"I don't think you want anything, Smith. That's the problem. You've got the bar, which is good. You've done a good job with it. But that's all it is to you—something to keep you busy."

"If you drove all the way out here to convince me to go back to riding, you wasted the gas."

"I don't want you to go back," she says. "I want you to be happy. You used to be so alive. Just being near you was enough to get me all fired up over nothing. I've been missing that all this time, and I think I gave up on ever getting you back, the old you. But last night when you rode that bull—you were the man I remember. And I don't care if you stay retired from the rodeo, I don't, but you gotta do something. You have to want something. You're thirty-two years old. You can't spend the rest of your life unhappy. I won't stand for it."

Smith turns around to make eye contact with Cooper, finds her face soft and earnest. She used to come see him on the circuit whenever she could, whenever he was in Wyoming or Montana. She'd drive hours to cheer him on in the stands when she was in college and when she lived in Laramie while Christa went to school. When she couldn't watch him, she'd call him on his event nights, or he would call her from the grounds, from hotels and motels and bars. She went to more of his adult rodeos than his parents did. He would search for her in the crowd on the weekends she showed up. Her smile was always the brightest thing in the stadium.

He's not sure how long they watch each other in the silence, the cold air rushing into the camper through the open door. Eventually, he says, "You talk like the only thing I've got to my name is the bar. But you're wrong. I've got you. And Christa."

Cooper doesn't quite smile. "Yeah, and you'd still rather live in this tin can than our house."

"That house belongs to you. This land belongs to me. Even if I slept in a tent, it'd still be good land. I don't want to give it up. Doesn't mean I have something against living with you."

She studies him without speaking for a moment, head tilted to the right. She's been giving him that look since they were kids, trying to figure him out. "You sure got something against rodeos. You ever going to tell me why?"

Smith tenses, feeling cornered in the camper with her blocking the only exit. He crosses his arms against his chest.

"Fine," she says. "But sooner or later, you're going to have to talk about it."

She turns and disappears out the door.

He follows her outside, a few paces behind her as she heads for her truck. "Hey," he says. "You mad?"

She stops and faces him. "No. You coming with us tonight?"

He hesitates. "No."

"Guess we'll see you tomorrow, then."

Smith nods.

Cooper gets into her truck, smiling at him over the wheel as she starts the engine, and he watches her drive away until she's gone.

*

The Cody Nite Rodeo runs every year from June first to August thirty-first, every night of the week, rain or shine. The gates open at seven o'clock in the evening, an hour before the rodeo starts. Cooper and Christa don't get there until ten before eight after having dinner at their favorite taco place. They buy beer from concessions, find seats in the covered stands on the south side of the arena, high enough up for a good view, and wait for the announcer to kick things off. Because the rodeo happens every night for three months, the stands are never full, but there's a pretty good crowd tonight, including locals, tourists, and people from neighboring towns. Everybody stands up as a teenage girl sings the national anthem, her voice filling the open air and the rhinestones on her pink cowboy boots twinkling under the white lights. As the girl sings, a woman on horseback rides through the arena bearing the American flag on a wooden staff.

The rodeo starts off with barrel racing, the safest category. Contestants ride their horses in a cloverleaf formation as fast as they can around three steel barrels positioned at corners of an invisible triangle. Whoever makes the fastest time wins, and a five-second penalty is applied for any barrels tipped over. In the pros and college rodeo, barrel racing is a women's event, but some amateur rodeos allow men to compete. Here at Cody's, it's women only.

First up is Rachel Bower, a twenty-two-year-old local with auburn hair pulled into a ponytail. She's riding a big dappled gray with the ease of someone who's been on horseback since childhood. She's one of those riders here who has no plans to go pro but who partakes in amateur rodeos for the fun of it, probably rode on her college team if she went to school in Wyoming and isn't ready to give it up now that she's graduated.

"So what's this party we're going to?" Cooper asks, glancing at her sister as Bower rides out of the arena.

"Darlene Tanner's throwing a rodeo party," says Christa. "Her boyfriend knows a bunch of the guys competing, so they're going to be there. Probably a whole lot of other people too."

"You know Darlene Tanner well enough she invited us?"

"I know Judy Baer, who's friends with Darlene. Darlene told Judy to invite whoever she wanted, and Judy invited me."

"Judy's kid is one of your students?"

"Yep."

Christa works full-time as a dance teacher at Cody's Rocky Mountain School of the Arts, Cody Center for Performing Arts, and Northwest College in Powell, a town half an hour northeast. She got a BFA in dance at Wyoming University in Laramie and started teaching right after she graduated. She began taking lessons herself when she was four years old and hasn't stopped dancing since.

Cooper's been to more dance recitals than anyone who isn't an actual dancer, been to more of them than rodeos—and she's been to a lot of rodeos. She lived in Laramie while Christa was in college, so they wouldn't have to be apart for four years, and attended her sister's college recitals as she had the high school, middle school, and grade school ones. Now, she goes to at least one recital a season, watching Christa's students.

Christa glances at Cooper after a minute or two of silence.

"Would you rather drop me off and go home? I could probably get a ride back."

"No," says Cooper. "I'll go."

"You're bound to know at least some of the people there."

"You mean customers?"

"You know people in Cody besides your customers," Christa says.

Cooper doesn't reply.

Enid Osgood rides into the arena on a black mare, long dark hair flapping behind her as she weaves around the barrels. She's not much older than Christa, maybe twenty-eight. By day, she's an architect with one of the firms in town. Amateur rodeo is a hobby she picked up in college after growing up on horseback on her wealthy family's ranch somewhere east. She has the face of a muse, but somehow, she's still not married. Instead, she's one of the most coveted single women in Park County.

"You think Smith's working right now?" Christa says, keeping her voice down so only her sister can hear.

"I have no idea," says Cooper, eyes tracking Osgood.

"You think he gets lonely?"

"Of course, he does. The real question is, does he mind?"

Everybody claps for Osgood as she exits the arena, and the announcer clocks her time. She's in the lead, but that's no surprise. She's won barrel racing the last four years in a row.

"Did he ever tell you about the man who came to the bar last night?" Christa asks.

"No. You?"

Christa shakes her head. "You remember seeing him compete?"

"I don't think so. Smith never introduced me to him, that's for sure. There were so many other rodeo guys over the years, maybe I've seen him before and I can't remember. Who knows."

"His name's John Henry?"

Cooper nods. "John Henry Walker."

"Smith didn't look happy to see him. But maybe he was just pissed over riding the bull."

"Pissed and full of beer."

"Maybe...maybe he was embarrassed," says Christa.

Cooper frowns at her sister. "Embarrassed? What the hell for?"

Christa shrugs a little. "I don't know. He used to be a big rodeo star, and now he's running a bar in Cody."

"Everybody retires from the rodeo, Christa. And they've all got to move on with their lives and make money some other way."

"I know. But don't you think Smith kinda feels like he should've moved on to better things? Or that he thinks other people expected him to?"

Cooper purses her lips and looks away in time to see the next barrel racing contestant gallop into the arena. When she spoke to Smith in the morning, she didn't mean to make him feel ashamed of what he's done with his life since leaving the rodeo. She's not embarrassed by him or disappointed, but he might've taken it that way if he already felt like an embarrassment.

The sisters don't talk again as barrel racing comes to an end and the rodeo clown returns to the arena to entertain before bronc riding starts. The Cody Rodeo features both bareback and saddle bronc riding, in that order. Bull riding, the main attraction, is always the last event of the night. Cooper and Christa like the bronc riding best, maybe because of the horses or maybe because Smith was usually the star rider in the category during his career.

They watch Burt Russell, #36, prepare to mount the bronco in the chute. He climbs up onto the high sides of the pen and gingerly swings one leg, then the other, inside. Other men surround the chute to make sure he mounts the bronco properly, and he waits until he gets the okay from one of the onlookers before dropping into the saddle. The horse jerks under his weight, jostling him against the chute sides, and Russell positions himself for the ride, boots in the stirrups, gripping the braided rein. The announcer introduces Russell to the audience, listing his season scores and mentioning his birthplace, age, and how long he's been competing in rodeos.

The gate on the chute swings open to the sound of an airhorn, and the bronco storms out, throwing his hips back and kicking his hind legs high. Russell keeps his left arm raised, gripping the rein white-knuckle tight with his right hand, rocking with the horse's violent seesawing. Together, they swivel in a half circle, Russell never quite coming out of the saddle only because he squeezes his thighs around the bronco hard enough to stay mounted.

The buzzer sounds at the eight-second mark, and Russell tumbles off the beast. He hurries toward the arena fence and climbs up onto it as the horse continues to buck. The handlers move to herd the animal back out of the arena while Russell checks the scoreboard over his shoulder and waits for his time to show up next to his name. Eight point two seconds. He nods, looking more relieved than pleased, and disappears behind the fence.

Cooper and Christa stop clapping, along with the rest of the audience, and wait for the next contestant to show up as a new horse is led into the chute. They glance at each other but don't speak—they've revisited memories of Smith's career enough times at the Nite Rodeo. Cooper attended dozens of his rodeos alone while Christa was in high school and college, but Smith's last night, they were both in the stands. Their whole family—their parents and Smith's parents and brother—watched as he rode his last bronco and bull. Cheered for him as he stood in the center of the arena next to the other winners with a wreath of flowers around his neck and drank in the moment, a sadness in his eyes that had never been there before. The Boones and the Roses hadn't been all together at one of Smith's rodeos for years before that night. They watched him win for the last time, knowing he was walking away from his childhood dream not with peace in his heart but anguish. Together, they grieved for him.

When Cooper and Christa do talk about Smith's golden days, they don't mention that night. They choose to remember his joy, his passion, his thousand-watt smile, and the way he rode horses and bulls like he was born for that reason alone.

*

Darlene Tanner lives with her boyfriend in a two-bedroom house just outside of town. She's in her early thirties, never married, no kids. She wears her dark blonde hair with tiny braids woven in near her face, usually with feathers attached. She's part hippie, part biker, part punk rocker, and the Boone sisters appreciate her presence in Cody mostly because she helps balance out the community culture. Most people living in and around town are older, wealthy types who retired early or middle-aged married couples with kids, all of them straightlaced and boring. Darlene sticks out like the Boones.

By the time Cooper and Christa make it to her place, they have to park several yards away in the empty lot adjacent to the house and walk past the other cars and trucks lined up near it. The front door's propped open behind the screen, and the double-hung windows are pushed open, too, country music and party noise wafting out into the night. People are standing outside on the covered ground porch, beers in hand. There's a cooler full of ice and Budweiser right next to the door with a sign taped to the wall above it which reads, Come in for Good Times!!! Cooper and Christa go inside, the screen door banging shut behind them.

The house is full, most people on their feet in the living room and kitchen. It smells like beer and liquor and marijuana, like the sawdust and dirt and livestock of the rodeo that riders have tracked in. Plenty of the men are wearing cowboy hats, and damn near everyone's in cowboy boots. Cooper and Christa push their way through the crowd to the kitchen because that's usually where you can find a party host. Sure enough, Darlene Tanner's standing in there holding a red plastic cup, wearing a pair of cognac-brown suede pants with fringe all down the outside seams. She sees the Boone sisters and raises her cup.

"You made it," she says.

"Did everybody here actually go to the rodeo?" Christa asks.

"I didn't."

Christa leans in toward Darlene. "Have you met my sister Cooper?"

"I've seen her around. She's probably worked on my truck before."

Cooper and Darlene shake hands.

"Thanks for having us," Cooper says with a smile.

"Thanks for coming," says Darlene. "There's more pizza on the way, about thirty minutes, so you just hang tight. Find one of the coolers lying around and get yourself a drink. I'd go outside if I were you, there are too many damn people in here."

The sliding glass double doors leading to the backyard have been left open. Cooper picks through the cooler next to the door, searching for craft beer or Corona, and comes away empty-handed. Christa takes a can of Coors Light and steps outside. Cooper follows when Christa points out more coolers and a table of liquor and 2-liter Coke bottles wait on the patio.

A handful of men and women are in the yard, some of them dancing to the music and the rest talking and drinking. There's a fire going in the pit and several people encircling it in foldout chairs—men with women in their laps, all of them drinking and some of them smoking too. Some are Darlene's biker friends. Others are rodeo riders and buckle bunnies.

"Where's Judy?" Cooper says to Christa, cracking open a can of Blue Moon.

"I don't know," Christa replies. "I haven't seen her yet."

She pulls out her cell phone and sends Judy a text.

"Well, look who it is," someone says.

The sisters turn their heads toward the man's voice. Big Bob Hartmann, who works part-time at Smith's saloon and drinks there, too, approaches them from over by the fire, his denim shirt tucked into his pants and his red bandana tied around his neck like always. He's a heavyset man with a beer gut and well-kept silver beard. He wears the same old hat everywhere he goes, a brown wide-brimmed gambler. He looks like something out of an old Western movie, a miner panning for gold.

"Hey, Bob," says Christa, comforted by a familiar face.

"Never would've expected to see you here," Cooper tells him.

"I'd say the same to you," he replies. "Is Smith with you?"

Cooper snorts. "Hell, no. We came from the rodeo."

She finishes off her beer and turns to toss it in the trash can behind her, then goes to the liquor table and mixes herself a Jack and Coke.

"Well, he ain't working," Big Bob says to Christa and sips on his Rainier.

"Who's bartending?" she asks.

"Georgeanne. She's got the rest of the weekend off on account of covering for us tonight."

Cooper comes back with her red Solo cup and hands Christa another beer.

"It's a good thing I'm bumping into you here because we need to talk about last night. That was one hell of a show Smith put on," Big Bob says.

"Yeah," says Cooper. "And?"

"I've been hanging around Bad Moon since he opened the place, and he's never been on that thing. Not even when the bar's closed. And I'll tell you something else—he had a better time for that minute and a half than I think I've ever seen him have in four years. I wasn't even sober, but I could see it."

Cooper and Christa give each other a look.

"There's no law against a rodeo rider coming out of retirement," says Big Bob. "I know he won't hear it from me, but he might listen to you two."

"Smith's not going back, Bob," says Cooper, resignation in her voice.

"Why the hell not? Someone with that kind of talent shouldn't keep it bottled up on the shelf at the bar he tends. Hell, there's money he could be making."

"He's thirty-two and five years out of practice."

"There are riders older than him who ain't as good in the pros right now."

Christa smiles sadly at Big Bob. "Smith won't even set foot on rodeo grounds to watch. You know that."

Big Bob shifts his attention away, at the people gathered around the fire, and drinks. He shakes his head.

The sisters stand with him in silence for a while, drinking and watching the people in the yard. They only recognize a few individuals but aren't friends with any of them. Christa figures she would have better luck inside, but it's too loud and crowded in the house for her taste. She checks her phone again and finds a message from Judy, to which she responds with her location.

"Why the hell did that boy retire?" Big Bob says, still staring at the fire several paces ahead of them. "He had more in him. Still does."

Cooper glances at him. "I don't think he did, Bob. Talent and heart are two different things."

He turns his head to look at her. "Do you know why? Did he explain himself back then?"

Cooper lingers on Big Bob for a beat, then refocuses on the yard. She doesn't answer at first, sipping on her Jack and Coke. She was one of the only people who knew in advance of the public announcement that Smith was going to retire, the first person he told. He kept his secret from Christa until Smith permitted her to tell. Cooper was shocked, no less than anyone else. She had expected Smith to stay in the pros until at least the age of thirty, maybe even longer. She couldn't imagine him outside of the rodeo back then. Riding broncs and bulls wasn't just something he did, it was who he was—ever since they were kids and she'd watch the televised PRCA events with him in his living room, at her aunt and uncle's house. When Cooper was twenty-five, the idea of Smith quitting rodeo was as unfathomable as the idea of Christa dropping out of dance. Now, she and Christa can't imagine him ever going back.

"My cousin is a man of few words," she says to Big Bob. "I reckon you know that by now."

Christa drains her first beer can and opens the second. She drinks a couple mouthfuls and glances at the sliding glass door in time to see Judy Baer emerge from the house. Judy sees her and smiles as she approaches.

"Hey, there," she says, leaning in for a back-patting hug. "It's good to see you."

"You too," says Christa, smiling back. "Thanks for the invitation."

"Oh, it's no problem; Darlene knows who you are. She's real welcoming when she throws a party as you can see."

"Judy, you know my sister, Cooper."

"Of course." Judy shakes hands with Cooper. "How are you? How's business?"

"Good," says Cooper. "How are you?"

"Happy about having a night out! My daughters are both sleeping over with friends, so Danny and I don't have to worry about going home early."

"Is your husband here?" Christa says.

"Yeah, he's inside somewhere, with some of his buddies. He doesn't get to go drinking with the guys that often, so he's as glad about this party as I am. Speaking of guys, have you found one to chat up yet?"

Judy gives Christa a saucy smile and taps her elbow.

"No," Christa says as she lifts her beer to her lips. "That's not on my agenda."

"Why not?" Judy replies. "Look at you, you're gorgeous. I don't know how you're still single. Have you dated anybody since you moved to Cody?"

Christa shakes her head. "Nope."

"Hey, I know pickings are slim around here, but that's exactly why you should take advantage of this party. I swear half the people here are from out of town, and I've seen some pretty cute rodeo boys."

"I just came to hang out," Christa says. "I'm really not interested in a hookup or anything."

Cooper stands next to her sister with a tight jaw. She doesn't say a word, nursing her drink until it's gone.

Judy checks her cell phone when it vibrates. "A friend of mine got here, so I'm going to meet her out front," she says to Christa. "But come find me when you want to, and I'll introduce you and your sister to her."

"Okay," says Christa. "I'll see you later."

"Later!"

Judy smiles at Cooper before she disappears back into the house.

As soon as she's gone, Cooper says in a lowered voice, "Why the hell is every married person in this town determined to see the singles coupled up?"

She turns and tosses her empty red cup in the nearest trash can, then pulls another Blue Moon from the cooler by the back door.

Christa gives her an empathetic look. "At least she didn't ask you about dating."

"Yeah, because she thinks I'm gay, like everybody else in Cody. That's why they don't ask. But people think you should be married. They think Smith should be too."

"Well," Christa says. "It doesn't matter what they think."

Cooper peers into her sister's eyes, unsmiling. Christa offers a reassuring expression, touches Cooper's elbow.

Eventually, Cooper averts her gaze and continues drinking her beer, sucking it down faster than she did the first. Christa drinks with her in silence until she's almost through with her third can. She could go mingle with people, but she doesn't want to leave Cooper alone. She doubts her sister would follow her if she went inside looking for someone else to talk to. Cooper hates crowds and uneasily coexists with most people in Cody, which is why Christa gave her the option of sitting this party out.

Dwight Yoakam starts crooning a slow song over the speakers, one of the Boone sisters' favorites. Cooper holds her hand out to Christa, and Christa smiles like her sister's being silly but lets herself get pulled along. Cooper leads her over to a clear spot by the fire, not far from where the couples are dancing. She holds Christa's hand up in her own and wraps her other arm around Christa's waist. Christa rests her free hand on Cooper's bicep and follows her sister's feet. They move in perfect harmony because they've done this before, swaying back and forth, and halfway through the song, one of them leans in closer. They rest their chins on each other's shoulder, holding each other close, and Cooper sings the song under her breath, so quiet the words get lost beyond them. They're both drunk enough, warm and happy about the stars.

In the darkness of the yard, someone watching from a distance could mistake them for another couple, Cooper for a man. She, in her slouchy jeans and T-shirt and lace-up boots, her hair cut close to the scalp, and Christa in her knee-short floral skirt and cowboy boots, reddish-blonde hair thick and long down her back. They dance through the next song, and when it ends, Cooper stops and pulls back, looking at her sister.

"I'm going to go get another drink. You want one?"

Christa shakes her head. "I've gotta sober up to drive us home. You go ahead."

They leave the dance floor together, and Cooper goes inside. Christa waits by the door, grinning to herself, hands on her hips.

A man steps out of the house and comes up behind her, standing at her right shoulder. She feels him and smells him before she sees him, like a fifteen-hundred-pound bull who's stepped too close, blowing hot breath against her.

"Hey, there, pretty lady," he says.

She turns to face glistening teeth, twinkling eyes.

"What's your name?"

He smells like whiskey and livestock. She doesn't have to ask him to know he's a rodeo rider, but she has no memory of him from earlier in the evening. He's tall but not as tall as Smith, maybe six feet even, and brawny. He's dirty blond, with several days' worth of facial hair. His plaid shirt is untucked with the sleeves rolled to the elbows, a pair of dusty jeans, and roper boots.

Christa doesn't want him to know her first name. So she says the first one that comes to mind: "Joy."

"You look like a Joy," he says, his tone suggestive. "I'm Buck. Buck Haley. Maybe you've seen me in the rodeo."

"The Nite Rodeo?"

"Yeah. Saddle bronc and bull riding. I'm there almost every night."

She nods, watching the yard and wondering where Cooper is.

"Did you go earlier?" he asks.

"No. I quit going a few years back."

"Really? Why? It's a pretty good show for the amateur circuit. Don't you live around here?"

Christa's about to lie again when Cooper shows up.

"Hey," she says, not missing a beat of the situation. "You ready?"

"Yeah." Christa looks at Buck and tells him, "Sorry, but I gotta go. Enjoy the party."

She doesn't wait for him to respond, giving him a wide berth as she follows her sister into the house.

The crowd is bigger now, the air inside thick with the smell of beer, tobacco, and sweat. More people are drunk than when the sisters arrived. Some of them are dancing while others talk with their voices raised against the music. A small group gathered at the coffee table in the living room share a joint, one woman half asleep slumped at the end of the sofa. There's a couple making out against the wall at the mouth of the bedroom corridor, another cozied up in the family room armchair. Darlene's sitting on a stool in the middle of the kitchen, smoking a cigarette and yapping to the men surrounding her. Judy is nowhere in sight.

The sisters make it to the front door and slip outside again into the cool night, their pace brisk as they pass people drinking on the porch and the lawn. Darkness envelops the property, no other homes or buildings nearby and no streetlights along the narrow access road that leads back to the highway.

"We're going home, right?" Cooper says.

"Yeah. I'm done."

"Sorry I took so long. There was a line for the bathroom."

Christa pauses, resisting the urge to check over her shoulder. "Did you get your beer?"

Cooper bounces the unopened can in her hand. "Yup. Want to hit the gas station and pick up a case? We could have our own party to make up for leaving early."

"No. I think I'm going to make myself some tea and go to bed."

They get into Cooper's truck, with Christa behind the wheel, and head off into the midnight blue.

*

Red Lodge, Montana—population 2,200—is hosting a private rodeo this weekend, one that's moved to a different location in the state every year since it started four years ago. Like most private rodeos, this one hasn't been advertised, online or off, but pro circuit athletes were notified to enter months ago via newsletters and word of mouth. Private rodeo sponsors usually recruit at least one or two competitors of their choosing, but the rest sign up, no different than in any other rodeo.

Smith never competed in private events though he was sought after by their hosts. There was good money to be won, but he never liked the idea of putting on a show for a bunch of rich people and their friends who felt too good to watch pro rodeo with the rest of the public.

When John Henry paid for his beer at the saloon, Smith caught a glimpse of the hotel key card he'd stuck into his wallet. The Comfort Inn, Red Lodge. John Henry only mentioned rodeos in Billings and Livingston, but neither of those events was scheduled for this weekend. On his lunch break at the bar, Smith called the Comfort Inn posing as an out-of-town rodeo attendee and got the event details from the front desk. He spent the rest of the afternoon trying to decide what to do.

He makes the hour drive north across state lines in forty-five minutes. He arrives at the rodeo grounds where the annual Red Lodge Rodeo was held last month, parks his truck at the far edge of the lot, and walks past the bevy of newer, fancier pickups and SUVs to the main entrance. He buys a ticket from the woman in the ticket box, who recognizes him with a big smile and assumes someone invited him. He heads into the stands hoping nobody else is an old fan of his and finds a seat halfway up, near the middle of the section.

Most of the spectators are dressed nicer than the crowds he's used to seeing at pro rodeos. A woman in one of the private boxes on the other side of the arena, dressed all in white with a hat, looks like she's at the Kentucky Derby instead of a little rodeo in Red Lodge, Montana. The crowd, spread thin across the stands, is small compared to public rodeos, even to the Cody Nite Rodeo. There are hardly any children, no rodeo clown to start the event, and instead of an ordinary person serving popcorn and Coke cans from a concessions tray, a couple women wearing black-and-white server uniforms go around asking people if they want wine, champagne, or cocktails.

Everybody stands for the national anthem, the men holding their hats to their hearts as usual. Instead of a live singer, they play an instrumental version over the speakers. Smith has heard the national anthem sung by every kind of person imaginable, male and female, all ages, in every kind of weather. He still remembers who sang it at his first national championship, what she was wearing, the sound of her voice. He remembers the girl who sang it at his last event too.

This rodeo only has four competitions: tie-down roping, bareback, saddle bronc, and bull riding. Smith spends the thirty minutes it takes to get through tie-down roping debating with himself about staying versus leaving. He ignores the feeling in the air, the women twittering, the condescending laughter of the rich and urban as they watch the cowboys wrangle the calves off their feet. Though he must have as much money as some of these people, sitting cold in the bank, he is not their kind.

Bareback bronc riding begins, and he almost gets up and goes. When the first man rockets out of the chute on a horse named Tilt-a-Whirl, nostalgia hits Smith, washing through him in waves for the longest eight seconds he's had in a while. The memories start rushing back when the next rider goes. He remembers with his whole body: his callused right hand gripping the strap, his knees digging into the horse's sides, his thighs clenched, his heart pounding, the blur of everything around him, the violent jerking, the primal fear overpowered by exhilaration. It's over as soon as it starts, the rider letting himself get bucked off and landing on his feet, then running out of the horse's way as the handlers move in.

Smith doesn't have time to figure out if he's sad because, in minutes, it's the next guy's turn. Hundreds of rides in dozens of different places come back to him in flashes. He closes his eyes a second before the buzzer signals the eight-second mark and doesn't hear the announcer's words, only his voice in the background.

When he opens his eyes again, John Henry's climbing into the chute, and Smith feels like he's having some kind of out-of-body experience. The gate flies open, and the bronco rages into the arena, back legs kicking high. The huge bay spins, and John Henry on its back looks like an illustration of Pecos Bill riding a tornado, come to life. Smith doesn't see or hear anything else but that man and horse, not until the beast throws John Henry off into the dirt as soon as he makes eight seconds.

After John Henry's first ride, Smith spends the rest of the rodeo with his head in his hands, except when John Henry reappears in saddle bronc and bull riding. He couldn't describe what he's feeling if somebody asked, but he does know that when John Henry is on the back of a bucking animal, it's all he sees and all he cares about. He holds his breath without realizing it, exhales the second John Henry's boots hit the ground. Each time, he's torn between John Henry and his own visceral memories of riding. Once John Henry's bull ride is over, the tension leaves Smith's body, and he slumps in his seat, giving himself a minute before he tries getting up.

His legs are weak, but he leaves the stands anyway, going straight to the men's room on the ground floor. He's alone, and in the silence, he can still hear the announcer and the crowd cheering and clapping. He paces in front of the sinks, trying to breathe and get himself together. He broke out into a cold sweat at some point after John Henry's first ride, and now his skin feels sticky with the drying perspiration.

Smith judges himself in the mirror, hands braced on the sink in front of him as he leans forward. His hair, long enough to tuck behind his ears, hangs in his face. He grew it out after he retired, maybe to separate himself from his old rodeo passport photos. He's clean-shaven, but he sports a five-o'clock shadow often enough, something else he never did during his rodeo career. His eyes are the color of the sea in a terrible storm, a bluish-gray, and they're full of trouble now. He looks at his hands, once always dirty and rough and tan from so much time in the sun, now clean and callused in the palms, too soft—maybe like himself.

What the hell is he doing here? What did he think was going to come from this? He swore he would never go back, he would never look over his shoulder at what he left behind, he would make a clean break from the rodeo world and everything in it. It was the only way to move on with his life, to find peace in retirement, and here he is like a damn fool, baited by a cowboy he hasn't even thought of in years.

And what is he supposed to say to John Henry Walker, if he talks to him at all? Everything that passed between them is ancient history. They have no reason to reconnect, no knowledge of each other's present life or person. Weeks from now, John Henry's going to return to wherever he came from, to the life he has at home, and Smith has no interest in bridging the distance any more than he does in calling up other old friends he's been out of touch with. Does he want to speak to John Henry? Or should he slip away undetected, get into his truck, and go back to Cody?

Smith takes a breath and turns on the faucet, washes his hands and face with cold water. He dries them with paper towels, runs his hands through his hair, and gives himself a last look as a couple men enter the bathroom.

He walks out before they have a chance to recognize him, hearing the rodeo announcer closing the event and thanking the audience for coming. He exits the arena and pauses a few paces outside the entrance, surveying the cars and the pale early night. The parking lot lights have already switched on, glaring white. He's alone, but pretty soon, the crowd will flood out around him. He could get into his truck right now and go home before anybody else emerges from the arena. John Henry would never know he was there.

Smith closes his eyes and takes a breath, bows his head. He knows better than this—but he wants what he wants.

When John Henry Walker steps out into the shadows of the arena's back exit, Smith's waiting for him.

John Henry stops in his tracks when their eyes meet. "I'll be Goddamned," he says, a smile spreading across his face. "What are you doing here?"

Smith says the first thing that occurs to him: "I owe you an apology."

John Henry raises his eyebrows. "You made the drive from Cody and sat through a whole rodeo to apologize to me?"

"Well, I don't have your phone number."

John Henry shakes his head. "All right, go on."

"I'm sorry I was a jerk to you last night. That's no way to treat an old friend."

John Henry pauses, then says, "I caught you off guard, in public. I shouldn't have done that. I probably should've just stayed away, like I have been. But it is good to see you, Smith."

Smith nods. He has no idea what else to say, so he stays quiet.

"You hungry?" John Henry asks.

Smith hesitates, then says, "I could eat."

They decide to have dinner at the Bear Creek Saloon, seven miles east of Red Lodge along Highway 308. They're silent in the truck, passing through the pitch darkness of the desolate plain. John Henry rides in the passenger seat with his hat in his lap. The radio stays switched off, and every time Smith thinks of something to say, he doesn't speak.

The saloon appears on the side of the road, looking like a haunt where men go to disappear, or the memory of a hundred other bars and restaurants all over the West where Smith used to eat his own victory dinners, drink too much, and make eyes at a woman or a man he'd later screw in his truck or motel room. A handful of vehicles, mostly pickups, line the front of the saloon, and the requisite hogs with their steel necks and handles gleaming in Smith's headlights, twenty-first-century replacements for horses at the hitching rail.

Smith orders the buffalo rib eye, medium rare, and the Red Lodge Ale on tap. John Henry orders the prime rib, medium, and a bottle of Miller High Life. There are a handful of other customers present, many of them older men dressed like cowboys—ex-rodeo riders or ranchers or common Montana citizens. Nobody pays them much attention, and their waitress is polite enough, reminding them the pig races start at 7 p.m. every night Thursday through Sunday if they want to come back before the weekend's over. The Bear Creek Saloon is the only establishment in the state that hosts pig racing, a weekly event starting in May and ending with Labor Day in September. Smith watched the race with Cooper and Christa one night a couple years ago.

"You ever miss it?" John Henry says.

"The rodeo?"

"All of it. Competing, traveling all over the country, the time in between events."

Smith doesn't answer at first. Plenty of mornings in the last five years, he's lain awake in his bed thinking about roots, wandering, two-lane blacktop cutting through the plains under blue sky, the time between weekly rodeos passing in miles on the odometer, the time between rodeo seasons spent like a caged dog, living days and weeks for eight seconds on a horse or a bull. He used to enjoy missing his cousins, thinking about them on those long drives, recapping victories to Cooper on bar room pay phones even when it would've been better if she'd seen them herself—all because the reunions were so sweet, that first hug after weeks or months of separation. People talk about "putting down roots" as if signing a marriage license and buying a house that takes thirty years to pay off is the same thing as planting a tree. If Smith can take root in anything, anywhere, it's only Wyoming soil and the Boone sisters.

"No," he tells John Henry. "I don't miss it."

John Henry gives him a skeptical expression. "When I knew you in the rodeo, you were happy. Now, you're not."

"You've spent all of three hours with me for the first time in six years, and you think you know how I feel?"

"Yeah," says John Henry. "I do. If you were happy, you wouldn't be able to hide it."

Smith doesn't reply, just glances away.

They're silent for a little while.

"I thought you were going to win out there," Smith says. "You're a better rider than the guy who placed first— unless something's changed since I retired."

"I wasn't supposed to win," says John Henry, not quite smiling as he drinks his beer.

"What do you mean?"

John Henry doesn't answer.

"Did you throw the ride?"

John Henry nods. "Yup."

Smith gapes at him, incredulous. "Why the hell would you do that?"

"I was asked to—by the hosts."

Smith pauses, hearing the whole story in those few words but not wanting to believe it.

John Henry was the only Black competitor in that private rodeo. Every other man was white.

"All those rich folks in the box would not have been happy to see me walk off with five grand," he says. "Especially if any of it came from them."

"You've gotta be kidding me."

"No, sir." John Henry pulls on his beer. "But the hosts paid me off, so it wasn't a total loss."

"How much?"

"Two thousand."

"That's still a three-thousand-dollar loss in my book."

"Yeah, and it's two grand I didn't have yesterday."

"Well, unless you plan on reentering in the future, I don't see the point of giving away three grand to avoid pissing off a bunch of racists."

"I like keeping my options open," John Henry says. "I could come back next year. And the year after that. As many times as I want."

"Why would you want to?"

John Henry pauses. "Not everybody can afford to act out of pride the way you can."

"It's not pride," says Smith. "It's dignity."

The waitress delivers their food, and John Henry orders another beer. They start to eat and lapse into a silence filled with other people's voices and the classic country playing on the stereo system. They take turns stealing glances at each other, avoiding eye contact.

"You still living in Missouri?" Smith asks about halfway through the meal.

John Henry nods. "In Jefferson City."

"Used to be St. Louis, wasn't it?"

"Yeah, last time I saw you. I've been in Jefferson four years."

"Is it smaller than St. Lou?"

"A lot smaller. But not small enough."

John Henry used to tell Smith about his dream of living on his own land, somewhere in the country. Starting a farm or a ranch, spending the rest of his life working with his hands outdoors, staying in the saddle after retiring from the rodeo. Back in the old days, he lived in St. Louis because that's where he'd gone to college and where he found a job after graduating, but he hated urban life and spent as much time as he could traveling to rodeos and training out of town.

It occurs to Smith he's got what John Henry wants: the land, the money, the means to build his own home and start his own ranch or farm. He never dreamed of these things during his rodeo career. He never thought about life after the rodeo when he was still in it, not even in the days leading up to his last ride. When he was twenty-five, he thought he would keep going for at least another decade—and that might as well have been forever, at the time. Now, he's got a life John Henry is still saving up for, and he doesn't know what he's doing with it or if he wants it at all. He doesn't know who he is, only who he used to be.

"What do you do when you're not on the road?" Smith says, scooping up baked potato with his fork.

"I'm still engineering."

"I'm surprised you don't already have that land you talked about. You always made plenty of money outside the rodeo, more than any other guy I knew. More than I ever made at a day job, hell."

John Henry grins at him. "What do you know about day jobs? You were a full-time cowboy as long as I knew you and even before."

"After high school, when I was starting out in the pros, I worked. I didn't win all the time right off the bat. There were dry spells."

"You were how old when you went full-time? Twenty-one?"

"Twenty and change."

John Henry shakes his head and drinks his beer.

"Why don't you have your farm?" Smith asks him. "Or do you?"

John Henry stares at him from across the table, pausing before he answers. "The land's not the only thing I'm buying if I start a farm. There's a lot of cost involved long-term, and I want to make sure my farm is going to be sustainable before I commit to it."

"Is that the only thing holding you back? Money?"

John Henry doesn't reply, reaching for another roll in the bread basket and wiping up the steak juice on his plate with it.

After they pay their bill and walk out of the saloon, they stand outside on the pavement before the entrance, stalling as they both try to decide what comes next. Smith admires the stars, thumbs hooked into his hip pockets. He feels a sense of peace, sudden and unexpected, settle over him like snow on an evergreen.

"I could go for another drink," John Henry says. "If you're interested."

Smith looks at him. "You want to get drunk together?"

"I didn't say drunk."

Smith starts heading for the truck, and John Henry follows a pace behind. They get in, Smith at the wheel and John Henry in shotgun, and sit there with the engine off.

"You trying to decide if you want it or if I do?" John Henry asks.

Smith focuses on the darkness ahead that lies beyond the saloon. "Both."

"I'll do it if you want. I'll be all right if you don't."

Smith pauses, still refusing to even glance at the other man, sticks the key into the ignition, and starts the truck.

They ride back west without speaking and without company on the road.

*

The Red Lodge Inn is a bare bones motel near the southern edge of town. They go there after stopping for beer at the only gas station convenience store open late in Red Lodge. Smith steps into the office alone to book a room with two queen beds while John Henry waits in the truck outside. They move the truck to a parking space right in front of their room and disappear inside with the beer, locking the door behind them.

They eye each other in the yellow light of the lamp, standing a couple paces apart.

"How long's it been?" John Henry asks.

"Since what?" says Smith.

"Since you been with a man."

Smith pauses, looking away. The last time was a one-night hookup in Sheridan, a man not much older than him from the casual encounters section on Craigslist. "Months. You?"

"About three," says John Henry. "You know, these days, you can find dudes in the stands with a thing for cowboys, easy. I been with more of them since I saw you last than other rodeo guys."

Smith hooked up with his share of rodeo outsiders when he was in the circuit—not men who came to watch but randoms who would approach him in the bathrooms and parking lots of dive bars and saloons, who'd look at him a certain way from across the room first and wait for him to look back before meeting him in the men's room or the parking lot. It wasn't all the time. He picked up more women than men during his rodeo career as there was never a shortage of buckle bunnies in any given town ready to ride every year. But when Smith wanted a man, only a man would do, and the sex was usually worth the risk. He always preferred to have an ongoing arrangement with someone he knew as opposed to one-night stands with total strangers, but it was hard to be friends with another rodeo man in public and keep the ongoing sex they had a secret. Plenty of times, Smith would fool around with a buddy just once, only for one or both of them to back off afterward like a skittish horse. John Henry was the last male friend he'd had a sexual relationship with, and they parted ways about a year before Smith retired.

"So you want to do this?" John Henry says.

"I'm here, ain't I?" says Smith.

John Henry nods, hands on his hips and weight shifted onto one leg.

Smith sets the six-pack on the short dresser, tosses a beer to John Henry, and pulls another one for himself. The hiss of the cans opening cuts through the still room. They stand there and drink, staring at each other, without breaking until the cans are empty.

Smith puts his empty can on the dresser and says, "Left something in the truck."

He leaves the room, exhaling in the cool night air, his hand shaking as he opens the cab door on the truck's passenger side and pulls the plastic bag out from under the seat. He pauses in front of the motel room door before going back inside, not sure if this is a good idea or a bad one.

John Henry's in the bathroom washing his hands. He meets Smith's gaze in the mirror.

Smith takes the box of condoms and bottle of lube out of the plastic bag and holds them up for John Henry to see.

"When did you get those?"

"Before I drove up here."

John Henry faces him and dries his hands with one of the towels hanging on the rack. He's amused, not quite smiling. "So you didn't come to catch up or apologize for last night. You just wanted to get laid."

"No. I wanted to be prepared."

"Sure."

John Henry steps out of the bathroom and passes Smith, who keeps his distance as John Henry sits on one of the beds to take off his boots. It's too quiet in the room, but turning on the TV would feel wrong. John Henry stands up, a few inches shorter on his bare feet.

"Come here," he says.

Smith hesitates for a split second, then goes to stand in front of him and drops the bag on the floor. They peer at each other in the dim light, close enough to feel each other's body heat.

John Henry makes the first move, lifting his hand to cup the back of Smith's neck and leaning in for a kiss. Smith's never liked kissing much, especially the sloppy kind, but he tolerates it better with someone he knows well. John Henry looks into his eyes again, then kisses him with more confidence. He doesn't pull back this time, following the second kiss with a third, opening his mouth enough that Smith tastes the beer and steak on his breath. Smith's got his eyes closed and his hands on John Henry's hips. John Henry starts to unbutton Smith's shirt but doesn't stop kissing him. He gets all the way down to Smith's belt and pulls the shirt out of his jeans, undoing the last couple buttons. Smith takes the shirt off and tosses it onto the second bed. John Henry starts to kiss his neck, which always makes Smith weak, and Smith leans into it, John Henry pushing his hands underneath Smith's white T-shirt and up his back.

Smith reaches for John Henry's belt buckle and snaps it open, head tipped as John Henry sucks at his neck. John Henry starts to pull Smith's T-shirt up, and Smith finishes the job, throwing it on the other bed. John Henry sheds his own shirt and tank, then starts kissing Smith again, hands working his belt open. He reaches his hand into Smith's jeans and boxer briefs and starts fondling him. Smith breaks his mouth away from John Henry's only long enough to gasp, his lips now tender, his pulse fast.

John Henry kneels on the carpet, pulling Smith's jeans and boxer briefs to his ankles, and takes Smith's half-hard penis into his mouth. Smith tips his head all the way back and bites his lip as John Henry sucks on him, hands gripping Smith's thighs, fingers pressed into the white flesh. After a few minutes, John Henry reaches between Smith's legs and starts to rub his hole. He pushes his fingertip inside Smith, and Smith's knees almost buckle as he leans forward and braces himself on John Henry's shoulders. Shoulders chiseled and bulky with muscle from a life of riding broncos and bulls, built in the seconds of holding on.

"Stop, stop," Smith says, breathless. "I'm going to bust if you keep going."

John Henry stops, mouth and hands falling away from Smith. He stands up, eye to eye with Smith again, his lips wet. Smith breathes, hand pressed to his belly, his body hot and his legs weak. His vision's fuzzy at the edges, only beginning to clear up after a minute or two of going untouched.

John Henry finishes stripping. He's already hard, and he strokes himself as he stands there in front of Smith.

"You topping?" Smith asks, his heart still fast in his chest.

John Henry nods. When they were in the rodeo together, he usually topped Smith. Not always but most times.

"Sit down," Smith says.

John Henry sits on the end of the bed, leaning back on his hands, and Smith kneels on the floor between his legs to blow him. Smith is not a fan of giving blowjobs to men, but oral sex is an expectation most guys have, one he feels obliged to meet. He grasps John Henry's hips and works his mouth on the other man's cock. John Henry sighs and hums as he caresses the back of Smith's head. It's an affectionate gesture that makes Smith feel at once appreciated and uncomfortable, a reminder this isn't a stranger with a fake name he's fucking but a former friend, someone he's been with many times before, someone who sees him as more than a hot lay.

"That's enough," John Henry says, his voice quiet and kind.

Smith stands up and wipes his mouth with the back of his hand.

"Lie down," John Henry tells him as he gets up and retrieves the plastic bag from the floor. "On your back."

He puts the box of condoms on the night table while Smith lies on the bed with his legs spread. John Henry's got the bottle of lubricant in hand as he sits on the bed, facing Smith.

"You don't have to waste time," Smith says. "I can take you."

John Henry gives him a look as he squirts some lube onto his fingers. "Either you're real desperate right now or you been fucking too many one-time guys off the Internet."

Smith keeps his eyes on the ceiling as John Henry fingers him, touching himself intermittently. It feels surreal, being here and doing this with a man he thought he'd never see again. John Henry bends down and sucks on Smith's cock a little bit, moving two fingers inside him, and Smith closes his eyes, mouth ajar. John Henry sits up again and takes his fingers out of Smith, adds more lube to Smith's entrance, then pushes three fingers inside. He sucks on him again, spreading his fingers and sliding them in and out. He's not doing this because Smith needs it but because he knows Smith enjoys it. Strangers never take this kind of care, this kind of time. Smith usually doesn't either, with them.

John Henry rolls the condom on. "You ready?"

"I'm ready." Smith swallows and tries to relax.

John Henry starts to push himself into Smith, going slow, and Smith breathes through the almost-burn of the stretch. John Henry pauses when he's buried in him all the way. He could come without even touching himself. He hasn't been fucked by a man in so long, he forgot how good it feels. Just as good as being inside a woman.

John Henry breathes, his voice paper-thin. "Shit. You good?"

"Yeah."

John Henry slowly pulls out of Smith until only the head of his cock is inside, then slowly pushes back in to the hilt. He does that several times, the room filled with the sound of the two men's gasping and grunting. Smith is torn between wanting more, wanting to be fucked fast and hard, and loving the dragged-out strokes, feeling every inch of John Henry moving back and forth inside him. If he wasn't completely hard when John Henry started, he is now—and he can't bear to touch himself.

John Henry starts to fuck him a little faster, finding the right speed and rhythm after a handful of thrusts. He's got Smith by the hips, his knees between Smith's legs. He alternates between watching his cock pumping into Smith's ass and tipping his head back, his eyes closed, lips parted.

After several minutes, they stop and change positions. Smith kneels at the top of the mattress, plants his hands flat on the wall above the bed. He can see into the back lot behind the motel through the curtains on the rectangular window above the headboard. John Henry enters him again and hammers into him, the mattress creaking under them, and Smith pushes his ass back into John Henry's thrusts, rests his forehead against the wall below the window. He's sweating, his face hot.

When he's tired of kneeling, Smith sinks back onto the bed, buries his face into one of the pillows, and wraps his arms around it. John Henry grinds his hips against Smith's ass, fucking him in slow, deep thrusts. He pushes Smith flat on the mattress, and covers him with his body, sucks and nibbles on Smith's neck. Smith turns his head in the pillow just enough to breathe, his eyes closed, his skin tingling. He's panting under John Henry's weight, rocking his hips and his ass in a small motion, wanting John Henry to fuck him harder and deeper. John Henry runs his hand up and down Smith's side, rotating his hips clockwise over and over until he starts moving in and out of Smith again.

"You miss me?" he says to Smith, his voice low and husky, words slurred. "You miss this?"

Smith doesn't answer, whining in frustration. He bends his knees underneath him to lift his body up off the mattress, and John Henry follows his lead, rising and pulling Smith with him. On his knees and elbows, Smith jerks back against John Henry's thrusts. It almost unsteadies John Henry, on his knees again with his hands on Smith's lower back. He reads the signal and starts pounding Smith with long, hard strokes, hitting the sweet spot nearly every time like the right angle is in his muscle memory. Smith moans, the sound guttural, his eyes closed and his hair hanging around his face.

"Yeah," John Henry gasps. "Fuck, yeah."

Smith moans again, his hands curled into fists, sweat dripping down his inner thighs, pleasure building from his prostate.

He shifts from his elbows to his hands, bracing his palms flat on the bed. John Henry leans his weight onto one knee, planting his other foot on the bed, gripping Smith's hips and pulling him into every thrust. He stays in that position for a while, going deeper than he was before.

Smith starts to whimper. "Oh, my God," he says, curling his fingers into the sheets. "Oh, fuck—shit! Jesus Christ, keep going. Keep—please, John. Fuck."

John Henry shifts back onto both knees. He's panting behind Smith, trying to reach under him to grab his cock but fails, swept away in the motion of thrusting, skin damp with sweat against Smith's. "What do you want?" John Henry's voice is ragged in Smith's ear. "Tell me how you want it."

"Deeper," Smith chokes. "Fuck me deeper. Please."

John Henry tries, slowing enough to move his hips in a scooping motion, driving as deep into Smith as he can before thrusting up inside him. They moan and groan, voices overlapping, not even trying to be quiet. Smith hasn't been fucked by a man like this in years, maybe not since the last time he was with John Henry. It feels so good, it's almost unbearable.

Smith resists the urge to jack himself off. He tries to jam his ass back into John Henry with every thrust, but his thighs are tired from holding up his weight, all his muscles prickly with tension. He sobs with his head bowed between his shoulders, squeezing his eyes shut, wanting more but feeling like he can't take it. John Henry grips his shoulder and his hip and fucks him, tipping his head back and closing his eyes.

Smith drops to his elbows and puts his head down in the pillow, muffling a long moan as his orgasm tears through him. The pleasure crackles through him, burns in the pit of his groin, more intense than he's felt in a long time. He shouts into the pillow, afraid he'll black out if he touches his cock. He almost collapses his lower half onto the bed, his thighs quivering and weak, but he stays on his knees as John Henry continues.

"Fuck, yeah," John Henry gasps. "I'm close. I'm close now."

Smith could cry at the relentless pounding of his overstimulated prostate, a small shock jolting through him every time John Henry hits it.

"Gonna come," says John Henry, his thrusts short and desperate. "Gonna fucking come. Shit."

Smith clenches around John Henry, his whole body loose and feverish, and John Henry groans, grinding his hips into Smith's ass, pulsing inside him.

"*Fuck*," he keens, long and drawn out. "Fuck, yeah, Smith."

He keeps going until he's bowed over Smith's body, chest hot on Smith's back, one hand on the mattress to hold himself up and his other arm wrapped around Smith. He doesn't stop until he's wrung every last second out of his orgasm, breathing hard in Smith's ear. Smith finally drops flat on the bed, and John Henry goes with him.

They lie there in silence for a while as John Henry calms down. Smith's drowsy, ready to pass out underneath John Henry's weight.

John Henry rolls off Smith and onto his back, lying next to him in the bed. He stares at the ceiling, then gets up, peels off the condom, and puts it in the trash can. He comes back with a beer and sits next to Smith, propped against the headboard.

Smith eventually rolls over and wakes himself up, figuring John Henry isn't going to just finish the beer and go to sleep without any conversation. He doesn't speak because he doesn't know what to say. John Henry drinks most of his beer and lights a cigarette from his pack on the night table.

"So when's the last time you been with a woman?" he says.

"Little while," says Smith. "You?"

"I got a girlfriend back home. She's the only woman I been with since we got serious."

"But you fuck men when you're on the road."

"You know how it is," says John Henry and takes a drag on his cigarette.

"No, I don't. Does your girl know you swing both ways?"

John Henry makes a face, part skeptical and part cynical. "What do you think?"

Smith shakes his head. "I wouldn't have done this if you'd told me about her first."

"Yes, you would've. And so what? We're not doing anything rodeo boys haven't done for a hundred years. I haven't seen my girlfriend in twelve weeks. I've been touring all summer. If I was home, I'd have sex with her, but I'm not home. So here we are."

"Don't give me that bullshit. Cheatin' is cheatin'. I've never done it to someone else, and I don't go trying to help other people do it either."

"You ain't that stupid," John Henry says. "You think the riders you screwed during your career were all single at the time? Give me a break."

Smith scowls, whips the sheet and blanket open, swings his legs over the side of the bed, and sits with his back to John Henry. He leans forward, elbows on his knees.

They're quiet, uneasy tension in the air.

"It's just sex," says John Henry. "It doesn't change the way I feel about her."

Smith shakes his head and runs his hands back through his hair with a sigh. After a pause, he says, "You going to marry her?"

"I've been thinking about it. Haven't bought a ring yet, but when I go home after the season ends, I think I will. She's a good woman."

"So all that crap at the bar about expecting me to have a wife and kids by now, that was you talking about yourself."

"No, I was being honest."

Smith doesn't reply. He stares into space, pensive instead of irritated. This was a mistake. He shouldn't be here, the sex never should've happened, he shouldn't have looked for John Henry at all. He's going to regret this whole night. He's starting to already.

John Henry sighs and puts his cigarette out in the ashtray on his night table. "You upset about me getting engaged?"

Smith wants to roll his eyes. "Jesus, why would I be? I haven't seen you in six years. You've got a life, and so do I. The only reason we're in the same room right now is because you decided to find me, not the other way around."

John Henry's quiet. "I didn't ask you to come to Montana. I didn't even tell you where I was staying."

"Yeah, well. I needed to get laid."

Smith finally gets up from the bed and walks over to the dresser, still naked. He opens another can of beer and starts drinking, avoiding his own eyes in the mirror.

John Henry watches him from the bed. "What the hell happened to you? The Smith I knew was a good guy. Now, you're acting like an asshole. As far as I can tell, you don't have anything to complain about, so what's with the attitude?"

Smith shoots him a bitter glare. "You don't know me anymore. You don't know anything about my life."

"I know you got your own business that's doing pretty well, some family living in the same town, and your health. Not to mention all the money you made in the circuit. That's more than a lot of people got. And the Smith I knew would've been happy to know all this is in his future."

Smith drains his beer and puts the empty can on the dresser next to the others. He opens his third.

John Henry sits up straighter, coming off the headboard. "Look, if you want me to leave, I'll get a ride back to my hotel."

"I paid for a double, and there's no way you're getting a ride from anyone in this town at two o'clock in the morning," Smith says and takes a drink. "It's fine. We'll just quit having this stupid conversation and go to sleep."

John Henry stares at him for a moment, then lies down again.

Smith sits in the faux-leather accent chair in the corner, on the opposite side of the room, and finishes his beer in silence. He pulls opens the blanket and sheet in the second bed and gets in, facing the wall with his back to John Henry. He falls asleep feeling lonelier than he has in a long time.

*

The Silver Dollar Bar is one of Cooper's regular haunts. She stops by for a drink after work some afternoons when it's dead except for two or three retired guys who treat drinking like a job. She doesn't come in at night unless she's in a mood, the kind where she feels like drinking without being prodded by her sister or her cousin. Nobody tries chatting her up at the Silver Dollar, not even on busy weekend nights when they're drunk, and she appreciates that as much as she does the bar's style. Cody being a small town, everybody knows who Cooper is and notices her in a room, but the same folks who try making small talk with her in Smith's saloon won't give her a second glance in the Silver Dollar.

She's playing pool by herself, moving her beer bottle around the rim of the table as she goes. She's still wearing her garage coveralls, the sleeves rolled to her elbows and the first few buttons undone. There's a name patch sewed into the front above her left breast, and the shop's name is printed in faded black letters on her back. The pant legs are tucked into her boots. The boots are big and heavy, their black leather faded and well worn, tongues curling over the laces a little. Circling the pool table in a slow shuffle, bending low to take her shots, she's a sight to see—a blue-collar butch woman, a dying secret of small-town America. The locals don't comment on her, but they look at her sideways when she passes by, when she has her back turned. They give her a wide berth, like she's some kind of animal to be careful around. She's the black bear in the mountains, sharing a delicate agreement with humans to keep a mutual distance.

She pops the eight ball across the table and into the corner pocket, then stands the cue stick on the floor and holds on to it as she finishes her beer. She puts the cue back into the rack and takes her empty bottle to the bar, sits on a free stool and orders another drink. The Silver Dollar's quiet, only a couple people at the opposite end of the bar and a few guys seated at the scraps table. The front door's propped open to let in the cool summer air and the sounds of an insect chirping and vehicles passing by every few minutes. There's something on the flat-screen TV, the volume low enough not to disturb anybody, but she's can't be bothered to figure out what it is. She nurses her beer and listens to the music playing on the stereo system, the kind of alternative country Smith plays in his saloon because he knows Cooper likes it.

Somebody slides onto the stool next to Cooper, on her left. Leeann Bernard.

"Hey, stranger," Leeann says, then asks the bartender for a beer.

Leeann is the only out lesbian in Cody. The only out lesbian in Park County, to Cooper's knowledge. She never wears makeup, her face dusted with light freckles and skin golden brown from her time in the sun. She's wearing a gray felt Western hat with a flat brim and a small pair of feathers tucked into the crown band. Her dark hair is grown out past her shoulders, but that doesn't make her seem any less like a lesbian. Cooper can't put a finger on it, the giveaway. It's something besides the way Leeann dresses and the work she does. Plenty of women in Cody and the smaller towns throughout Park County and Wyoming dress in jeans, boots, and flannel shirts. Plenty wear cowboy hats, like the men. Plenty work and play outdoors, do manual labor uncommon amongst city women. But they come off feminine in a way Leeann never does.

"What are you doing here on a Sunday night?" she asks.

"Same thing you are, apparently," says Cooper. "Drinking."

"Where's the rest of the clan?"

"Christa's home. Smith is AWOL."

There is a pause of silence, the two women drinking side by side. Leeann watches the TV with no real interest.

"Where you coming from?" Cooper asks.

"My shop." Leeann refers to the smithy she built on her property. "I've been working the last several hours. There was no beer in the fridge, so I thought I'd pick some up at the liquor store, but then I remembered I hadn't been to the Silver Dollar in a while."

"What are you working on?"

"A giant iron pussy."

Cooper snorts.

"I was commissioned by the county courthouse."

"No, really."

Leeann grins and takes a drink.

They're quiet again for a minute, listening to the music.

"So tell me what's on your mind," Leeann says.

Cooper glances at her. "Nothing in particular."

"Liar."

"I'm sitting here, having a beer."

"You're brooding."

Cooper keeps her eyes ahead, muscle in her jaw twitching.

Leeann knocks her elbow into Cooper's on the bar. "Come on. You know I won't judge you."

Cooper hesitates, still not looking at Leeann. She shakes her head. "It's nothing. Just shit I can't do anything about."

"You're going to have to be more specific—because there's a lot of shit you can't do anything about."

Cooper smiles for a second. "I'm thinking about my family. If they're still going to be here in ten years or if they're going to move on—from me. And if they do, what am I going to do? How am I going to handle...being alone?"

Leeann gives her a look. "I think you've had too much to drink."

"I'm not drunk," Cooper says. "And this isn't the first time I'm having these thoughts."

Leeann pauses. "What do you mean by move on?"

"Get married. Shack up with somebody romantically. The standard shit."

"Smith and Christa aren't dating anybody, are they?"

"No. They're not."

"And they haven't since you all moved to Cody, have they?"

"Nope."

"Why the hell are you worried then?"

"Just because they've both been single a while doesn't mean they will be forever. It doesn't mean they want to be."

"Well, no, but it's also not a given that either one of them's going to end up married. Have they told you they're hoping for it?"

"No."

"Then how do you know they are?"

"Most people hope they end up with that kind of life, don't they? Most people end up married at least once, even if it doesn't work out. And the ones who don't tie the knot usually fall in love with somebody and move in with them, at least."

"Yeah, but you're not in here moping about most people. You're in here moping about your sister and your cousin. The way I see it, what most people do or want has nothing to do with Christa and Smith. The only way to know what they're after is to ask them."

Cooper doesn't answer, taking a drink instead. Leeann's right, but Cooper can't bring herself to ask her sister or her cousin about marriage and romance. She's too afraid of hearing what she doesn't want to hear. Every time this fear of losing Christa and Smith surfaces, she drinks her way through it in solitude and waits for it to pass.

Leeann gives her a couple minutes, pulling on her own beer and watching the television. The guys who were at the game table are gone now, and the Silver Dollar is empty except for Cooper, Leeann, and the three other people seated at the opposite end of the bar.

"So, you don't want your cousin or your sister to fall in love."

Cooper purses her mouth. "I don't want them to leave me. I don't want to lose what we have. I don't want Christa to move out... But I don't have the right to ask them to stay single with me. If they want to get married one day, I don't have the right to hold them back."

"Hell, Cooper, it's not about having the right. You feel how you feel. You want something for yourself, and there's nothing wrong with that. You may not be entitled to ask your family to sacrifice what they want to make you happy, but you get to want what you want." Leeann pauses to drink. "You love your sister and your cousin a lot, and that's good. They love you back. I could be wrong, but I don't think love is as fragile as you're making it out to be."

Cooper doesn't know what to say, so she downs the rest of her beer and sets the empty bottle near the opposite side of the bar. She sets her eyes on the bartender until she sees her and lifts a finger to signal she wants another drink.

The bartender comes over. "More of the same?"

"No," says Cooper, voice low and husky. "I'll have a whiskey. Maker's, please."

"You got it."

The bartender turns around and fetches the bottle of Maker's Mark from the liquor stock. She brings it to the bar, flips a clean glass up from under the bar top, and pours Cooper two fingers of whiskey. She asks Leeann if she's good, then leaves the women alone again.

"You're determined to torture yourself about this all night, aren't you?" Leeann says to Cooper.

"I didn't ask you to watch," Cooper says.

Leeann pauses and pulls on her beer. "I don't see what the point is in getting all worked up about something that might happen one day. Because it might not happen. And even if it does, it isn't going on right now, so why be upset in advance?"

"Is this your way of comforting me? Because if it is, it's not working."

"Smith and Christa have no idea how you feel, do they?"

"How I feel about what? About the possibility of them coupling up with people? No."

"Well, I find that pretty damn screwed up, considering how close you are," Leeann says. "You should talk to them about it. Clearly, trying to handle it by yourself isn't working too good."

"So you're moving on from comfort and giving advice now," says Cooper, sipping on her drink.

"They deserve a chance to put your mind at ease, is all I'm saying."

"They can't. They can't promise me anything, and I don't have a right asking them to."

Leeann's quiet for a beat. "It's not so bad, you know."

"What?"

"Being on your own. Because that's the other thing you're afraid of, isn't it? Not having anybody you're close to, the way you are with your family, ever again."

Cooper doesn't answer. She's lived here four years, and Leeann is the only person she can call a friend. And they don't spend a whole lot of time together. Cooper spends most of her free time with Christa and Smith, but she still isn't independently connected to any of their friends, not that they have many. People are nice enough when she fixes their cars or when they see her at Bad Moon, but friendliness hasn't grown into friendship.

"How old are you?" Leeann asks even though she knows.

"Thirty," says Cooper and sips her whiskey.

"Thirty years old and you act like you'll never make another friend as long as you live. I know the booze is making it worse, but damn, Cooper. Don't be so pessimistic."

"What friend am I going to make in Cody who doesn't hold me at arm's length because she's married? God knows I'm not going to meet another person who's single for life in this town, that's for sure."

"Hey, I'm single," Leeann says. "I've been single three years already. And I'm older than you."

"You're single because you're gay in a town full of straight people. Not because you got a problem with romantic relationships. Which means you aren't going to be single forever."

"I don't have a problem with being single either. If I did, I'd move to Cheyenne or Billings or fucking Seattle. Would I like another girlfriend someday? Sure. But romance isn't more important to me than my life here. It's not more important than my work and my home, this land. I would never leave Wyoming country for a woman. And what I'm trying to tell you is your family could feel that way about you. I wouldn't be surprised if they did."

Leeann finishes her beer and flags the bartender for another.

"What a person says when she's single don't mean shit," says Cooper as she lifts her glass to her lips. "Falling in love changes you. Changes everything. Makes people unrecognizable. And that's one reason why I won't talk to Christa or Smith about this bullshit. They could tell me one thing now and mean it, but if either one of them meets somebody, all bets are off."

"I think you're exaggerating," Leeann says, starting on her second beer. "And generalizing. Falling in love is not that dramatic for everybody. Some people never quit acting like they're in Goddamn high school, I'll give you that, but it is possible to be levelheaded and involved with somebody at the same time. Promise."

Cooper's whiskey is almost gone, the last of it lingering at the bottom of the glass. She's drunk now but not drunk enough. All her worry's going soft in her mind, blurring out of focus, and she feels a little better than she did before.

"I don't know how you do it," she says.

"What?"

"Live here. In Cody."

"It's a good town. Far as towns go."

"People look at you different. Treat you different. Like you're an outsider, even though you've lived here for six years. They do it to me, too, and I'm fucking sick of it. I'm not even gay. They just think I am."

"It's a damn shame you're not, let me tell you."

Cooper gives her a look. "Yeah, well. If I have a sudden lesbian awakening one day, you'll be the first person I call." She finishes off her whiskey and knocks the glass onto the bar top.

Leeann breaks out a pack of cigarettes and an old Zippo. She lights up and tucks the lighter back into her breast pocket, leaving the pack on the bar in front of her. She hunches forward, both elbows on the bar top, and glances toward the bartender to see if she's going to get told off for smoking inside. The bartender doesn't seem to care.

Leeann offers the cigarette to Cooper. "Want a drag?"

Cooper takes one drag and gives the cigarette back. "Seriously," she says after a long pause. "You could have lesbian friends, a lesbian community, be surrounded by straight people who treat you like one of them. That's all in addition to romance you don't have to drive an hour or more to find. Why wouldn't you choose that instead of this?"

"Well, first of all, there is no such thing as a straight person who treats gays the same as straights," Leeann says. "And second, I already told you—I love living here. I got a good job, I make good money, I got my own house and two acres and my shop all set up. I got fucking Yellowstone in my county. I don't need everybody here to like me or approve of me to be happy with my life."

Cooper looks at her. "I don't either. But that's not the point."

Leeann turns her head to make eye contact, the slightest of smiles on her face. "No, it's not. So ask me the real question."

Cooper stares at the other woman, feeling transparent and hating it. She faces the bar again and drinks. Leeann does the same.

Cooper has never wanted a lover. She's never had a crush. She's never seriously dated anybody because she's never been interested. All she's ever wanted is a few good friends, Christa, and Smith. She could live with her sister for the rest of her life and be happy—and sometimes, she daydreams about Smith moving in with them for good. She imagines a bigger house somewhere, maybe on

Smith's land, and the three of them together—until they're old, until they drop dead one by one. She's been following them her whole life, from Casper where she grew up to Laramie where Christa went to college, then to Cody after Smith settled down here. She's wondered before if they would follow her or if she's on the wrong side of a one-sided commitment.

Two more people trickle out of the Silver Dollar, leaving one man at the bar besides Cooper and Leeann. Closing time is coming up soon. Cooper's probably too drunk to drive, but she's got a key to Smith's saloon where she can sleep on the couch in his office.

"I'm worried about Smith." Cooper signals to the bartender, who comes over and pours her a shot of whiskey at Cooper's request.

"Something wrong with him?"

"He's unhappy—ever since he retired. I feel like he's holding himself back, like he still hasn't moved on from the rodeo."

"Why did he retire?"

Cooper glances at her. "Personal reasons."

"Well. If he's not happy with the way his life's going, he can do something about it. He's a grown man. It sure as hell isn't your job to do it for him." Leeann takes a long drink, cigarette tucked between two fingers on the bar.

Cooper throws back her shot, body warm with it. She gets an impulse to call her cousin, but she won't do it when she's feeling like this. He would know something's wrong, hear it in her voice. They know each other too well to get away with lies.

"So, you need a ride home?" Leeann asks, turning toward Cooper. "Because I can't let you drive anywhere."

Cooper weighs the temptation of sleeping in her own bed against the possibility of Christa being awake to see her drunk, the convenience of walking over to Smith's saloon to crash in his office against the consequence of having to explain herself in the morning. Comfort wins.

"Yeah, I guess you can take me home."

"All right," says Leeann, raising her hand at the bartender for her bill.

*

Monday evening, after her last dance class, Christa heads over to the Wild Horse Cafe to pick up dinner. The Wild Horse Cafe N' Gift Shop is a small diner on Highway 14, across from the rodeo grounds. The cafe's name is painted in white capital letters above the overhanging patio roof, and the wooden hitching rails are painted brick red to match the building front. A sign advertising the cafe stands in the grass before the dirt parking lot, paired with a wagon wheel and a model pinto horse reared up on its hind legs next to a cowboy figure. The Stampede Park stadium is in clear view on the other side of the road, and on summer nights like this one, cafe patrons can hear the rodeo as they get in and out of their vehicles. Christa hears it, on her way inside—the announcer over the loudspeaker, the cheering crowd.

The restaurant's interior looks like somebody's grandmother decorated. Mismatched knickknacks are everywhere, including an assortment of dolls. Framed prints of horse paintings hang on the walls, and fake plants sprawl across the wall-length shelf above the front door. There are lace curtains in the window and another wagon wheel set against the base of the hostess podium.

To the right of the entrance, in the tiled section of the restaurant, an open counter fronts the kitchen, allowing customers to see some of the cook staff and servers. A white board hung below the counter lists the daily specials. Near the counter and next to a pair of refrigerators, a glass display case is full of pies and raw fruit and gallon jugs of juice and water. There aren't many tables, three of them already taken for dinner, and at the unoccupied ones, red plastic glasses stand flipped onto their rims. The carpet is a dark blue-green, the walls painted beige.

Meredith, one of the cafe owners, sits behind the hostess podium. She stands up after Christa comes in, putting her mug on the podium.

"Well, hey there, Christa," she says, face crinkling with a warm smile.

"Hi, Meredith." Christa smiles back.

"Are you dining alone tonight?"

"Actually, I'm ordering to go."

"Do you need to see a menu?"

"Sure, why not."

Meredith hands Christa a menu: four printed pages on white paper stapled together, already turned to the dinner section on the last page.

Christa looks it over and orders the fried chicken with mashed potatoes, corn, and side salads for herself and Cooper. She pays the bill and goes outside to wait for the food. Sitting in one of the chairs on the cafe's covered porch, she watches the highway and the stadium, the night sky open and clear above the rodeo lights. Not many vehicles pass by on the road even though it's the main drag cutting through Cody. September through May, it's dead quiet out here. That's one thing she didn't anticipate before she moved to Park County—how quiet it is everywhere, all the time. Only birdsong breaks the silence outside of town. She's lived in Wyoming all of her life, but she grew up in cities. Casper, the Boones' hometown, has about sixty thousand people in it. Laramie, where she went to college, has half as many. They may not be Seattle or Portland, but compared to Cody, population 9800, they were noisy.

A truck pulls into the lot, headlights flashing in Christa's eyes as it turns into an empty space. Two men get out and approach the cafe entrance. She checks the time on her cell phone and figures she has another five minutes to her wait.

"Joy?"

Christa looks up and sees Buck from the party, standing there with another guy who's about to pull open the door. She freezes.

"I'll be damned, it is you," Buck says, too pleased for her comfort.

Buck's friend glances from Christa to Buck and says, "I'm going in and gettin' a table."

He disappears inside, leaving Christa alone with Buck.

"So you do live around here," Buck says to her, putting his hands on his hips.

She feels the same way she did the night she met him—unsettled, the fine hairs on the back of her neck bristling. She doesn't want him knowing where she lives. She doesn't like being alone with him, even here, within other people's earshot.

"Why aren't you over there?" Christa asks after an awkward pause, glancing at the stadium on the other side of the highway. "I thought you said you were in town for the rodeo."

"Well, I am, but not many guys ride every single night of the week. At least not the out-of-towners."

She doesn't know what to say, so she gives him a tight smile without speaking.

"You waiting for someone?" he says, glancing at the parking lot.

"I ordered something to-go," she replies, checking the time on her phone again. She should probably see if her order's ready, but that would require getting past him.

"Your boyfriend waiting at home?"

He asks the question in a gentle, prodding tone any man would use to find out whether a woman he just met is available. So far, he hasn't displayed any objectively questionable behavior, but Christa's got a bad feeling about him.

"Not exactly," she says, thinking of her sister.

"Does that mean I can ask you out?"

Christa doesn't know how to reject him politely, so she stands up. "I better see if my food's ready."

She goes inside, Buck following, and sure enough, there are plastic bags packed with Styrofoam cartons on one of the tables behind the hostess podium. Meredith gets up from her chair again to give Christa the bags.

"There you go, honey," she says. "You and Cooper enjoy."

"Have a good night, Meredith." Christa's aware of Buck still standing somewhere behind her. When she turns around, he's got his fingers in his hip pockets. "Good luck at the rodeo," she tells him.

"Thanks," he says. "Good seeing you again."

Christa smiles and exits the restaurant, clutching one bag of food in each hand. She walks fast to her RAV4, puts the food on the floor of the passenger side, checks the cafe door as she rounds the SUV to the driver's side, starts the engine, and peels out of the parking lot onto the highway.

The Cody Nite Rodeo has another six weeks before it ends with the summer. If Buck stays in town that long, she has no idea how she's going to avoid him.

*

Smith, Cooper, and Christa drive up to Powell for the annual Park County Fair on Saturday, the three of them snug on the bench seat in Smith's truck. Powell's only twenty or thirty minutes northeast of Cody, depending upon how fast you drive, and they all spend time there, Christa most of all because she teaches dance at the college. Sometimes, Smith or Cooper will go up alone, just to get out of Cody, hang out in a different bar than the usual. Powell is smaller than Cody by about three thousand people, but there's always a big turnout for the county fair. People come from all over western Wyoming and Montana, and tourists passing through the state on road trips stop too.

The Park County Fair has cowboy country character, thanks to the livestock showmanship contests that take place in the mornings before the fair's main attractions open in the afternoon. Most of these contests are youth only, with a few open-class competitions that include adult farmers and ranchers from all over. Contestants show their beef cattle, dairy cows, pigs, lambs, sheep, chickens, rabbits, and goats, and Saturday afternoon, people can buy some of the animals at the youth livestock sale.

The arts and crafts exhibits feature pieces by both adults and kids, everything from landscape paintings to third-grade drawings to needle work to leather and metal.

Judges award ribbons—first, second, and third in each category divided by age range and medium. Smith follows Cooper and Christa to the tent where they find a three-foot-tall, wrought iron doe with a blue ribbon tied around the neck. Leeann's entry.

Each night, the fair has a different main attraction: pig mud wrestling, demolition derby, medieval knights jousting on horseback, a country musician's concert, and a motor cross competition. Chuck wagon races and figure eight racing happen every evening, and horseshoe pitching contests are Friday and Saturday night only.

One of the cousins' favorite things to do at the fair is to see who can hit the most targets at the shooting gallery. They've been around guns since childhood and go shooting with the real articles on Smith's land, so it's always a tight competition at the fair. When they arrive at the gallery, only two of the six stalls are occupied, so they pay the booth man and line up next to one another in three of the available stalls, taking up the toy guns with the same stance and posture they've each used since they were barely tall enough to aim over the booth front. The plastic guns resemble short, small rifles. The stationary targets are staggered across four stacked rows at about a yard's distance, and each target is worth five points redeemable at the big prize booth. A shooter is only given one round per target in her section, so if she misses a target or uses more than one round to hit a target, a perfect score is impossible.

"All right, now," says Smith, aiming at his first target. "Get ready to lose gracefully."

Cooper snorts and gives her sister a skeptical look. Christa smiles and prepares for her own shot.

The metal targets snap backward and collapse as the cork rounds ping against them, the chorus of the three shooters' landing hits loud enough to startle a toddler in a stroller wheeled past the booth. The cousins take out whole rows in rapid-fire shots, each of them not to be outdone by the others, and pause together when only a handful of targets remain, most of them on the top row.

Smith examines Cooper and Christa's sections. "We oughta come back after we've had a few beers."

"Why?" says Cooper. "So I can prove once again I'm the best drunk shot?"

"When has that been proven?"

"Are you kidding?" Cooper gawps at Christa, then back at Smith. "Only every time we've decided to shoot shit after one too many beers on the land. And that's in the dark, usually."

"I have no memory of you winning the last drunk shoot, and it wasn't even that long ago."

"Then your memory sucks. I won. I always win. Tell him, Christa."

"I think she's right, Smith," Christa says. "But you might've won a few times."

Smith turns to face his remaining targets again. "Well, that's it, then. Tonight, after the fair, we're going to my place with a case of Coors, and we're doing best two out of three with the Henry's."

"You're on," says Cooper.

"Guys, it's going to be late by the time we leave here," says Christa, not quite whining.

"It's a Saturday night. You can sleep in tomorrow."

Smith fires his toy gun and hits one of his top row targets, then sets his sight on the next one over. Christa and Cooper resume their own shooting, now taking their time along with Smith. When they're all out of rounds, Christa has two targets left, Cooper has one, Smith zero.

He puts his gun on the counter and turns to his cousins. "You two can split my tickets at the prize booth, unless you want me to pick something out for you."

"Is that your idea of winning gracefully?" Christa says, more playful than sarcastic.

"You just wait 'til I kick your ass later at the real thing," Cooper tells him.

They collect their prize tickets from the booth operator, handfuls of them, and move on.

They get on the Ferris wheel and admire the fairgrounds and the town sprawled out below them, the dark and empty land stretching far beyond Powell's edges. They go one round in the bumper cars, picking on one another more than anyone else. They ride the small roller coaster twice because it's Cooper's favorite. Cooper and Christa watch as Smith rings the bell on the high striker, swinging the mallet the same way he does an axe when he chops wood. They visit the livestock pens and spend some time on the dance floor at the smaller live music stage, Smith pairing up with each of his cousins for one song. He whirls them around, moving his feet in an easy combination of steps he learned in high school for his prom, pretending not to notice the women who eye him from the grass.

At eight o'clock, they head over to the food stands for dinner. The sisters buy hotdogs and large lemonades and split a pretzel, and Smith orders two boats of fries with his bacon cheeseburger because Cooper and Christa always pick at his fries when they don't have their own. They sit at one of the many picnic tables in the dining area, Smith on one side of the table and Cooper and Christa on the other. A few people who pass by wave at Smith, and he nods with the slightest smile of acknowledgment. Some small-time local band plays on the stage in the distance, a song they've heard in a couple different bars here in Powell. When they've eaten their dinner, Cooper gets her own beer, and Christa buys a bag of kettle corn. The cousins hang out at their table a while longer, in no hurry to move.

"I ran into that guy again," Christa says. "From the party."

"Where?" says Cooper.

"Wild Horse. The night I picked up dinner there."

"Did he ask you out?" says Smith, sipping on his cold, overpriced beer.

"I didn't really give him the chance... But I think he wanted to."

"What'd he say his name was?" Cooper asks.

"Buck. I told him my name is Joy."

Cooper smiles. "You used your middle name? Why?"

"I wasn't going to give him my first name and make it easy for him to ask about me. He's in the rodeo. Which means he's going to be in town for a few more weeks, and that's plenty of time for him to look for me if he wants to. I hope to God we don't run into each other again..."

"Hell, Christa, if you run into him again, just tell him you're not interested in a rodeo fling," Smith says. "Riders hear that from women on the road all the time."

"Was he a jerk to you?" Cooper asks her sister, turning her head to Christa.

"No. But he gives me a bad feeling. I thought maybe it was because I was a little drunk when I met him at the party, but I didn't feel any better when I saw him at Wild Horse."

"Well, I wouldn't worry about him. He doesn't know your first or last name, and in all likelihood, he's going to find himself a buckle bunny who actually wants to screw him and forget all about you."

Cooper bumps her shoulder into Christa's and plucks a couple fries from their boat.

"You wanna go soon?" Smith says, crumpling up the napkin he just used to wipe his mouth and dropping it on his tray. He checks his watch.

"Yeah," says Cooper. "I want one last ride on the roller coaster, then we can cash in these tickets and go."

"Are we still drunk shooting at Smith's place?" Christa asks.

"Hell, yeah, we are."

"You don't have to, Christa," says Smith.

"Oh, believe me, I'm not," Christa says. "Somebody has to make sure you two don't shoot the dog or each other."

Smith shifts his eyes to the right as he pulls on his beer and sees a woman standing several paces away, watching him.

He stands up and takes his tray as a pretense, slides the trash into the nearest garbage can, and leaves the tray on the shelf. He pauses by the can, looking at the woman, who continues to watch him.

Jordan Lange wears her long dark hair swept back in a ponytail. She stares at him with bright eyes the color of coffee grounds, eyes shaped like half-moons rimmed with black eyeliner. The long fringe on her chocolate-brown suede jacket trembles along the outer seams of the sleeves, and a pair of soft, loose pants billows around her legs in the breeze. Her tattoos are hidden under her clothes, but Smith still remembers them: the moon cycle arching above her shoulder blades, just below the base of her neck; a quote written in Shoshone under her left collarbone; a smiling black bear on the inside of her right forearm. He has traced those shapes on her light-brown skin, kissed the words he can't read and the full moon in its perfect circle, let it disappear again behind a sheet of black hair.

Smith goes to her, taking his time, meeting her in the open grass before the picnic tables.

"Hey, stranger," she says with a smile.

"Hey," says Smith. "It's good to see you."

"Is it?"

He pauses, eyes resting on her, allowing her to see through him the way she always did. "Yeah. It is."

Her smile deepens. "It's good to see you too."

"Are you here alone?"

"No. My friends are picking out prizes or something. We're about to leave. We're going to go drink at my place."

Smith nods. He doesn't know what to say to her; it's been so long since they talked for more than five minutes. With anyone other than Cooper or Christa, he's a man of few words. Jordan is the closest thing he has to a friend in town though they haven't spent much time together in the last two and a half years.

"Are your cousins well?" Jordan asks after letting the silence stretch a little too long.

"Yeah. They're good. How's work?"

"I've been spending a lot of time on the road. I've been up in Billings every month since March, I think, for a week at a time. But I've started getting some people who come to Cody just to see me, from Cheyenne and Sheridan. So, that's pretty cool."

"You still have clients on the rez?"

"Of course."

Jordan is half-Shoshone, with a white father who disappeared from her life after her parents divorced. Her mother still lives on the Wind River Reservation where Jordan was raised and where she returns many times a year. "Lange" is her mother's English surname, the family's Shoshone name a secret Jordan keeps from whites.

She's a tattoo artist with her own high-end ink parlor in town, a woman with a fine art degree who got into tattooing to make a steady living. In addition to working at her shop, she travels around western Wyoming and southern Montana, visiting other tattoo shops as a guest inker, and sells her drawings online for supplemental income.

Smith met her six years ago when he was in town for the Stampede Rodeo, the summer before he retired and moved to Cody. They had a weeklong fling and didn't see each other or speak again until a year later when he bought his piece of land in Park County and opened the Bad Moon Saloon in town. They had an on-again, off-again sexual relationship for a few months during Smith's first year as a resident and stopped for good because he didn't want romance. They stayed friends, and Jordan married some dude, then divorced him earlier this year. They didn't speak to each other much during her two-year marriage because their friendship made her ex-husband jealous, and they've been slow to spend time together or talk since the split.

"Listen," says Jordan, taking a step closer to Smith. She sticks her fingers into her front pockets, hunching her shoulders up. "I've been thinking about you. I've wanted to call you or drop by the saloon, but I didn't know if you would want to talk to me again. I miss you."

"I'm always willing to talk to you," he says. "But if you're asking me on a date..."

"I'm not asking you on a date."

Smith stares at her, silent and skeptical.

"I'm not looking for a boyfriend," says Jordan. "I'd like to be your friend, Smith, that's all. We were good at friendship. Weren't we?"

"Yeah. I guess we were."

"So—do you want to get a drink sometime? Or coffee?"

"How about you come to the saloon one night, and we'll go someplace?"

She smiles. "Deal."

Smith nods. "I better let you get back to your friends. My cousins are waiting."

"I'll see you soon," Jordan says.

They turn away from each other and go two different directions, Smith now seeing Cooper and Christa watching him from their picnic table. When he reaches them, nobody speaks for a beat as he sits next to Cooper on the table with his feet on the seat beside hers. He drinks the last few drops of beer out of the bottle and dangles it between his knees. The air feels cool and pleasant against his skin, the county fair lights shining behind them.

"She want a rebound man?" Cooper says.

"No. She wants to be friends again."

"I always liked her," says Christa.

"Me too."

The cousins make the drive back to Smith's land, passing through the pitch-black night in between towns, cutting through Cody and leaving it behind again. They don't talk the whole way, listening to one of the Americana mix tapes Smith keeps in his truck—songs they know all the words to because they've heard them a thousand times. They reach the boundary of Smith's land and roll through the only entrance in the fence, past the No Trespassing sign, their headlights the only interruption of darkness for the ten minutes it takes them to arrive at Smith's campsite.

Smith starts a fire in the firepit while Christa dumps a bag of ice and half the case of beer they picked up into Smith's portable icebox. Cooper digs the Henry rifles out of the old wooden trunk under Smith's bed and brings them outside, along with a box of ammo. Smith empties his recycling bin of the empty beer cans and bottles and arranges them at a fair distance from the campfire. Christa curls up in one of the beach chairs by the fire, wrapped in a blanket with her feet on the seat, and prepares to watch over Smith and Cooper as they shoot. She has her cousin's old wireless radio near the firepit, tuned to their favorite country station, and the dog lies next to her chair, watching Smith and Cooper too.

The beer cans and bottles explode into clouds of white smoke, the sounds of the gunshots echoing throughout the wide and silent plain amidst the noise of glass shattering. After a few more drinks, Smith and Cooper holler after every target they hit, raising their voices when they talk. They lie on their bellies like soldiers in training, side by side in the dirt, trying to make each other laugh before each shot, trying to make each other miss. Sometimes they succeed: Cooper bursts into a loud laugh as she fires a shot that brushes past her target and knocks it over; Smith sniggers and buries his face in his arm at something she says just before he makes a shot so off he'd be embarrassed if he was sober.

When he nails one of the more distant cans he could barely see, Smith gets on his feet and raises his rifle above his head in one hand, triumphant. Cooper takes a shot from beside the beer cooler, standing and squinting into the darkness at what she thinks is a can glinting in the starlight. At the metallic sound of the bullet shredding the can, she lowers her rifle with a smug grin and picks another Coors out of the cooler.

Once all their targets are conquered or disappeared, they put down their rifles, and Cooper jumps onto Smith's back. He carries her around the campfire in a wide circle, his arms hooked under her legs where they encircle his hips, both of them too drunk to see straight. Christa plays at being a rodeo host and comments on her sister's ride as if Smith is a bull or a horse.

"That's it! Eight seconds, ladies and gentlemen, it's all over! Boone is the new Park County all-around champion!"

Cooper thrusts both her hands in the air above her, and Smith sinks to the ground with her still on his back. They sprawl apart, and Christa shakes her head at them, smiling.

When dawn begins to break, turning the eastern sky a milky, starless blue, Smith wakes up outside on his bedroll with the dog warming his left side, no memory of how he set himself up there. The camper door is shut, and he gets up to go inside, looking for his cousins. He finds them asleep in his bed, heads turned toward each other, Cooper's left arm tangled with Christa's right. He smiles to himself, then goes back outside to his bedroll on the ground and passes back into sleep until the sun is too bright for him to stay there.

*

The Shoshone National Forest stands between Cody and Yellowstone, stretching from Wyoming's northern border as far as South Pass City in Fremont County. The road there from Cody cuts through flat plains before climbing into the mountains of the forest. Smith winds through the fir and spruce trees in his old pickup, careful on the switchbacks through Dead Indian Pass, taking the time to slow down and peer through his window at the Absaroka Range spread out in the distance. He drives through a long green valley, listening to Waylon Jennings and trying not to feel wistful.

He meets John Henry at Painter Outpost, an RV park and campground over an hour northwest of Cody, deep in the Shoshone woods. They rent one of the dry cabins for one night, parking their pickup trucks right outside of it and dumping what little they brought with them inside. The outpost has a convenience store, gift shop, and restaurant only open during the summer. There are other people there, campers and RVers and two other parties renting cabins, but Painter Outpost is the kind of place Smith can be sure nobody will recognize him from Cody or ask him questions about what he's doing, where he's going, and where he's from. Most of the guests are gone when he and John Henry arrive, their tents and RVs left behind while they spend the daylight hours hiking, horseback riding, kayaking in the nearby river, fishing, and ATVing. The campground is quiet in the late afternoon, nothing but the gentle buzz of insects breaking the silence as Smith and John Henry walk down the road away from it.

"Do your cousins know you're here?"

Smith pauses before saying, "No."

"They know about the other night?"

"Nope."

"You going to tell them?"

"Probably."

"I could've sworn they knew about you."

"They know."

"So why haven't you told them about us?"

"Because when I do, they'll probably think I'm a dumbass."

John Henry smiles, his hands in his hip pockets. "A dumbass for foolin' around with me?"

"For foolin' around with a guy from my past who's got a girlfriend waiting for him back home."

The two men fall silent, passing through the trees.

"If it's such a bad idea, why are we here?"

"I like a good lay."

John Henry shoves him playfully.

"Don't pretend you had a better reason for agreeing to meet me."

Once the sky starts to dim, they turn back, arriving at the outpost's little restaurant called Clark's Fork and Spoon. They go inside and sit down, the only guests except for a pair of old women who must be RVers.

They order halibut burgers with French fries and bowls of beef stew and cold beer in bottles. They don't talk much, letting the restaurant's television fill the quiet of the room. The old women don't speak either, finished with their dinner and sipping on their drinks.

"How do you like Cody?" John Henry asks.

Smith glances at him, spooning the last of his stew out of the bowl. "It's all right."

"Did you realize it's nickname is 'Rodeo Capital of the World' when you moved in, or did that somehow escape you?"

Smith purses his lips at the sarcasm and doesn't answer.

"I just think it's interesting you quit the rodeo, swore off it forever like something that did you wrong, then decided to go live in a rodeo town. Either you love torturing yourself, or you don't want to leave the life behind as much as you claim."

Smith eyes him. "You realize the irony of you saying that to me, in our current situation."

John Henry grins. "Seeing you ain't torture."

"Exactly."

"So you admit you have a hard time letting go of the life you claim to hate."

"Never said I hated it."

The old women leave. Smith and John Henry finish their food and order more beer, drinking it just slow enough to close down the restaurant. The host looks bored and ready for bed, watching the TV from behind the counter toward the front of the room.

"Have you dated anyone since you left the rodeo?" asks John Henry.

Smith glances at him. "No."

"Why not?"

"Because I don't like being coupled up."

John Henry pauses, glancing away. "I guess I could tell you some kinda bullshit about meeting somebody special one day who changes your mind, but I don't think you want to hear it. And it's not my business anyway."

"You're right, it's not."

"You at least been getting laid regularly?"

"I get laid."

"I bet you had women showing up at that bar of yours like moths on a light bulb, your first year in business." John Henry smiles. "Smith Rose, the rodeo star. Twenty-seven years old, with the short haircut you used to have and the five-o'clock shadow. Good-looking single guy, with no ex-wives and no kids. Christ."

"You realize most of the women in Cody are married or old enough to be my grandmother, right?"

"Married women cheat, and being older ain't the same thing as being dead."

Smith shakes his head.

After a pause, John Henry says, "And the men?"

Smith blinks at him. "What about them?"

"You know what."

"If you're asking whether I've been hit on by a man in Cody, the answer is no. If you're asking whether I've screwed a man in Cody, the answer is no."

"You can't be the only guy in town who swings both ways. Or even just the one way. Cody's not that small."

"I'm not stupid enough to try finding out."

"So you travel for sex. It's the rodeo all over again."

"No, it's not."

John Henry pauses and considers Smith. "Yeah, I guess it isn't."

Walking the short distance from the restaurant to their cabin, they're almost uneasy together. They don't say a word or look at each other. They know what happens next—the sex is planned this time—but they're not tripping over themselves in a rush to get there. All their conversation and having dinner seem like pretense now, and maybe they're a little ashamed by the feeling.

When they reach the cabin doorstep, they don't go inside. Smith breaks out a cigarette from the pack he bought the day after their last encounter. He's not a regular smoker, but sometimes, smoking calms him. He hasn't had a cigarette out of this pack since the day he bought it. Now, he lights up. John Henry is a casual smoker, but he declines the pack when Smith offers it.

They stand outside for a while as Smith smokes. Nobody else is here as far as they can see. The moon is country bright, only a sliver of it missing, the sky sugarcoated with stars. Smith gazes at them as he takes a drag on his cigarette, thinking about Cooper and Christa and how the three of them lie in the bed of his truck some summer nights to look at the sky. He catches himself in a smile and smokes it away.

"Why did we quit talking?" he says to John Henry.

John Henry glances at him. "You mean when we quit fooling around?"

"Yeah. You can't blame it on me retiring. I stayed in the rodeo a whole year after we stopped."

"That's the way men do things in the circuit, isn't it?" John Henry says, searching the night sky. "You quit screwing and pretend you never knew each other, so nobody gets any ideas. You didn't stay buddies with every other rider you screwed, did you?"

"No. But you and I were friends. All that time we spent together—it wasn't just about sex. Was it?"

"Does it matter now?"

Smith pauses. He looks over his shoulder at John Henry, cigarette in his lips. "You must get some kind of satisfaction out of not answering questions."

"I'm following your lead for once."

Smith peers back into the darkness, at the silhouettes of treetops. He sucks on his cigarette, calmer than he was before.

"It was safer to quit talking," John Henry says. "I don't know what else to tell you."

Smith regards him but doesn't answer.

They stand there in silence until he finishes his cigarette.

When they go inside, they leave the lights off in the cabin. It's easier that way. They take off their boots and leave them near the door before moving toward the queen bed pushed against the left-hand wall opposite the bunk beds on the right. The smell of cigarette smoke on their clothes remains distinct through the mustiness of the cabin. They don't say a word because it feels too dangerous now, like they might back out of this if they do anything in this room that isn't sex.

They stand in darkness broken only by the moon's milky light filtering through the window, kissing until their bodies are flushed with arousal. There's no romance in it, and that's why Smith is here, doing this again. They touch like old friends, fuck like men who don't have a future together and no promises between them. They're doing this the same way they always have, without expectations or longing. It's safe in a way Smith has always wanted sex to be—caring and honest, more than sheer lust but less than whatever John Henry has with his girlfriend back home.

Smith breaks away from John Henry's mouth, starts kissing his neck. He breathes in the other man's scent, all that faded sawdust and earth, shivers when John Henry's hands slide under his shirt, up his back. They look at each other for an instant, exposed as they can never be in daylight, noses almost touching. Smith snaps open the first few buttons of John Henry's shirt and kisses his collarbone, his chest, smelling him as if, decades from now, the scent will be what he remembers about this night. Kisses him all the way down his belly, splitting buttons until he unbuckles John Henry's belt, unzips his jeans, springs him loose.

John Henry runs his hands through Smith's grown-out hair while Smith kneels there on the floorboards—and it's something he never did when they were last together, when Smith kept his hair short. But he does it now like he's always done it. Smith wants John Henry to remember the softness of his hair, how long it lasts in his fingers.

This time, the sex is slower. There's a kindness, without all the tension of their last meeting. A kindness that feels so much like friendship, it's like they're not attracted to each other at all, just having sex out of mutual loneliness, trying to get back what's long gone, trying to prove they still care.

"You all right?" John Henry says after his first few thrusts, petting Smith's side.

"Keep going," Smith says, almost whispering. He reaches behind him to find John Henry's hand and brings it to his hip.

They're quiet, so quiet the only sounds are the frogs singing outside, their own soft breathing, and the mattress creaking under them.

John Henry presses a kiss to the back of Smith's shoulder. Smith is surprised, but he juts his ass back into John Henry's groin even though he knows the kiss wasn't meant to be sexy. A well of loneliness opens in him, deep and wide, as he lies with his face in the pillow. John Henry reaches between his legs, hand gliding along Smith's inner thigh before stroking his cock. Smith lifts himself off the bed, on his hands and knees for a couple minutes, trying to block out the lonesome feeling and focus on John Henry pumping into him.

"Stop," he says.

John Henry stops, then pulls out of him.

Smith glances over his shoulder. "I want to lie on my back."

"Okay," John Henry says.

Smith lies down, spreads his legs, and cants up his hips.

John Henry gets near him, runs his hands over Smith's chest, then guides himself back inside him

Their eyes finally meet, the knot in Smith's gut only a little loosened. John Henry starts to fuck him again, calm and steady, missing Smith's prostate as much as he hits it. But Smith is in no hurry to orgasm. He wants this to last, the closeness, the sense that John Henry cares about him. He hasn't had sex with someone who cares in years, hasn't had a close male friend since he left the rodeo.

Is this the only way two men can connect? The only way they can be close?

John Henry plants his hand on Smith's chest, right over his heart. Smith watches him close his eyes, the moonlight splashed across his upper arm and back, beautiful black skin drawn taut over rippling muscle. He wishes there was a mirror opposite the foot of the bed so he could see John Henry's backside, those powerful thighs, sculpted on bulls and broncos, still going strong as John Henry kneels between Smith's legs.

John Henry looks at him again, moves his hand off Smith's chest onto the mattress, and leans over him. Smith scoops his hips up and wraps his legs around John

Henry, pulling him in deeper, changing the angle of John Henry's thrusts. Now, John Henry hits the sweet spot every time, and Smith inhales a sharp, hissing breath. John Henry makes a low, clipped sound in the back of his throat, hanging his head between his shoulders. John Henry's breath is hot on Smith's face and heat pools just above his groin.

"You son of a bitch," John Henry gasps, humping him with a little more force now.

Smith wants to ask what he's done, but it feels wrong to speak.

John Henry sets his elbows on either side of Smith and grabs his face in both hands, touching his forehead to Smith's. They're close enough to kiss, but they don't, lips parted with silent cries. Smith grips John Henry's ass with both hands and pulls him in as John Henry pushes.

"Oh, fuck," John Henry whispers.

He's barely pulling out of Smith now, his thrusts short as Smith keeps him buried. Smith clenches his ass around John Henry's cock every other second, panting as his hip joints tingle and the heat spreads through his groin.

"So close," John Henry says.

"Me too," says Smith, voice raspy and paper-thin.

They come within seconds of each other, mouths open with shuddering breaths. Smith squeezes John Henry's ass, a whimper dying in his throat before it can escape, and John Henry ruts against him, erratic and needy, until Smith wants to shrink away from him up the bed because he can't take it. Everything in Smith's body seizes up, a scream frozen in his chest, his abs clenching until his orgasm ends. John Henry drops his head into Smith's neck, pumping into him until he's squeezed every last drop of pleasure out of his climax.

When they finally stop, they don't speak, trying to catch their breath. Smith rests his hands on John Henry's lower back. John Henry lays his head on Smith's shoulder, facing away from Smith's neck. The world outside is quiet, the air inside their cabin thick.

Smith lies there under the weight of his old friend and tries to imagine what life would be like if he had this for more than a few weeks—a sexual friendship with someone he cares about, one which never approaches romance because his friend is as happy without it as Smith is. He has no idea what would happen if John Henry were single and lived in Cody, and they were both out as bisexual, if John Henry would want them to be a couple and quit the sex or the friendship once Smith turned him down, or if something else would unfold. What if John Henry married his girlfriend and moved to Cody with her and she gave them her blessing to fool around? Smith wouldn't mind that at all. Wouldn't mind having that with someone other than John Henry, man or woman.

If people in town knew he was thinking it, they'd say he's nuts. John Henry probably would too.

Smith doesn't move when John Henry rolls off him and throws away the condom. Doesn't move when John Henry gets back into the bed, lying next to him in the too-little space Smith leaves on his left. John Henry turns his back on Smith, settling on his side. They don't speak.

After a minute or two, Smith turns toward John Henry and throws his arm over him. He passes out quick.

*

Christa sits on the floor with her back to the mirrors, watching as her three- and four-year-olds practice the ballet routine they've been working on for the last few weeks. Tonight, she's at the Rocky Mountain School until eight o'clock. Her summer schedule is lighter than the rest of the year, without having to teach at Northwest College and with fewer classes in Cody. Most of her summer students are under the age of ten, registered by mothers who want them out of the house for at least a little while during their time off from school. Some of the girls are students during the fall and spring sessions, too, and others are summer-only dancers.

Christa calls out praise and instruction as she scans the twelve girls during their performance, voice raised over the music. With kids this young, she cares less about perfect form and execution and more about basic understanding of the steps. She wants to see each student remember every part of the routine after practicing it for three or four weeks. Whenever she teaches preschoolers, she is aware some of them will potentially become long-term students of hers—the kind of dancers who, like Christa herself, start early in life and finish high school having become skilled enough to pursue professional dance if they wish. She was four years old when she started. Her parents enrolled Cooper in dance, too, but it didn't stick. The memory of her now short-haired, brawny, auto mechanic sister in a leotard and tights at age eight makes Christa almost laugh.

She turns off the music as the girls hold their finishing position and claps for them.

"Good job, everybody," she says. "Very good."

She turns her head toward the classroom door at the sound of it opening. A man wearing a uniform shirt tucked into his jeans and an Accents Floral hat comes into the room, carrying a box and a clipboard.

"Christa Boone?" he says.

"That's me," she says, glancing from his face to the long, narrow box cradled in his arm.

He crosses the distance between them and offers her the box. "These are for you."

She takes it in both hands and lifts the lid to peer inside. Long-stemmed red roses.

The delivery man holds out a clipboard and pen. "Sign here, please."

Christa juggles the box into her left arm and signs the delivery confirmation sheet.

The man nods with a polite smile and turns to leave the classroom.

Christa, forgetting she has twelve little girls watching her, returns to her spot on the floor again and sits down. She sets the box in front of her, opens it, and takes out the bouquet. The girls gather around her, some of them dropping to their knees and others staying on their feet, ogling the roses with starry-eyed appreciation.

Christa picks the card out of the ribbon tying the wrapped stems. It reads:

Your real name is even prettier than your fake one.
Buck
806-682-1428

She feels a cold, hard weight sink into the pit of her stomach, like a stone.

"Is that from your boyfriend?" Erin Andrews asks.

"No," says Christa, her voice low and somber. "I don't have a boyfriend."

She holds the bouquet in the crook of her arm the way she used to hold the bouquets her parents gave her at the end of every dance recital in grade school, the way she held the bouquets Cooper gave her at the end of her college recitals. She doesn't know what else to do in front of her students, who eye the roses with a little envy and admiration.

"My mom only gets roses on Valentine's Day," says Judy James as if impressed a man likes Christa so much to give her flowers in July.

"Who gave them to you?" Lynn Darby asks.

Christa tries to get a hold of herself and shake off the unease. She shouldn't be upset in front of the girls. She can't explain this to them. "I don't know; he didn't sign his name. I guess I have a secret admirer."

A few of the girls coo while others smile at Christa and one another.

Christa sets the roses on the floor and stands up to close the class. The girls scatter in anticipation of their final exercise as she tells them to get in their lines. They stand in three rows of four, and Christa leads them in their cooldown: folding over at the waist and letting their arms hang limp; rising back up with a deep breath, reaching for the ceiling; and finally, sitting with their legs in butterfly pose, soles of their feet together. When she dismisses them, they leap up and bound out of the room to change into their street shoes and meet their parents.

Christa, who usually follows them into the hall and the school lobby right away, lingers in the classroom. She stands alone, staring at the roses at her feet with one hand pressed to her forehead. She lifts her eyes to look at herself in the mirror. How the hell did Buck find out her real name and where she works? He must've talked to someone in town who knows her or knows of her, someone who recognized her by the description he gave. Maybe he asked Meredith, that day at the Wild Horse

Cafe. She would tell him all about Christa, not knowing any better.

Christa steps out into the lobby to see her students off, going through the typical string of good-byes with them and their mothers. She hangs around until the last girl is gone and tells Marianne at the front desk she'll lock up. She goes back into her classroom, which is now vacant and too quiet for how bright the lights are. The roses are where she left them on the lacquered floor, deep red like a puddle of warm blood. She tosses the box into the big trash can, gathers up her bag and the roses, and switches off the lights before leaving the room.

The parking lot is deserted, silent except for the distant whirring of cars. Hers is the only vehicle in the lot, standing like a lone buffalo on the plain. She pauses halfway to her SUV, listening, surveying her surroundings—half afraid Buck is there, watching and waiting for the right moment to reveal himself. The trees lining the edge of the parking lot rustle in the breeze. The sky is a monochromatic wheel of purple shades, fading toward the horizon line where a thin peel of orange lingers like the slow-burning edge of the world. One star glimmers in the lavender haze.

Christa gets into her SUV and locks the doors. She puts the flowers on the passenger seat, starts the engine, and pulls out of the parking lot onto the road.

She checks her rearview mirror every other minute as she drives home. She doesn't see him.

*

It's after hours at Steel Saddle Automotive, and Cooper's alone in the garage. The office door is locked, the Open sign switched off, but one of the garage doors is still raised to let in the air and light. She's got the stereo tuned to the classic rock radio station and the volume turned up loud enough to fill the garage with Great White singing "House of Broken Love."

Her motorcycle is back on the bike lift. A bunch of her tools are set out on the nearby tray. She's replacing the tires today after finally receiving the brand-new ones she ordered from the motorcycle tire supplier Steel Saddle partners with. The new rims came in a week ago from a discount Triumph parts shop on eBay. Changing out the tires is easy enough but involves a lot of dismantling and reassembly. Because she's replacing both the tires and the rims, she gets to take off the old ones and toss them without removing the tires from the wheels. All she needs to worry about is putting the new tires on the new rims, then installing them on the bike. Once the new tires are on, she'll balance them.

The restoration job is almost finished. She repainted the bike's fuel tank, oil tank, and parts of the main frame, and re-chromed the fenders, headlight, and most of the original engine parts. Cooper chose to repaint the fuel tank in the original Alaskan white with Grenadier Red stripes edged in bronze down the top. The side cover and oil tank were repainted black. She replaced the battery, the fuel filter, the spark plugs, brake pads, hoses, shock absorbers, and the fuel line; cleaned the fuel valve, the carburetor, and chain; fixed the transmission; and rebuilt the engine with new seals and gaskets. She gave the bike a new seat only because she managed to find one online though the original seat was in decent condition.

Cooper has worked on plenty of motorcycles in the ten years she's been a mechanic, but she's never restored one, much less a classic like this Triumph. She bought the bike for two hundred bucks from a guy out in Ten Sleep who had a bunch of old motorcycles locked up in a storage shed on his property, motorcycles he'd been collecting since the '70s because he used to ride a lot. The Triumph had belonged to an ex-girlfriend of his and hasn't seen much road since the '80s. It caught Cooper's eye even though it didn't look like much, collecting dust in the shed. She bought it because she wanted a side project and figured maybe if the restoration turned out well, she could sell the bike and make a decent profit—but now she wants to keep it, wants to wander Wyoming and Montana on the back of it. All she needs is a helmet.

Cooper gazes out at the long driveway and sees a woman walking toward her, a familiar parked car in the lot behind her. Tallulah Pace, who goes by "Lou." She's wearing a button-down sundress in a small floral print, the hem falling a few inches above her knees. She looks like she got out of the shower and decided to let her strawberry-blonde hair air-dry without combing it. It's still damp and wavier than usual. The heels of her cowboy boots click on the concrete as she comes up the driveway, her necklace glinting in the sun.

Lou is thirty years old, like Cooper, and one of the few single women in town. She's never been married and has no children, and as far as Cooper knows, she hasn't had a romantic relationship in the four years Cooper's lived here. Cooper's always found that hard to understand because Lou's pretty and sweet and just the kind of woman in small-town Wyoming who marries young and usually has three kids by now. The dating pool is small in Cody, but there must be men who have asked Lou out during the last four years.

Lou smiles when she reaches the garage, crossing the door's threshold.

"Hey," Cooper says.

"Hi," says Lou. "I was hoping you'd still be here."

"Is something wrong with your car?"

"No. The car's fine."

Cooper blinks at her. She and Lou are friendly whenever they bump into each other or when Lou brings her car in for service, but they don't talk or spend time together socially. For a split second, she wonders if Lou came to talk about Smith. Maybe she's finally decided she wants to go out with him and came to ask Cooper to set it up. Cooper's lost count of how many times women have asked her and Christa to play matchmaker for them with Smith.

"Nobody else is here, right?" Lou says, glancing at the office and the lobby.

"Just us," Cooper replies. "What's going on?"

Lou stares at her boots and wipes her hands on her thighs, over the skirt of her dress. She starts to wring her hands a little bit and turns away from Cooper, taking a few steps away.

Cooper sets her hands on her hips, watching Lou's back and feeling more unsettled by the minute.

"This isn't easy for me, so I should probably spit it out." Lou turns back to face Cooper. "I really didn't want this to be weird, but I don't know how else to do it, so... I came to ask you if you want to go out some time. For coffee or a beer or dinner? It doesn't really matter what, I just— I wanted to ask. And I don't see you around town much, and when I do, it never feels like the right time."

Cooper stands there dumbfounded, silent for too long. "Are you asking me out on a date? Or are you trying to be friends?"

"I'm asking... I guess I'm asking you out on a date. If you want it to be a date. It doesn't have to be."

Cooper watches her, sees all that nervous energy in her body and the cautious hope in her eyes, registers Lou had to work up the courage to do this, and has no idea what to say.

"I'm not a lesbian" is the only thing that occurs to her.

Lou's face crumples. "Oh," she says, her voice small. She takes a step back, looking horrified. "I'm sorry."

She starts to flee, but Cooper follows and catches her by the wrist.

"Wait, wait, wait," Cooper says. "Hold on. You don't have to apologize. It's okay."

Lou looks afraid of her—or maybe afraid of Cooper telling the whole town.

Cooper lets go of her wrist. "I understand why you assumed I'm gay."

"I didn't mean to offend you," Lou says.

"You didn't offend me. I thought you were straight, so we're even on the wrong assumptions."

Lou averts her eyes. "I'm so embarrassed."

"Don't be. You were really brave to come here and ask me out. Most people wouldn't have the guts. I'm sorry I can't say yes."

Lou considers her with a mix of disappointment and disbelief. "So you're straight?"

"No. I'm not anything."

"What do you mean?"

"I mean, I'm not interested in people. Like that." Cooper's voice softens as she says it for the first time to someone who isn't Christa or Smith.

Lou pauses as if she's processing this information. "You've never wanted to date anyone?"

Cooper shakes her head. "No." She digs her hands into the hip pockets of her jumpsuit. "And I never have, not really. I guess you could count the one week I went out with Justin Berry, sophomore year of high school, but I never actually liked him."

Lou pushes a lock of hair behind her ear and takes a step forward. "So—you've never had a crush? You've never...been with anybody? I'm sorry. It's none of my business."

Cooper gives her a reassuring smile. "It's okay. No, I haven't had a crush. I've never wanted to get somebody into bed. I came close to trying a few times, just because I felt like I should, but I never went through with anything."

Lou looks at the floor. "Well, I feel like an idiot. You never gave me a sign you were interested in me, and I knew that but... I thought maybe you figured I was straight, and if I asked you out... *God*."

"You're not an idiot," says Cooper, studying the other woman in the light of the long day behind her. The sun is a deep golden color, sitting low in the sky, and it casts a halo along the edges of Lou's body, dusting her bare skin and her red hair with light. "Most people in Cody think I'm a lesbian. I don't know if it's a rumor people gossip about, but I know what I see in people's eyes. I can't blame them. The way I look—and I've never been on a date or hooked up with a guy since I moved here? It makes sense."

Lou wipes her hands down the skirt of her dress again, still hanging her head.

"I'm sorry I can't give you what you want," Cooper tells her. "I'm sure I'd be lucky to have you for a girlfriend. I can't imagine why you'd want to go out with me, of all people."

Lou peers at Cooper with shy eyes. "My sixth sense tells me you're a good person. And you're cool."

Cooper laughs. "I am?"

"Yeah, you are."

"Well, thank you. I got a feeling you're a good person too."

Lou smiles. "I guess I better go home. I'm sorry again, for putting you on the spot."

"Don't be."

Lou turns around and heads for her car.

Before she exits the garage, Cooper says, "Hey, Lou."

Lou stops and peers over her shoulder.

"I won't tell anybody."

"Thank you. I won't either."

Cooper nods. "If you want to get a drink sometime as friends, just ask."

Lou smiles at her and leaves.

Cooper watches her disappear, a bittersweet feeling washing through her.

*

Jordan comes in after hours, the way she used to—when he would sit her on the pool table and kiss her as the jukebox filled the whole saloon with slow Americana. Walks in like she belongs here as much as he does. And seeing her here again, Smith wonders why it took him this long to ask her to come back.

He's sitting on a bar stool, his back against the bar and one arm stretched along the edge. She doesn't sit down, just stands off to his left and smiles at him.

He smiles back, because he can't help it. "Hey."

"Hey. I'm following through on your invitation."

"I'm glad. Want a drink?"

"Not now."

He blinks at her in that owlish way of his, and she passes him on her way around the bar, her bootheels knocking on the floor. She stands behind the bar across from him, and Smith swivels on his stool to face her, sliding his glass in front of him.

Jordan flips a clean glass onto the bar top and fills it with ice and water, then drinks from it. He watches her, trying not to be obvious, admires the way the light moves in her straight black hair and the shape of her shoulders, the line of her arm, the way her jacket fringe quivers against her.

"What are you thinking about?" she asks, peering at him and bringing back the feeling she always gave him. Like she can see right into the deepest part of his soul and understand.

Smith pauses, dropping his gaze from her face. "A man."

"What kind of man?"

"The good kind." He lifts his glass to his lips and tastes the warm, familiar burn of his favorite whiskey.

Jordan's quiet for a moment, looking at him. "Is this man your friend? Or something else?"

"He's my friend. And something else too."

She pauses again, then says, "Are you in love with him?"

He meets her eyes and finds no judgment, jealousy, or disgust. Just earnest curiosity. "Why do you ask that?"

"Because you sound sad. Like you love something you can't have."

Smith thinks of the rodeo, of his glory days and the way they made him feel. It occurs to him, for the first time, that falling back into this two-step with John Henry might be about more than the man himself. Maybe his feelings toward him aren't the only old feelings he's chasing.

"I guess I love him. But I'm not in love with him."

"You sure?"

He gazes into her dark eyes, unguarded. "Yeah. Pretty sure."

"So—why are you sad?"

He blows out a breath and shakes his head. Takes another drink. "I miss him. I miss how things used to be."

"You mean all of it? Your old life?"

"Yeah. But there are a lot of things I'm glad I left behind. I retired for a reason. And the reason hasn't changed. I know it hasn't. I don't want to go back to that shit."

"What reason?"

He bites his lower lip, eyeing her as he hesitates, and she waits for him, the way women have been waiting for him all his life. His cousins included.

She already knows the reason. He sees it in her eyes. Maybe she knew all along.

"I got tired of hiding. Tired of being afraid someone would out me and destroy everything I was. Everything I built."

"So you destroyed it first."

"I didn't destroy my career. I pulled the plug. With my reputation intact."

He finishes off his whiskey, tipping his head back as he drains the glass.

"But Smith," she says. "Just because you retired, doesn't mean your secret's safe. Any guy in the circuit who knew could still tell. And if someone did, you would still take a hit to your reputation. Your legacy."

"I'm five years gone, Jordan. I'm old news. And none of those guys I screwed would tell because then they'd be ruined too. It wouldn't be one of them. It would be someone who saw something or heard something he wasn't supposed to. I was always careful as hell, but I got tired of being careful. I'm still tired of it."

It isn't until he says it that he realizes how he's been feeling.

"You've been hiding here the same way you did in the rodeo," Jordan says. "What's changed? Maybe you have less to lose, fewer chances of being found out. But you're keeping the secret, and it's still holding you back."

"So what am I supposed to do? Come out? Risk everything I got in this town?"

"You have this bar, which you don't love. And you have your cousins, who already know you. And you have a piece of land you can keep or sell, no matter what anyone in this town thinks. The only thing you have to lose is your image. And that hasn't made you happy in the last five years, has it?"

Smith doesn't know what to say, so he pushes his empty glass toward her. Jordan pours him another whiskey. She remembers what he likes, and he isn't surprised.

"Can I ask you something?" He hunches toward her with his elbows on the bar top.

"Of course."

"What'd you think when I first told you?"

"When you told me you're into men?"

He nods.

She gives a small shrug. "I was a little bit surprised because I had never seen any signs. But that's all."

"It didn't bother you? Knowing you'd been with a guy who's been with men?"

"Why would it bother me? It's not like you gave me some kind of disease. You didn't hurt me, cheat on me, leave me for someone else."

Smith sips on his drink and starts hankering for a cigarette. He's already loosening up—from the whiskey and Jordan's company—and he knows if he keeps drinking with her, he could end up telling her things he doesn't even know he ever felt. It was always like that with her. Comfortable and freeing. He's not used to being so open with people, and it scares him a little how she can draw things out of him.

Jordan finally pours herself a glass of red wine, and they let a silence settle between them like the first snow in pine woods. As easy as it is to talk to Jordan, it's just as easy to be silent with her.

"Not many women would be with a man, knowing he's attracted to men too," Smith says, thinking out loud.

"I didn't know you were when we were involved. But you could've told me then. I would've had the same reaction."

He looks at her in a kind of disbelief though he knows she isn't lying.

"Were you talking about other women, in the future? If you came out?"

"No. I was talking about you."

She's leaning on the bar now, bent at the waist with her elbows on the bar top. She glances at him over the rim of her glass as she drinks more wine.

"Who ended your marriage?" Smith asks.

"You sure know how to be direct when you want to be," Jordan replies, smiling. "I did."

"Why?"

She doesn't answer him at first, looking off to the side as she thinks. "I wasn't in love with my ex. And eventually, I realized he wasn't good for me. So I cut him loose."

"Why'd you marry him if you didn't love him?"

"I don't know. We didn't put a whole lot of thought into it. We were in Cheyenne together, and he just asked me out of nowhere. So we went to city hall and got married. One of those stupid things you do when you're young, I guess."

"You're not a reckless person. You must've cared about him a lot to say yes. Even if you didn't love him."

"Or I was lonely."

Smith tilts his head to the side in surprise. "Were you?"

She gives him a different kind of smile as if maybe she's embarrassed to admit she's capable of loneliness. She was twenty-six when she married her ex-husband, twenty-nine when she divorced him a year ago. But she has always seemed older than her age to Smith, possessing a maturity and wisdom he never has. In combination with her independence and free-spirited nature, her maturity and wisdom make it hard for Smith to believe she would marry a man she didn't love out of loneliness.

Jordan drinks more of her wine, straightens up. "Can I be honest with you right now?"

"I hope you're always honest with me."

"When you and I broke it off for the last time, it made me doubt I could end up in a long-term commitment with a man. I doubted I could find someone who was right for me in that way. I still doubt it. So when I married Brett, I didn't expect it to last forever. And when I left him, I wasn't that disappointed or upset our marriage hadn't worked out. I wanted to see what it felt like to be someone's wife. Now, I know."

Smith sits dumbstruck on his barstool, staring at Jordan with his whiskey forgotten between them. For a moment, he feels responsible for her low expectations in men, thinking it's his fault for not being the marrying kind. But he realizes there wasn't blame in her voice.

"Why would you have doubts about the right man being out there for you? Look at you. You're beautiful and kind and fun to be with. Smart, got a college degree and all. You make your own way in the world. You're a good person. The only way you'll grow old single is if you want it that way."

Jordan ducks her head at the stream of compliments, smiling with the blush of wine in her cheeks. After a long pause, she says, "I didn't say I felt unworthy or unwanted. I said I don't think there's a man out there who's so right for me, we can be happy together forever. Maybe I will get married again someday. But even if I do, I don't think it'll last. That's not necessarily a bad thing."

Smith watches her finish her wine and, after a beat, finishes his whiskey. Their empty glasses stand on the bar, and they stare at each other, a spark of attraction flashing through their eyes and disappearing back into memory.

"Think you'd ever marry a man?" she asks.

"Ha! Yeah, right, and we'd get the fucking local TV news station to cover the wedding. Ex-All-Around Rodeo Champ Smith Rose Gets Gay Married. Bonfire of his old title belts at the reception. Come toast marshmallows in the flames of his former glory."

Jordan laughs. "I didn't know you could be such a drama queen, Smith."

"Well, I've had two whiskeys, and that is the most ridiculous idea I've ever heard in my life. So consider what I just said sarcasm, not drama."

"I don't think it's a ridiculous idea."

And he can tell she means it.

"I don't want to get married. To a man or a woman."

"You're only thirty-two. You could meet someone who changes your mind."

"And you could meet someone who proves you wrong and stays married to you for fifty years."

"I didn't mean to be dismissive. It's fine if you don't ever sign a marriage license. I'm just saying, you could be with a man if you wanted. Not in secret. Out in the open as real partners. That's not ridiculous."

But the idea of living in Cody or any other town in Wyoming, shacked up with a man who everyone knows is his lover—might as well be the flat-earth conspiracy. He can't even imagine people knowing he's bisexual, let alone coexisting with them while he's got a boyfriend.

"How long are you going to let other people control your life, Smith?"

He looks at her and lets the question pierce him. He doesn't answer it.

She takes a step back from the bar, breaking the tension. She puts her hands on her hips. "I better get going."

Smith doesn't move, still leaning over the bar with his eyes fixed on her. "I missed you. Didn't know how much until now."

Jordan smiles, the light reaching her eyes. "I missed you too."

Smith bobs his head. "I know I probably don't deserve it, but I'm asking you to be my friend again. For real, this time. And if you say yes, I'll do my best to be the kind of friend you deserve."

She pauses, regarding him with a soft smile. "You deserve it."

"Is that a yes?"

She nods. "Yeah."

He smiles at her now, just a little. "I'm a whole lot better at being a friend than a boyfriend. I'll show you."

"All right."

She comes to his side of the bar, back out onto the floor, and he gets up from his seat to walk her to the door. The alcohol hits him once he's on his feet, like a warm wave washing over him. The multicolored string lights lining the walls look hazy now, her sheet of black hair even softer than it typically appears. He follows her until she stops in the doorway and turns to face him.

They gaze at each other in silence, close enough for Smith to feel her body heat. She's seeing something in him, some truth he's not trying to hide in this moment, and he lets her see it though he doesn't know what truth it is. He stares at her, aware of his loneliness skulking at the edges of his heart like a starving coyote, waiting for her to leave him.

Whatever she sees, she keeps to herself.

She pulls him into a hug, and he wraps his arms around her reflexively. They stand there, holding on to each other until the loneliness wells up in him and grabs him by the throat. He leans into her, weak in the knees, and he can feel her sense that loneliness in him. She doesn't shrink away from him, doesn't flinch at his weight. She holds him with the strength and steadfastness of a tree, unmoved by his human weakness. He breathes in the smell of her hair, the memory of their old affair coursing through him. He realizes he still loves her. Always did.

*

Smith goes to his cousins' house for dinner on a Thursday night. He usually joins them at home at least once a week. Cooper and Christa would have him eat here every night, but Smith likes sitting out on his land alone for dinner, especially in the summertime. They rib him about eating out of cans and the microwave because he lives in a trailer, but he's a decent cook who has no trouble with the stove, the oven, or a campfire. Half the week, he ends up eating at the saloon anyway, where his cousins often join him.

The Boone house is tucked away on a street shared with only a few other homes. There's enough space on the lot to give Cooper and Christa a sense of privacy. Behind a soft green lawn and trees, the blue-and-white house looks like something out of a dream, with a raised porch under a gabled roof. The porch ceiling is adorned with rows of string lights the sisters often switch on at night. The white rocking bench and the baskets of red geraniums hanging from the ceiling beam makes the porch feel more Deep South than Wyoming. An old leather saddle salvaged from Smith's rodeo days straddles the balustrade, and a wagon wheel leans against the wall beside the front door, giving the house's exterior a western touch Cooper insisted on.

Inside, the house is cozy, thanks to the money Smith gave his cousins out of his rodeo winnings. Deer antlers adorn the mantle above the living room fireplace, and a large painting of pink, white, and purple flowers hangs on the wall. A dark-brown, distressed leather couch and a baby-blue, velvet armchair face the fireplace. Another, shorter couch in cognac leather with a colorful Southwestern throw draped over the back faces the window next to the front door. The coffee table in the living room and the dining room table are both thick, sturdy wood with a rough finish. A chandelier hangs above the dining table, and there are candles all over the house, in white and pale pinks, that Christa often burns.

The kitchen walls are painted pastel yellow, and the shelves above the sink are decorated with small potted succulents. They have a vintage General Electric refrigerator and a small, white round table at the far end of the kitchen where the sisters usually eat unless Smith comes over. The kitchen's sliding glass doors let out onto the back deck, Cooper's favorite spot to spend summer nights drinking beer and watching the stars and the trees in the yard. The wood pile stacked against the back wall of the house is more for decoration than practical use: come winter, Smith will chop fresh wood on his land for his cousins to use in their fireplace.

The house has three bedrooms and three bathrooms, including two showers and a stand-alone bathtub in the master suite. The third bedroom belongs to Smith, although the sisters would use it as a guest room if they ever had overnight company.

Christa has a cream-colored bedframe with long, sheer curtains hanging from the canopy and a dusty-pink pincushion bench at the foot. An oversized vintage mirror with an ornate frame stands in one corner of the bedroom, and in another corner is a peach upholstered chair. She had the walls repainted in a honey-milk white to bring out the warmth in all the other colors. The cream-colored window curtains have a pink rose print. There are fat, white candles all over the room and a huge print of Georgia O'Keefe's *Flower of Life II* painting on one wall.

Cooper's room is all dark woods, a rifle and a tomahawk on the wall above the bed, her favorite cowboy hat hooked on the back of the door, a fur skin blanket draped over the forest-green chair. There's a bookcase about four feet tall, full of Western paperbacks. The white comforter and sheets on the bed deepen the browns of the wood floor and furniture. She has framed photographs of Christa, Smith, and herself scattered all over the room: Cooper and Smith at one of the rodeos he won when he was twenty-four, Cooper and Christa on the day of Christa's college graduation, the three of them at Bad Moon right before Christmas two years ago. The photo she keeps on her night table was taken in the spring of 1992. Smith was eight years old, Cooper six, and Christa two. They're all smiling, openmouthed and gleeful, hanging onto one another. Cooper's in the middle, her knees bent, one arm around Smith, who's leaning toward her a little, and the other arm around Christa.

On this Thursday evening, Smith sits outside on the back deck while Cooper grills fish next to him. His dog Scooter lies next to his chair. The kitchen's glass door is open with the screen door shut, allowing Christa to hear them talking while she watches the rice and the steamed broccoli. After seven o'clock, the sky is only paled with waning daylight, sunset at least an hour away. Smith sips on his beer with his back to Cooper and the grill. He stares at the lone star twinkling above the horizon line and wonders if it's a planet. Christa's playing music in the kitchen, loud enough for Smith and Cooper to hear it.

"So," Cooper says over the sizzle of the fish filets. "Somebody asked me out the other day."

Smith peers over his shoulder at her. "Who?"

"A woman."

Smith grins and looks away again. "Did you say yes?"

"Of course, I didn't. Why would I?"

"You going to tell me who it was, or am I going to have to guess?"

"She's not out, and I promised I would help her keep it that way."

"I won't tell anyone."

"I know you wouldn't. But it's not my place to out her, even to you."

Smith drinks some of his beer and reaches down to pet his dog's head. "You're not a little bit curious? See what it's like?"

"What? Dating? No. I'm not having sex, and I'm not coupling up. End of story."

"All right. I was just asking."

"You're the one who likes screwing around. If anyone was going to go on dates here, it would be you."

"Yeah, well. You know how I feel about that."

"Yeah, I do. And I'm no different."

Smith looks at her over his shoulder again.

Cooper makes eye contact.

Christa slides open the screen door and leans in the doorway with her own beer in hand. "Is that a meaningful silence I hear, or you two run out of things to talk about?"

Cooper and Smith shift their attention to her.

"You hear Cooper got asked out on a date?" Smith says. "By a woman?"

"Yeah," says Christa. "She's been asked out before."

"Did she tell you who it was?"

Christa glances at her sister. "No."

"Now I'm gonna think it could be any single woman in town," Smith says.

Cooper turns her back on Christa, flipping the fish again.

"Coop, you ever go on a date in high school?" Smith asks. "I can't remember now."

"I dated Justin Berry about a week when I was fifteen."

"That's right. I hated that kid."

Cooper smiles at Smith. "Really?"

"Hell, yeah. You don't remember? We were having lunch together one day, in the cafeteria, and he came around and tried to get you to sit with him and his friends. He made it obvious he didn't like me. Maybe he was jealous. He wanted you to give him all your attention and not talk to any other guys, including me."

"Well," Cooper says, her voice softened with affection. "I don't remember those parts exactly. I'm just glad I dumped him before anything sexual happened."

"You never told Mom and Dad about Justin, did you?" Christa says to Cooper.

"No. I didn't want them to know before I was sure I liked him." Cooper switches off the grill. "All right, this fish is done."

"It smells good," says Smith, getting up. "Let's eat."

They have dinner in the dining room because the kitchen table is only big enough for two people. They have buttered bread with their meal. Smith and Cooper open second beers. The dog lies under the table next to Smith's chair, hoping for scraps he doesn't get. The radio's still on in the kitchen, too quiet for them to make out the songs unless they really listen in silence.

When they're almost finished eating, Christa sets her silverware down and takes a breath.

"Buck sent me flowers," she says.

Cooper and Smith look at her.

"Buck from the party?" Cooper says.

Christa nods.

"How'd he send you flowers?" says Smith.

"I got a bouquet of roses at work on Monday night. It had a card with his phone number on it. He found out what my real name is somehow. My first name."

Cooper frowns. "What the hell?"

"He must've asked somebody about you," Smith says to Christa. "Someone who was at that party or someone at Wild Horse, the day you bumped into him."

"I don't know what to do," says Christa. "I don't want to go out with him. I don't even want to talk to him. I've had a bad feeling about him since the party... Now he knows who I am and where I work. If he can find that out, he can probably figure out where I live. What if he shows up at one of my dance studios?"

"You want me to track him down? Talk to him?"

Christa gives her cousin an uncertain look and reaches for her water glass. "No. I mean, he hasn't done anything wrong. And I should be able to turn a guy down myself, not have somebody else do it for me. Maybe he thinks he's got a chance because I wasn't straightforward about being uninterested. Maybe he'll back off if I'm honest."

Smith glances at Cooper, who shifts her eyes from Christa to him with an uneasy expression.

Christa drinks some water, puts her glass on the table. "Am I making a big deal out of nothing?"

"He found you," Cooper says. "He doesn't even know you, and he has no reason to think you're interested in him. But he found you anyway and sent you roses like you're already dating. That's completely out of line."

"He could be a romantic," says Smith. "If he's only in town until the rodeo ends, he might figure he's got nothing to lose by coming on strong or doesn't have enough time to waste any. I don't know. Maybe he's just pushy. Pushy doesn't always mean dangerous."

Cooper gawks at him in disbelief. "Are you kidding?"

"I'm not saying Christa should be happy about what he did. I'm saying it may not be time to break out the shotgun, that's all."

"He probably did ask about me at Wild Horse, and Meredith knows where I work. All he had to do was swing by the schools to find out when I teach," Christa says. "So it wasn't hard for him to find me and send those flowers. But I had a bad feeling about him before I got the roses. Now, it's worse."

She drinks the last of the water in her glass and gets up to go to the kitchen. Cooper follows her and leans back against the doorpost, watching as Christa takes the pitcher of lemon water out of the fridge. Smith lingers in the doorway, close enough to touch Cooper, and sips on his beer.

"You should trust your instincts," Cooper says. "I don't like this guy knowing where you work. Maybe you should carry the Ruger until the Nite Rodeo's over and we know he's gone."

Christa eyes her sister. "You think so?"

"I'd have some peace of mind if you did. Wouldn't you?"

"Yeah," Christa says, sounding unsure. "I guess."

She sips from her glass, standing barefoot on the clean tile.

"It's not a bad idea," says Smith. "You got a holster?"

Christa nods.

Cooper stares at her sister, hands on her hips. She chews on her lower lip, then says, "I almost want to go find him at the rodeo and tell him to leave you alone."

"Don't do that."

"Why not?"

"Because it's too much. All I have to do is not call him, and if he shows up to see me when I'm working, I can tell him I'm not interested."

Cooper doesn't reply, her arms crossed over her chest now. After a pause, she turns her head toward Smith, and he shrugs at her. He steps back into the dining room when Cooper moves to get past him and waits by the doorway for Christa to join them.

Christa brings the water pitcher to the table and takes her seat again.

"All right," says Smith, moving to stand before his chair. "I got something to tell you."

He pauses with his beer still in hand, and Cooper and Christa look up at him.

"You remember John Henry? The man who came into the saloon to see me, the night I rode the bull?"

"Yeah," says Cooper.

"Not really," says Christa. "But go ahead."

"John Henry's a rodeo man. We knew each other when I was still in the life; we were friends for a couple years. He and I used to...used to fool around sometimes. He came to see me because he heard I was in Cody, and he's been competing in the area. I guess he wanted to know how I was doing—where I'd ended up. After that night, I went to see him in Montana."

Smith pauses again, concentrating on the table now. He's got his free hand on his hip, his weight on the other foot.

"I slept with him. And last weekend, when I was out of town Friday and Saturday, we met up and had sex again. Pretty sure we're not done either."

Smith swallows and glances at Cooper, then Christa, like he's waiting to field their condemnation.

"Okay," Cooper says. "So is there a problem?"

Smith doesn't answer right away. He runs his hand through his hair, pushes it back out of his face. "He's got a girlfriend back home. And he's thinking about marrying her."

Cooper and Christa trade a look, then return their attention to Smith.

"I know I'm a bastard for helping him cheat," Smith says. "I'm not proud of it. And if he wasn't disappearing back to where he came from in a few weeks, I wouldn't be doing this. I would've cut him off after he told me about her."

After a moment of silence, Smith sits down again and takes a long pull on his beer.

"Is he gay or bisexual?" Cooper asks. "I mean, is he with his girlfriend because he wants to be, or is she a cover?"

"He swings both ways. And he's in love with her."

"Were you...a couple, in the rodeo?" Christa asks. "Or was it just sex?"

"We weren't a couple. We started out friends, and the sex became a thing because we both screwed guys in the circuit. My friends were straight as far as I knew. They didn't know what I got up to with men. I didn't know the guys I slept with all that well, and I never tried making friends with them. We were all too skittish about getting caught. But with John Henry, it was different. We didn't start fooling around until after we'd been hanging out a while. We kept doing it until we quit being friends."

"So the two of you sleeping together now, it's not because you have feelings for each other?"

"Not romantic feelings," Smith says.

"You still care about him," says Cooper, her voice softened.

Smith meets her gaze and hesitates. "I miss him. Or I miss having a friendship like the one we had. Whichever one it is, it doesn't help that the sex is just as good as it was before."

"He must still care about you too," Christa says, her tone encouraging.

Smith doesn't answer, sitting in his chair, pensive and wistful.

"Is he out?" says Cooper.

Smith shakes his head.

"Then you've got to be careful for your sake and his."

"I know," says Smith.

The cousins are quiet for a beat. An insect buzzes outside through the screen door in the kitchen.

"When is he going home?" Cooper asks Smith.

"August."

"Are you going to be okay when he goes?" says Christa, gazing at Smith the way she used to when she was four years old, big blue eyes ready to well up if he cried.

Smith smiles at her. "Yeah. I'll be fine."

Cooper scrubs her hand down her face and takes a drink. Smith told Cooper he was bisexual when she was twenty years old. He was twenty-two and had just started fooling around with men. She was the first person he told, and she's been keeping the secret ever since, the last ten years. He asked her to keep it from her sister until Smith gave her permission to tell—after she and Christa moved to Cody. Cooper never cared that Smith has sex with men, but even at twenty, it was clear she knew other people would. Smith's parents, her parents, everyone who knew their family in Casper. She watched Smith become a rodeo star, a household name in Wyoming and in the national rodeo circuit, and knew the secret would ruin his reputation and maybe even his career if it got out.

Now, here he is, five years retired, and she's still worried about it.

"Wanna see what's on TV?" Christa says.

Cooper glances at her, then at Smith.

"Sure," he says, finishing off his beer. "I'll do the dishes. You two go on."

While Smith washes the dishes, Cooper sits next to her sister on the living room sofa as Christa channel surfs, thinking about Buck and the roses and Smith sneaking around with a taken, closeted man. She doesn't see how she's supposed to get any sleep until the summer's over and the rodeo takes all this mess away with it.

The cousins watch a movie, and by the time the credits roll, it's dark outside.

"Think I'll stay here tonight." Smith does that sometimes, sleeps over at the Boone house, but Cooper wonders if this time Buck has something to do with it.

"You know where the clean sheets are if you want to change the bed," Christa replies.

"Yes, ma'am." Smith gets up from the sofa and stretches before leaning down to kiss both women at their hairline. "G'night. I'll see you in the morning. Come on, Scooter."

The dog follows him to the spare bedroom.

Cooper and Christa stay behind on the couch, eyes glazed on the TV for a minute. Cooper turns her head to Christa.

"What'd you do with the roses?" she says.

"Gave them to our old lady neighbor," says Christa.

Cooper redirects her attention to the TV. "Take the gun with you. Tomorrow."

"I will."

They're silent again for a little while, listening to the sounds of the television and Smith brushing his teeth in the guest bathroom.

"Do you still pray?" Cooper says.

Christa looks at her. "Only on occasion."

"I wish I did. I wish I believed in something I could pray to."

"Why?" says Christa.

"So I could pray for you. And Smith."

Christa doesn't respond. After a long pause, she moves to lean against her sister and lays her head on Cooper's shoulder.

*

John Henry was a boy who lined up his toy horses on the floor of his bedroom and pretended to herd them on some faraway range. He gave each horse a name and a personality, and he spoke to his one and only cowboy figurine about the ongoing business of keeping them. The cowboy was a white man, so John Henry imagined him as a friend and ranching partner instead of projecting himself onto the figure. He named the cowboy Pecos because he loved the Pecos Bill character from the American tall tales book he found at the local library.

His parents couldn't afford to pay for riding lessons when he was in elementary school, and they assumed he would grow out of cowboys the way other boys abandoned superheroes. He didn't know about the rodeo then. It would take him until age twelve or thirteen to discover it on someone else's TV and realize he could ride broncos and bulls if he trained, even though all the professionals he saw were white guys. Once he made the rodeo his reality, he started thinking he could have that horse ranch he used to dream about, too, or a cattle ranch or a farm. If he won enough events and saved as much money as he could, one day he could have his own land—something no Black person he knew had managed to achieve.

He didn't even think about girls or dating until he was seventeen, a senior in high school, and by then, he was already starting to compete in amateur rodeos. The sport consumed all of his free time, all of his thoughts and energy, and he didn't immediately realize the pretty girls who began to make eyes at him in the school hall were attracted not just to his looks but to the novelty of him. He was the only rodeo boy in school, the only Black rodeo boy they'd probably ever heard of. Somehow, word got out when he began to compete, and he graduated with a nickname: Chaps.

He took that nickname with him into the pros. John Henry "Chaps" Walker, the announcers called out when it was his turn to jump in the chute. The more other riders heard it, the more they called him by the nickname. It wasn't until he was well into his career that he realized his high school nickname reminded him of where he'd come from and who he was. No matter where he went, what prizes he won or lost, he was a kid from New Iberia, Louisiana, and it was a miracle he'd made it as far as he had, college degree and all.

"You do make 'em look good," Smith told him once, admiring him in some arena locker room while John Henry checked himself out in the mirror. It was the first time Smith had ever openly flirted with John Henry, the first signal he dropped of his attraction to men. They'd been friends for about a year at that point, and John Henry had never suspected Smith of being anything but heterosexual. He didn't believe he'd heard the tone of Smith's voice right, at first.

Men hadn't occurred to John Henry until he was a junior in college, stone drunk and making out with AJ Porter, one of his closest male friends. They never talked about it, but found themselves drinking together alone more often.

John Henry graduated and went on the road full-time for the rodeo, descending into the rabbit hole of anonymous sex with men he'd pick up in nameless bars, his secret entirely compartmentalized from the rest of his life. For years, he didn't dare try anything with other rodeo riders, already too conspicuous in rooms full of white men. He was always looking over his shoulder, checking the rearview mirror to make sure he hadn't been accidentally followed by another rider on his way to the nondescript bar or Motel 6.

He did have girlfriends and casual sex with women all over the States, but like Smith, he filled the time in between women with men. Every few months, he'd sneak off to some local clinic to get tested for STDs, waiting alone for the results in silent fear. He second-guessed signals from male strangers, sometimes too afraid he was misreading to make a move. He found himself attracted to a few of his rodeo friends and distanced himself from them, paranoid about raising suspicion.

He never told a soul what he did with men. He got so used to hiding it, so used to carrying the secret, he had himself convinced he wasn't really "that man." The sex took on a surreal quality, and he believed, without realizing it, that it somehow didn't count.

Things were different with Smith. After Smith. They knew each other, liked each other, trusted each other. When they had sex, it wasn't a careless, anonymous fuck where John Henry could pretend to be someone else. Smith knew who he was and cared about him. He cared about being safe, cared about John Henry's comfort, cared about him when they weren't having sex at all. John Henry had never experienced that with another man, nor has he since his falling out with Smith in 2009.

Smith doesn't seem to understand what their falling out was about, to this day. John Henry was never honest with him. Their friendship had been sexual for about two years, unlabeled and unexclusive, with no expectations or rules. They weren't always in the same place at the same time, during rodeo season, but when they were apart, they'd call each other up to figure out when they'd cross paths again at a competition. They'd talk like old friends, trading scores and stories from their latest events, and it wasn't any different than their friendship had been before the sex.

It was simple and comfortable, until it wasn't anymore. John Henry found himself imagining the two of them in the distant future, living together on a ranch somewhere. It started to bother him whenever he thought about Smith having sex with other people when they were apart. And when they were together, sometimes he wanted to kiss Smith on the forehead or the cheek and cuddle him in bed without doing anything sexual.

He knew in his heart he wanted Smith to be his boyfriend, his partner, but he couldn't admit it to himself, let alone speak the wish aloud. It scared the shit out of him. Made him dread seeing the other man as much as he longed for it. Having a private sexual relationship with the same man was one thing, but having a boyfriend he told people about? That was something else. He couldn't do it. He could never be that guy. It didn't matter what he wanted. He had a career, parents who would never accept a bisexual son, friends who would reject him.

When John Henry told Smith he didn't want to have sex anymore, Smith seemed only a little disappointed and way too understanding. John Henry expected him to cut off their friendship, too, but Smith did no such thing. He acted as if nothing had changed apart from the sex, and that hurt John Henry even though he was grateful for their ongoing friendship. He told himself he could keep being Smith's friend; they would both move on to new lovers and one day remember their brief affair the way so many other older men must remember their distant youth and its secrets. He tried having sex with other men, but it felt empty and wrong. He tried finding a girlfriend, but his heart wasn't in it, no matter how right the women were. Months passed during which he'd go weeks without seeing Smith, but every time they met again, there was the feeling in the pit of John Henry's stomach. Love. Love tangled up with fear, denial, and realism.

"Listen, man," he'd said to Smith on a chilly night in Minot, North Dakota. "I don't think I can see you anymore."

The look in Smith's eyes came back to him many nights in the following six years when John Henry lay alone in motel beds failing to fall asleep. All the years they'd known each other, he'd never seen hurt and betrayal on Smith's face until he was the reason. And Smith didn't argue. He didn't ask why. He just turned and walked away, the sight of him leaving for the glaring white lights of the arena seared into John Henry's memory forever.

John Henry doesn't know why he drove down to Cody that night last month. He's been close enough at least once a year since Smith retired, but it never occurred to him to go looking for the old star. Why now? He can't explain it. He doesn't know what he was expecting, but when they were finally face to face again in the middle of the Bad Moon Saloon, John Henry felt that love come alive as if no time had passed at all.

*

Christa dances alone in her classroom at the Cody Center for the Performing Arts, the second school she teaches at in town. Her workday is over, but she lingers in the empty room to dance out her feelings the way she always has, getting out of her head and into her body. She's been through three songs already, and the fourth is almost over. She doesn't watch herself in the mirror, moving on instinct without thinking about what she's doing or what she looks like. She leaps through the air, spins, comes back to the floor over and over. She doesn't have the words for how she feels—for her fear and dread and the sensation of being trapped—but she has her body and everything it can do.

She doesn't reflect on the fact that her body is the reason Buck hunts her. He doesn't know who she is and doesn't care. If she had a different appearance, he might've passed her over at that party, never giving her a second thought. He might've seen her and forgotten her by the end of the night. If she had a different body, a different face, maybe she wouldn't be afraid now. If she were a man, she wouldn't be afraid.

She stops when the song ends and stares at her own reflection in the silence. Her bare, white skin and her flushed face, her slender arms and narrow shoulders, the lines of her torso in the leotard and her legs in the tights. She didn't ask for this body. She didn't ask for this face. She shouldn't have to live her whole life in dread of the next violent, predatory man.

Christa suddenly remembers John Henry. She can almost see him in the mirror, standing next to her—his gentle eyes, his powerful shoulders, his dark skin. He lives with his own fears, on the run from his own predators. As many men in the world as she has to flee, doesn't he have his own? Men who would kill him for being Black or having sex with other men. Or both. Maybe he doesn't have to lose sleep over the threat of rape the way she does, but he must've spent enough nights in motel and hotel rooms all over America, wide awake at two in the morning because someone might've seen him go in with another man. There must be roads all over this country he drove too slowly, too carefully, to make sure the nearest cop didn't have a reason to stop him.

But John Henry hasn't crawled into a hole and withdrawn from the world. He hasn't stopped seeing men. He hasn't quit going where he wants to go. He hasn't abandoned his home the way Christa has wanted to since Buck started stalking her. John Henry persists as much as he can, with just as much to lose as she has. She doesn't know how—but he does it. If he can face the men who threaten him day in and day out, maybe she can too. Maybe she should try.

Jenny from the front desk pops her head into the room.

"I thought you might still be here," she says. "There's a phone call for you."

Christa follows her out to the lobby and picks up the desk phone from its receiver. "Hello, this is Christa Boone speaking."

"I was hoping you'd answer," says Buck on the other end. "I'm free tonight if you are."

Christa slams the phone onto the hook.

Jenny gapes at her wide-eyed. "Who was that?"

Christa takes a step back, and her eyes flit toward the glass doors of the building entrance, heart pounding. Is he out there, waiting for her in the parking lot?

"Are you okay?" Jenny says.

"Yeah," Christa replies, eyes fixed on the darkening world beyond the building entrance. "I'm fine."

Jenny watches her, but Christa doesn't pay attention to her. She turns on her heel and heads back to her classroom to retrieve her bag.

She walks out into the parking lot with her gun in her hand.

*

Smith borrows a couple horses from Pete Bachman, who runs one of the horseback riding schools for kids in Cody. Smith loads them up in a trailer and drives them out to his own land. By the time John Henry shows up, the horses are saddled and waiting, tied to the back of the trailer still hitched to Smith's truck. Smith watches John Henry drive toward him from his chair outside, near the firepit. John Henry parks not far from the campsite, and Scooter stands up to greet him when he gets out of his truck and approaches.

John Henry stops to pet the dog and surveys the campsite. "You've been living like this for the last five years?"

"Yup," says Smith, eyes half closed in the muted sunlight.

John Henry gives him a disbelieving, judgmental look. "You got how many acres of land and how much in rodeo winnings saved up?"

"I ain't ashamed of living a simple life."

"If that's what you want to call it."

They mount the horses and start to ride west, their pace unhurried. Scooter follows them for a little bit until Smith turns in his saddle and tells him to stay.

The land unfolds in green flats and fields of yellow grasses dotted with sagebrush, a cluster of low rolling hills, the mountains blue and misty in the distance. They ride through treeless meadows and thickets of pine, the air clean and pure. They ride under an overcast sky that feels closer to the earth than usual, the sun small and shrouded in washed-out clouds. They cross the creek cutting north-south through a stand of Douglas fir trees and rocky banks and ride back into open plains. They don't speak, Smith keeping ahead of John Henry as he leads them to the spot he picked out.

They stop in a clearing surrounded by Engelmann spruce that feels farther away from civilization than it is, observing the land and listening to how quiet it is without the sound of their horses walking. They ride back out of the clearing and into another stretch of treeless plain.

Smith dismounts and takes the blanket he rolled up and packed, throwing it open and laying it on the ground. John Henry watches him, still in his own saddle, and Smith glances his way as he retrieves the canteen he put in his saddle bag, along with the condoms. He drinks with his back turned on John Henry, then throws the canteen and condoms onto the blanket. He looks over his shoulder, and John Henry finally gets down from his horse, then leads both horses several yards away from the blanket.

Smith gives him a skeptical look as he returns. "What's the matter? Don't want them watching?"

"Horses talk, you know."

John Henry steps right up to Smith, toe to toe, and pulls the cowboy hat off Smith's head before he kisses him. Reaches up and combs his fingers through Smith's hair, curling his hands shut around it and tipping Smith's head back enough to kiss his throat.

"You kiss every guy you screw this much?" Smith asks.

"No," says John Henry. Then kisses his mouth again, slow and gentle. "I'll quit if you want."

"It's all right."

"I kiss you because I don't want you to feel like I'm just using you for sex."

"You're not using me for sex? That's news."

John Henry smacks his arm.

Smith smiles.

They strip off their clothes piece by piece, taking their time. Watching each other, touching. Pressing a kiss to each other's neck, brushing noses. Running their hands over each other's skin. Their boots, belts, jeans, shirts, undershirts, socks, and finally their underwear litter the ground and the blanket all around them, and they stand there for a few more minutes, touching with gentle affection.

Smith feels vulnerable, naked with this other man in broad daylight, out in the open with nowhere to hide. But there's a rush of freedom too. He knows they're safe here; they can do anything they want, make all the noise they want. He's never been this free having sex with another man. He's always had to be careful, quiet, sneaking around in the dark, looking over his shoulder in the morning. It's always been like that for John Henry too.

They kneel together on the blanket, facing each other, kissing and touching for a few minutes. Smith runs his hands down John Henry's back and over his ass, squeezing it. John Henry sucks on Smith's neck, stroking Smith's sides.

Smith lies on his back, his knees up, and John Henry gets between his legs and starts blowing him. Smith lifts his eyes to the sky, his breathing like rustled tissue paper, his hands flat on the blanket.

John Henry crawls up over him, bracing his hands on the ground and looking at Smith. "I want to feel you inside me. I'll still fuck you after."

Smith swallows, making eye contact with him. "Okay."

John Henry reaches for one of the condoms, opens it, and rolls it onto Smith. He climbs on top of him, knees on either side of Smith's torso, and reaches behind him to find Smith's cock.

"You don't want to stretch first?" Smith asks.

John Henry shakes his head. "I'll be fine."

He guides Smith to his entrance, takes a breath, and pushes back.

Smith inhales sharply when he enters John Henry. "Shit," he whispers.

John Henry closes his eyes and takes several deep breaths as he slides back onto Smith, taking him inch by inch until he's sitting on Smith's thighs. He opens his eyes and gazes at Smith.

"You okay?" Smith says, his voice already rough.

John Henry nods and breathes again. He doesn't move for a while, allowing his body to adjust. Smith lies still, so turned on he's light-headed. When John Henry's ready, he plants his hands on Smith's chest, shifts his weight forward onto his knees, and starts to hump. Smith doesn't move, letting John Henry set his own pace. When he's more comfortable, John Henry ruts against Smith with longer, faster strokes. He closes his eyes, fingers curled over Smith's shoulders, mouth open as he pants. Smith slides his hands up John Henry's thighs and rests them on his hips, watching the other man's face.

"Fuck," John Henry whispers.

Smith squeezes John Henry's hips.

John Henry drops his head between his shoulders and rides Smith like he means it. He's breathing heavy, gripping Smith's shoulders tight. "Fuck me," he says.

Smith bucks his own hips, helping John Henry work less, sweating already with the effort of moving underneath one hundred and eighty pounds of cowboy.

John Henry begins stroking his own cock, eyes shut.

Smith watches him, trying his best to pump into John Henry. "Am I hitting it?"

John Henry nods, rubbing himself and rocking on Smith, one hand still on Smith's shoulder. He whimpers, then tips his head and looks at the sky.

Without warning, Smith rolls John Henry onto his back, pushes John Henry's knees up with his hands, and starts fucking him hard and fast.

"Oh, shit. Oh, God," John Henry says.

"Don't you come," says Smith, breathing hard between the words. "Not yet."

John Henry stops touching himself, moaning as Smith thrusts into him. "Smith... Fuck, Smith. Just like that. Please."

Smith drives into him, his whole body hot and sensitive, the air now cool against his bare skin. He leans down, one elbow on the ground next to John Henry's side, and sucks on John Henry's neck. Bites his collarbone.

John Henry sobs and throws his arm over his eyes, letting Smith take him, motionless. He wraps his legs around Smith, his thighs quivering. "Oh, God," he says, voice higher than usual. "Oh, God."

Smith considers making him come like this, but he wants John Henry to fuck him more. Usually, Smith bottoms with men, but he relishes the feeling of being inside another man when it happens. It's nothing like being inside a woman, which he loves just as much.

Right when an orgasm starts to crest, Smith pulls out of John Henry, then takes John Henry's cock into his mouth. John Henry cries out and grabs the hair at the back of Smith's head in his fist. Smith sucks on him, and John Henry groans with the unrestrained volume of a man who doesn't have to worry about being heard.

When Smith stops and sits up, they're both breathing heavy, his heart beating fast. They're sweaty, still hard, their skin prickling in the open air. They look at each other for a moment before Smith lies next to John Henry on his back.

John Henry rolls toward him and fondles Smith's cock, kissing his neck. Smith passes him a new condom, and John Henry puts it on, then kisses Smith on the mouth as he jerks him off. He runs his hand all over Smith's chest and side, rubs his belly, thumbs his nipple. He stops kissing him and pushes Smith onto his side, facing away from John Henry. He slips a finger inside Smith, moving it in and out, then another, but he doesn't use any lube this time. Smith's already a little loose, his whole body relaxed.

John Henry strokes himself a couple times before entering Smith, both of them sighing as he slides in to the hilt. Smith lifts his top leg, and John Henry tucks his hand underneath Smith's knee before moving. He fucks Smith slow and deep. Fucks him like he wants Smith to remember every thrust, like he wants Smith to feel it for days and weep with need by the time he finally comes.

Their voices overlap, the two of them grunting and gasping. John Henry's breath is hot on the back of Smith's neck, the heat of John Henry's body against his own. Lying here like this, Smith's never been more exposed, but he knows John Henry's got him.

Smith sees the horses grazing and smiles, openmouthed and panting. The animals don't pay the men any attention. A bead of sweat rolls out of his hair and down his face. John Henry reaches for Smith's cock and rubs it, slowing the pace of his humping, and Smith reaches behind him and plants his hand on John Henry's buttock, gripping it just enough to hold on. He tries to grind his ass back against John Henry, tries to pull him closer and deeper.

John Henry huffs behind Smith's ear, grabbing Smith's hip. He pumps into him with more force. Smith strokes himself, getting close to the edge. He's sweating and shaky, grunting and groaning the way he wanted to the last couple times they had sex. John Henry sucks and nibbles on the back of his neck, and Smith groans louder as a shock of electricity shoots from his neck straight to his groin. He shivers, his eyelids fluttering shut.

He moans John Henry's name as his orgasm swells from his prostate like a wave, and when he finally ejaculates, he's silent, his mouth open and body trembling. His mind goes blank, whites out, and for a few seconds, he forgets where he is and who he is and who's with him.

John Henry fucks into him faster, desperate, hugging Smith tight under his arm and grinding against him. "Fuck, yeah, Smith. Shit, I'm going to come. Shit. Oh, my God."

Smith is limp, the aftershocks of his orgasm washing through him as John Henry pulses inside him. John Henry yells as he comes, thrusting into Smith as his body stiffens and squeezing Smith's hip hard enough to bruise. He doesn't stop, bucking into Smith through his orgasm and for a few moments after it ends.

When he's completely spent, John Henry pulls out of Smith and rolls onto his back next to him. They lie there for a while, waiting as their breath and pulse even out. Smith turns toward John Henry and drapes his arm over him, rests his face against John Henry's shoulder. They doze in a light sleep under the wide blue sky, the sun warm on their skin, undisturbed by the soft sound of the breeze ruffling the grasses and the horses grazing.

Smith sits up and considers the land—all of it his except for the mountains in the distance. After a minute, John Henry gets up and heads for the horses, walking gingerly on bare feet. Smith watches him, admiring his body. He was always more attracted to John Henry than to most other men he screwed. Those muscles, the shape of his ass, the breadth of his shoulders, the curve of his back, his powerful thighs, hands made for growing things. He has a face Smith wants to touch, trace over with his thumbs, kiss over and over.

Smith turns his head away when John Henry comes back with a cigarette lit in his mouth and the pack in his hand. John Henry sits next to him on the blanket, facing the same direction. They're quiet until John Henry speaks.

"So what are you going to do with this land?"

Smith doesn't answer.

"You must've had plans for it when you bought it."

"I planned to live on it. That's what I'm doing."

John Henry gives him a look. "A man doesn't buy twenty-five acres for a trailer and a dog."

"Looks like I did."

John Henry pauses as he takes a drag on his cigarette. "What's going on with you?" he says, his tone gentle and friendly.

"What do you mean?"

"This isn't you. Any of this. When I heard you were retiring from the rodeo, I thought you'd just had enough, and you wanted to move on to something different. Maybe you got an idea, got interested in something else. But it's like you dropped out of life. You bought a bunch of land you ain't doing nothing with. You're living in a trailer all by yourself, in the middle of nowhere. You're running a bar. I don't mean to offend you, I'm sure it's a pretty good bar, but—you never talked about wanting one. I guess I can't believe you're living like this because it makes you happy."

"Why else would I do it?"

"Because you're unhappy. Or because you don't know what you want. I don't know. That's why I asked."

Smith doesn't speak for a long time, weighing his desire to open up to John Henry against his instinct to guard himself. John Henry smokes beside him without impatience, keeping the cigarette butt between his fingers even once he's finished because he doesn't have anywhere to put it.

Smith glances at him. "Gimme one of those."

John Henry gives him the pack and the lighter, and Smith lights a cigarette of his own. He used to do this when he was in the rodeo—bum a smoke from John Henry after sex. Not any other time.

"You're right," Smith says, keeping his eyes on the land. "I'm not happy."

John Henry's eyes settle on him. "Okay."

"I haven't been since I retired. Since before, I guess. My last year in the rodeo, after we quit talking, I wasn't happy. I thought maybe if I left, I'd feel better, but leaving made it worse. Better in some ways, I guess, but worse too."

Smith puffs on his cigarette, gathering his thoughts. In a few weeks, John Henry's gone, so Smith doesn't have anything to lose being honest with him.

"I just got tired of it. Rodeo culture. But I love riding. I love the adrenaline and the animals and breaking my own records. I love the crowds and the competition, feeling like I'm cheating death all the time. There's nothing like it. Not here, not in the outside world."

John Henry looks away again. He waits a spell, then says, "You ever think about coming back?"

"A thousand times." Smith considers the mountains lining the distant horizon. He takes a breath, then a drag on his cigarette. "But I always knew if I did, I'd be right back into all my old complaints. Sooner or later, everybody's got to move on anyway. If I can't learn how to do it now, why would doing it later be any easier?"

"If you quit too soon, if you really aren't done, that'll keep you from moving on. You were in your prime, Smith."

"Yeah, and now I'm thirty-two and five years out of practice. I'd make a fool of myself, going up against a bunch of twenty-five-year-olds who eat and breathe the life the way I used to."

"Most of the kids in the circuit are never going to be as good as you. On their best day, they're not going to come close. You'd make fools of them, going back and winning."

Smith smiles and shakes his head, holding the cigarette in between his thumb and forefinger and smoking it like a joint.

They fall into silence for a couple minutes, the sun warming their shoulders.

"So what are you going to do?" John Henry asks.

"I don't know. Keep running the saloon, I guess."

"You got to want something, Smith. You got to find a new thing to be fired up about if you're really done with the rodeo."

"Why?" Smith turns his head to John Henry. "Why do I have to love something else, the way I loved riding broncos? Plenty of men in this world work jobs they don't love. I don't know why you're so Goddamn adamant about convincing me to change my life."

"Everybody needs something to keep them going. You deserve to be happy, Smith. Why don't you believe that?"

Smith lowers his gaze between his knees, then lifts his head again and smokes.

"It doesn't have to be a job," says John Henry. "It could be a hobby or a cause or a family. But something. Something that makes you want to live."

"I have a family," Smith says, his voice soft.

"Your cousins?"

"Yeah."

John Henry thinks for a minute, and Smith doesn't interrupt, smoking the last of his cigarette.

"I know you have them, but that's not what I meant."

"I know what you meant. I already told you, I don't want all that."

"No marriage, no kids, nothing?"

Smith pauses, then says, "I never really wanted kids."

"So you want to spend the rest of your life living alone in a trailer."

Smith doesn't quite roll his eyes. "Would you quit hounding me about the Goddamn trailer? I get enough grief about it from Cooper and Christa."

"Oh? You mean, they want you to build a house on this twenty-five acres too?"

"Yes, they do."

"Maybe you should listen to them, then."

Smith doesn't respond, and they stay quiet for a while.

"Just because I don't want to get married, doesn't mean I want to be alone." Smith glances at John Henry, who looks back at him.

"Go on," John Henry says.

"Why are those the only two options? Marriage and being alone? Why's the only family that counts the kind involving marriage and kids? I love Cooper and Christa. I love my parents and my brother and his kids, I care about being a good friend, and I care about this town. It's not my fault if everybody else doesn't give a damn about those things. It doesn't mean I want to be alone."

John Henry bobs his head, gazing into the distance. "All right. I hear you."

Smith scrubs his hand over his face, then runs it through his hair. "Shit. Maybe that's why I've been so damn bothered the last five years. Maybe it's got nothing to do with the rodeo."

"What do you mean?"

"I mean, people. Relationships. I've lived here that long, and I don't have a community. I don't have close friends. I've got Cooper and Christa, but besides them, nobody knows me. They just know of me. Maybe what I really miss about the rodeo is the feeling of being a part of something. Having a tribe."

John Henry arches his eyebrow and gives Smith an amused look. "Were you always this much of a hippie?"

Smith bumps John Henry's shoulder with his own.

"Does it occur to you maybe the reason you don't have friends here is because you won't let anyone be your friend?"

Smith rests his eyes on him, turning his head and resting his chin on his shoulder. He doesn't answer. The two men stare at each other until John Henry takes the cigarette stub out of Smith's fingers and gets up to bring back the horses.

Smith lies on the blanket and stares at the sky, trying to picture his life ten years from now. He doesn't see anything.

*

Cooper goes back to Stampede Park stadium alone for the first time since she moved to Cody five years ago, waiting in the stands for Buck to make his appearance. She's been checking the rodeo lists every day since Christa told her about him. She could've found him at whatever hotel or motel he's staying in—there are so few in town, it would've been easy enough to search them all—but she wants to see him in action, size him up when he's at his most vulnerable. She sits and stands and sits again through the national anthem and the first few categories, not registering any of it. Her muscles are tight from her neck to her feet, fists almost clenched, her spite heavy and glowing in the pit of her stomach like a hot coal. Christa hasn't mentioned the man again since she told Cooper and Smith about him the first time, but a couple nights ago, when Christa came home from work, Cooper could feel something was off. Christa didn't say anything about Buck, but Cooper knew in her gut he was the reason for her sister's quiet, troubled energy.

"Hey," comes a female voice.

Someone touches Cooper's arm, and she jumps, then sees Lou next to her, looking startled.

"Shit," says Cooper. "It's you."

"Sorry," Lou says. "I didn't mean to scare you. I said your name, but you didn't hear me."

Cooper's heart beats fast in her chest. "It's all right. I was—I was just thinking."

Lou offers a small smile. "Must've been thinking pretty hard to miss your own name. Everything okay?"

"I don't know yet." Cooper checks the arena again to make sure Buck isn't there, then turns toward Lou. "Are you here alone?"

"I met a friend of mine and her husband and kids, but then I spotted you and decided to come over in case you wanted company." The hint of a blush surfaces on Lou's face as if she only realized once she spoke the words aloud how they might be taken.

Cooper tries to smile a little to be encouraging, but her mind and heart aren't in it, eyes and ears stealing away every few seconds to look for Buck's name on the board and the man himself in the chute.

"I don't want to keep you from your friend," she tells Lou. "But I don't mind if you stay."

Lou isn't going anywhere. That much is clear.

The two women sit, close enough to brush against each other, and Cooper decides not to dwell on Lou's physical nearness. It's a reminder of Lou's attraction to her, of her own guilt and remorse at disappointing the other woman. Cooper hated how she felt after Lou left the garage the afternoon she stopped by. The last thing she wanted was to hurt another woman, and she'd done it just by being herself.

She can't think about it again now, watching and waiting for Buck.

She hears the announcer say his name, then sees it on the board.

"All right, everybody, next up we have Buck Haley all the way from Amarillo, Texas. Let's see what he's got."

Buck climbs up one side of the horse chute, surrounded by other men in cowboy hats, and lowers himself down into the saddle with the same caution Cooper's seen thousands of times in her cousin and other rodeo riders. She recognizes the shape of the bronco jerking around in the chute under Buck's weight, already pissed off at the whole game. The announcer never gives the audience the riders' heights and weights, but Buck seems as tall as Smith and has a stockier frame. She wouldn't be surprised if he's pushing two hundred pounds.

The chute gate opens, and the horse takes Buck out into the arena, pounding the dirt with his front hooves, throwing his back legs into the air over and over. Buck holds on to the rope and does his best to stay on the animal, shifting to the left in the saddle instead of maintaining an upright position—which usually doesn't bode well for a rider's time, in Cooper's experience.

The bronco makes it to the eastern side of the arena, trying to throw Buck off, the pair of pickup riders following him astride their horses. Buck slides off the left side of the bronco and tumbles onto the ground, quickly crawling away from the horse as the pickup riders instinctively ride around him in pursuit of the bronc.

Cooper looks up at the score board as the announcer reads the score: 9.3 seconds. She feels a burning sense of disappointment. She didn't want him to make the cutoff.

"Do you know that man?" Lou must see something in the way Cooper watches him.

"No. He's an out-of-towner. I just heard about him."

"What'd you hear?"

"Nothing good."

Buck disappears, going back where he came from on the opposite side of the arena fence, and Cooper only waits a second before getting on her feet. Lou stands up with her.

"I think I'm going to go," says Cooper. "If you don't mind."

"Is something wrong?" Lou peers at Cooper with those blue eyes the color of morning glories.

Cooper shakes her head. "I didn't plan on staying through the whole show tonight, that's all. Sorry. I'm not trying to ditch you, I swear. I just—I've seen all I want to see."

"It's okay." Lou gives her a determined smile again. "I don't want to keep you if you don't feel like being here."

"Maybe we can get together some time soon," says Cooper, not expecting Lou to take her up on it. "If you want."

"I'd like that," Lou says, face full of sincerity.

Cooper nods. "You know where to find me."

She leaves Lou behind and goes out to the parking lot, gets into her truck, and sits at the wheel. She doesn't start the engine right away, taking a minute to think. Buck Haley isn't the first man to show an interest in her sister since the Boones moved to Cody, but he's the first one to set off Cooper's protective instinct. Her intuition is too strong for her to rationalize away.

Cooper may have just laid eyes on a man she's destined to kill.

*

Christa's at the grocery store on a Tuesday night, inspecting the heirloom tomatoes. She picks them up one by one, testing their firmness in her hand, setting aside the tomatoes she wants on the neighboring pile of cucumbers. She puts her basket on the floor and pulls a plastic bag off the roll, places her tomatoes inside, and ties the bag with a twist. She's going to use them in a salad with watermelon and goat cheese. Something she saw on the menu of a restaurant in Cheyenne when she was browsing the internet for recipes.

She glances up and freezes when she sees Buck across the store in the meat section. He's not paying attention to her, but it's a small store. If she doesn't leave now, pretty soon, he's going to notice her.

She heads straight to the registers, hiding herself behind the shelves next to the produce section, and picks the first empty checkout lane she sees. She puts her basket on the conveyor belt, not even sure she has everything she wants, and tries not to look in Buck's direction to see if he spotted her. She gives the cashier a forced smile, fishes her wallet out of her purse, and pays for her groceries. She hurries outside without looking back, trying not to run to her RAV4.

She throws her groceries in the backseat and gets behind the wheel, locking all the doors and starting the engine. She peels out of the parking lot and onto the road, checking her rearview mirror every other second.

About ten minutes after she leaves the store, she peeks into her rearview mirror and sees him, driving his truck right behind her. They pass under a streetlamp for a split second, and she sees his face behind the truck windshield in the orange light. She tells herself not to panic; he probably doesn't know she's in the RAV4, he's behind her by coincidence and not because he's following her.

She considers getting off this main road even though it's the fastest way home and taking side streets instead. If she does that and he follows her, then she knows he's doing it deliberately. She's afraid of the confirmation, but she doesn't want to lead him to her house.

Maybe she should call Cooper, but she doesn't want to worry her. What can Cooper do for her anyway? If Buck's following Christa, there's nothing she can do about it except try losing him. She doesn't want to lead him to Cooper, doesn't want him knowing where they live. She could drive out to Smith's land, but it's almost thirty minutes away, in the opposite direction. And she doesn't want to lead Buck to Smith either, even though her cousin can defend himself.

She checks the rearview mirror again, the truck's headlights still shining back at her. She's gripping the steering wheel too hard, doing the speed limit only because she doesn't know where she's going.

She stops at a red light, the intersection deserted except for her and Buck. Outside the scope of the streetlamps, they idle in pitch blackness, now past the town center and in the surrounding residential area. It's quiet, except for the faint buzz of insects. Christa stares at the red light, which seems to last longer than it ever has before, and steals a glance at her rearview mirror. Buck doesn't seem to watch her, sitting at the wheel of his truck with a nonchalant expression. For a split second, she feels the urge to get out of her car and go talk to him—

But the light turns green.

She starts to drive through the intersection, then checks her mirror again and sees Buck turning right, disappearing into the darkness as he heads south. She takes a deep breath, all the tension seeping from her body, and her eyes sting and blur as she keeps going east.

When she finally pulls into her driveway and parks her car, Christa sits behind the wheel for a minute. She takes a breath, glances into the mirrors again and finds nothing. The porchlight is on even though the last of daylight still clings to the sky, outlining the mountains like pale yellow smoke. She pulls her bag into her lap and takes out the gun, weighing it in her hands.

Cooper's sitting on the back deck with the sliding door open. She glances over her shoulder when Christa enters the kitchen, carrying the groceries.

"Hey," she calls.

Christa doesn't answer, leaving the food on the kitchen counter.

She goes to her bedroom with the gun. She digs one of her suitcases out of the closet, brings it back to the bed, and flips it open.

"What are you doing?" Cooper asks from the doorway. She's already changed out of her work uniform into sweatpants and a T-shirt.

Christa looks at her, standing next to the bed. "Buck was at the grocery store just now. I thought he was following me, on my way home. I don't know if he knew it was me in front of him or if it was a coincidence we were going the same way for a while...but it scared me, Cooper. I didn't know what to do. I didn't want to lead him here."

Cooper frowns.

"Maybe it's better if I stay out of town until the rodeo's over," Christa says. "I can go stay in Powell, at my friend's house. It's just for a few weeks."

Cooper comes into the room and stops at the foot of the bed with her hands on her hips. "No," she says.

"No?"

"You're not going anywhere. This is your home, your town. He's the outsider. He's the one who needs to get the fuck out."

"He's not leaving until the rodeo's over. There's nothing I can do about that. What I *can* do, is make myself scarce until he's gone."

"Why didn't you call me? When you thought he was following you."

Christa stares at her, quiet. "I didn't want to scare you. There's nothing you could've done anyway."

"I could've stayed with you! You didn't have to be alone. If you were scared, I could've been there for you. I can't be with you in Powell. You know I can't."

"I don't have to worry about him in Powell. He won't have any idea I'm there. And I won't be alone. I know plenty of people."

Cooper moves around the corner of the bed to stand in front of her sister. She takes Christa by the shoulders. "Christa. Don't go. We can tell him off. Smith can tell him off. We can protect you."

Christa looks into Cooper's eyes, feeling stupid for overreacting but afraid enough to run away. "I don't want Buck coming after you," she says, her voice now fragile.

"I don't care if he does. Don't leave, Christa. If you go, I won't be able to sleep or think straight until you come back."

Christa doesn't want to make her sister worry for the next three weeks, but everything inside her wants to leave Cody until Buck's gone. She's tired of feeling like she can't go anywhere alone besides work, constantly watching out for Buck in public places, dreading another encounter with him. She's tired of being afraid he's going to show up at the dance schools when she's teaching or send her another unwanted gift or find out where she lives. Even with the gun, she wants to stay home until he's gone, and she's afraid home won't be safe much longer either.

Her eyes burn as they well up, and Cooper pulls her into a tight hug. Christa holds on to her, face pressed into Cooper's shoulder. She doesn't cry, only because she fights it.

"It's okay," Cooper says. "I won't let anything happen to you. I promise."

Christa presses her hands into Cooper's back, squeezing her in reply. She doesn't want to spend three weeks in Powell without her sister, not when she's feeling vulnerable and afraid. But she doesn't want to stay in Cody while Buck's here either.

"I love you," Cooper says, her voice tender and earnest. "I'll keep you safe. Whatever it takes. I'll follow you everywhere, if that's what you need. Don't go where I can't protect you."

Christa is silent for a long beat, then says, "Okay."

Cooper pulls back from the hug and looks at her, holding Christa's hands in her own. "You'll stay?"

"I'll stay."

Cooper nods, looking relieved. "You want me to make dinner?"

Christa sniffs, shaking off the emotion. "No, I'm fine. I'll do it."

Cooper lets go of her and turns to leave the room.

"Cooper," Christa says when her sister reaches the door.

Cooper stops and turns back.

"I love you too."

Cooper nods and disappears.

*

John Henry's drinking at the unmarked dive along the North Fork Highway because his paranoia hasn't changed in ten odd years of rodeo life. He doesn't want to draw attention to himself and Smith, doesn't want people asking questions about Smith in particular, so he's staying out of Cody as much as possible. He's got a week before his next rodeo in West Yellowstone, Montana, which means too much time to think and get used to being with Smith. He's already two beers deep and mulling over the idea of competing in the Cody Nite Rodeo while he's here, just for the hell of it, but maybe doing that would show him too much of what could be... Living on Smith's land, throwing his hat into the Nite Rodeo ring every summer like a ritual and searching for Smith and the Boone sisters in the stands, going for a free drink at the Bad Moon Saloon afterward.

John Henry tries to shake off the fantasy before it sucks him in too deep. He finishes off his beer and considers ordering another or having a whiskey instead. He's more relaxed now than he was when he first walked into the dive, feels less like everybody else is watching him. He's the only Black person here, surrounded by white folk, which is par for the course in Wyoming country. It doesn't matter too much when he's in a rodeo stadium, but everywhere else, it sets him on edge.

Smith mentioned this place as the one spot in Park County where men can take a chance at picking up other men. The kind of place where people mind their own business and that business is usually the type unfit for polite society. John Henry tries and tries not to imagine Smith coming here alone to meet strange, harsh men who will fuck him out in the parking lot or the bathroom or on the side of the road a few miles down from the bar. Every single search like playing a game of Russian roulette, hoping the man really did give the signal and he doesn't live in town and no one else in the room is paying attention to Smith's face. John Henry can't help but feel anxious on Smith's behalf, but his turmoil is more than that too. He has a hard time thinking of Smith with other men in general.

The corner table of men playing cards erupts in a chorus of hollers, making John Henry jump a little on his stool. The bartender takes that as a cue to ask him if he wants another beer. John Henry nods, peering over his shoulder at the rowdy card players once the bartender slinks off to retrieve a bottle of Miller High Life from the icebox. He grabs the beer as soon as the bartender sets it in front of him and drinks the whole thing in one, long motion.

He goes to the bathroom to use the toilet and look at himself in the mirror, into his own dark eyes full of doubt and fear he hates acknowledging. He's spent most of his adult life so far wondering if the whole world can see right through him, see what he is and what he does with men in secret, despite all of his caution and public flirtations with women. He sees his own face in the dim, rose-gold light of a single bulb, and feels exposed. He stands there, wondering how to hide, listening to the slow classic country playing over the speakers until another man enters the bathroom.

Instead of returning to the bar, John Henry steps out the back door for some fresh air and a cigarette. He checks his cell phone and finds the signal weak again, no messages. He takes a deep breath, already feeling better now he's alone, and looks at the night sky arching over the land in star-speckled midnight blue. So many stars, he would lose his place quick if he tried counting them. A handful of vehicles huddle in the dirt parking lot like sleeping cows, not a single electric light in sight except the ones belonging to the bar. He lights up one of his Marlboros and waits for the act of smoking to calm him down, checking his watch and wondering if it's late enough to go back to Smith's camper.

He hears the pack of men coming around the corner before he sees them, their voices splitting the quiet of the outdoors, sprinkled with laughter. They come from the dive bar's front entrance, their faces obscured in the dark. John Henry counts five men, and he can tell they're young, probably in their twenties. He lingers in the shadows next to the bar's back door, trying not to draw attention to himself as they pass by a few yards away.

"Hey, who the hell is that?" one of the men calls out in John Henry's direction.

The pack slows to a stop, except for somebody continuing on to a pickup truck.

"I can't see a damn thing out here," says another man. "What are you talking about?"

"That guy by the door. Hey! What are you doing out here all by yourself, huh?"

John Henry doesn't answer. He considers going back inside to wait for the men to leave, then decides to give it a minute.

One of the men breaks away from his friends and approaches, stopping once he can see John Henry enough to satisfy his curiosity. "I think it's the Black guy," he says. "No wonder I can't see his face worth a damn out here."

The other men laugh.

"What are you waiting for, cowboy?" one of them says to John Henry.

"Probably his drug dealer," another man replies, quieter than his friend but loud enough for John Henry to hear him.

The group laughs again.

John Henry keeps smoking his cigarette, trying to play it cool, but feels acutely aware of his gun where it waits on his hip.

"You better be out here for drugs, bro," says the man closest to John Henry. "Because all the white pussy inside, that's not for you. Understand?"

"Hey, I'm fucking leaving in the next thirty seconds, with or without you," the man in the truck says, raising his voice. "Hurry the fuck up."

The three men closer to the truck move to hop into the bed, but the man near John Henry doesn't turn away from him yet.

"I don't care if buckle bitches want to throw themselves all over you for being in the rodeo," the man says, a slight slur in his voice. "They're not for you. So keep your dick in your fucking pants, all right?"

The man in the truck starts the engine and honks the horn, the headlights cutting through the darkness and illuminating both John Henry and the confrontational white guy.

"You better run along if you don't want to get left behind," John Henry says, his voice controlled.

The white guy scowls at him, backlit, and spits on the ground in John Henry's direction. He turns and heads for the pickup, climbing into the passenger side of the cab. The truck doesn't pull out of its parking space at first, the lights still on John Henry. He drops his cigarette stub and squashes it under his boot, giving the darkened truck windshield a chilly, defiant look. He's not going inside now. He won't back down from these fools. He stands there and hopes they can see the hilt of his gun winking in the headlights.

The truck finally rolls out toward the edge of the lot, and John Henry watches it pull into the road, eastbound toward Cody. He breathes a little easier once it disappears behind the bar, then heads for his own truck, wishing he'd stayed on Smith's land with a six-pack and the dog instead of coming out here.

A few paces from his truck, John Henry stops when he hears squealing tires and a growling engine.

The same pickup full of white men peels back into the lot, the three men in the bed and the one in the passenger seat firing their guns into the air and yelling as the truck circles the parked vehicles and John Henry. The truck makes three rounds, leaving tracks in the dirt, as John Henry hurries to get into his own pickup and start the engine. He stares at the back door of the bar, waiting for someone to come outside to see what all the commotion is about, but nobody does.

For one of the longest moments of John Henry's life, he sits behind the wheel of his truck, ready to draw his gun out of the holster, and wonders if the white men are about to ambush him or shoot him as they drive past.

But after the third circle, the truck hightails it back onto the highway and leaves John Henry behind, echoes of *fuck you* and the N-word swirling in the air like dust.

He waits five minutes before leaving the bar, giving the pack of men enough of a head start that they won't see him following the same eastbound route toward Smith's land. One man emerges from the bar's back door to give the parking lot a cursory glance, then goes inside again.

John Henry speeds on his way back to Smith, not slowing down even once he's off the main highway and on the desolate, no-lane road leading to Smith's property. When he finally sees the little camper's light in the middle of solid darkness, his eyes well up with tears, and he sniffs and swallows them back.

"What happened?" Smith says, standing up from his lawn chair as soon as he registers John Henry's face.

John Henry doesn't know if he can explain without sounding like he's making a big deal out of drunken harassment. Maybe he's overreacting.

"Jesus, are you shaking?" Smith says once John Henry gets up close to him. Smith touches him as if to confirm what he sees. "John, what's going on?"

"You got whiskey?" John Henry says, heading for the camper.

"Yeah," Smith replies, following him. "On the liquor shelf."

John Henry pulls the bottle of Bulleit from its place next to the gin and vodka and pours himself a glass on the kitchen counter. He downs the whiskey in one gulp.

"You need to tell me what the hell's got you so upset," says Smith, standing between John Henry and the open door.

John Henry just stares at him, the whiskey starting to kick in, then crosses the distance between them and flings his arms around Smith. Smith hugs him in return, no hesitation, and John Henry almost starts to cry at the sheer relief he feels.

"Okay, okay," Smith says, voice gentle and quiet. "I've got you. I've got you."

They stand there for a long time, holding each other in silence.

*

The garage closed two hours ago, but Cooper's still here, drinking straight from a bottle of Bulleit in the scrapyard. The August sun is finally beginning to slip toward the horizon, and because she's too drunk to drive, Cooper will soon start to walk to Smith's saloon to meet her sister. She has to keep the promise she made: She won't leave Christa alone after dark unless Christa gives her permission. Not as long as Buck's in town.

Cooper's been working on another restoration project since the beginning of the year, something she started before she found the Triumph in Ten Sleep. An old '70 Chevy Malibu, nothing more than a paint-stripped hunk of metal when she first saw it out here. Now, about eight months later, the car almost runs the way it should, and the exterior only needs the powder-blue coat Cooper's had planned all along. The Malibu is the excuse she gave herself and her sister for staying at the garage this late, and she's barely touched it since the shop closed at five o'clock, sitting on the hood drinking instead.

She's got her coveralls unbuttoned down below her breasts because there aren't any men around. The air's cooler now as dusk sweeps over Wyoming but still warm enough that Cooper keeps her sleeves rolled to her elbows. She slouches against the car under the weight of her loneliness and despair, far enough into the whiskey bottle that she'll be hungover tomorrow if she doesn't quit now.

She thinks about Lou in her floral-print dress and cowboy boots, coming to her here a few weeks ago, and she thinks about Leeann expecting to fall in love again one day even if she never leaves this town. If Cooper were like them, if she could just be like everyone else in the world and want a lover, she wouldn't have to face being alone forever. She wouldn't care if her cousin and her sister leave her behind for marriage. Even if she were a lesbian, she could have hope of companionship. She could've said yes to Lou. She could ask Leeann on a date.

Instead, Cooper fears the day when she has to pack up her half of the house on Farm Road and move into a one-bedroom apartment because Christa wants to run off with a man. She dreads a future where Christa and Smith are both out of reach, holed up in romantic bliss with their respective spouses, too busy or too addicted to their lovers' company to see Cooper one-on-one. Unanswered, unreturned phone calls and years of weekends spent alone—that's what she sees when she imagines her future. Maybe Christa and Smith will leave Cody altogether, and Cooper will wander Wyoming, the West, by herself until she's too old and tired to keep running away from her own solitude.

Her eyes fill with tears, and she grits her teeth, refusing to cry. She takes another drink and starts pacing around the car.

Why can't she be like everyone else? Why does she have to be so strange? Why can't she want what everyone else wants?

And why can't other people be like her?

She thinks she can hear the faint sounds of the Nite Rodeo in the distance, the announcer on the speakers and the crowd cheering. Is Buck competing tonight, the son of a bitch? She might go down there with her gun and find him, shoot him in front of the whole damn audience if she didn't need to go be with Christa.

What is she supposed to do for her sister now? What else can she do but kill the man? Nothing else is guaranteed to stop him from raping or killing Christa or both. Maybe Cooper can find out what motel Buck's staying in, break into his room at night, and shoot him in the bed. She has to do something. She can't resign to powerlessness.

Her eyes catch on the crowbar she left on the ground the last time she worked on the Malibu. She takes another drink, staring at the piece of metal like it's got something coming.

Cooper picks up the crowbar in one hand, staggering on her feet, and turns toward the Malibu. She sets the bottle of Bulleit on the ground and grips the bar in both hands as she approaches the car. She gets into a batter's stance, hesitating for a moment, everything slowed down in her whiskey haze.

She swings the crowbar hard into the front passenger window, smashing it all over the seat, the sound piercing the silence of the scrapyard. She starts beating the hood of the car, denting the bare metal over and over, swinging until her shoulders burn and her arms are too tired to keep going. By the time she quits and tosses the crowbar away, tears stream over her hot face, and she's panting, whimpering, sweating.

*

Smith is alone in the saloon on Tuesday night, polishing the bar and drinking beer. He's got the jukebox going, singing the lines he knows to the old country songs he used to hear in the back of his father's truck when he was a boy. He and his older brother would be quiet while their mother sang along with her favorite folk songs when they played on the radio. The one on the jukebox is one of her favorites, one of Smith's, too, a Judy Collins tune about a rodeo man the woman speaker loves.

He stops rubbing down the bar when Christa walks in and comes to stand before it, smiling as she listens to the end of the song. They look at each other, soulful and somber, his troubles and memories converging with hers in their eye contact.

"Hey, CJ," he says.

"Hey, cowboy," she replies.

Smith goes over to the jukebox and turns it off as Christa sits at the bar. He comes back behind it and sets the polishing rag aside.

"Can I get you a drink?" he asks.

"Beer, please," says Christa.

He knows what she likes, and he serves it to her, leaving the bottle cap on the bar top and picking up his own unfinished beer. She sips from her bottle and it's clear she has something on her mind. Smith waits for her to speak, watching her face. She puts her beer down and looks at him, the way she used to when they were kids and he wouldn't leave her alone until she told him what was wrong. She would lie across her bed on her belly, and he would kneel on the floor next to it, their faces mere inches apart. Staring at each other. She always told him what ailed her eventually.

This time, Christa reaches into her bag, pulls out her gun, and sets it on the bar. Smith eyes the gun but doesn't touch it, peering up at her to see if she's going to explain.

"I don't want to need that," she says, her voice thinning out and cracking. "But I'm scared. And I don't know what to do."

Smith feels his heart wrench and almost hops over the bar right then to hug her.

"I don't know what to do," Christa says again. "I could be imagining danger where there isn't any, or I could be right about him. But either way, the damn gun doesn't make me feel any safer, even though I know how to use it, and I'm a good enough shot. I don't want to have to shoot him—but I've been sleeping with the gun. Last night, I dreamt I was running with it in my hand. I want to put it down."

"You just did," he says, his tone as soft as hers.

Her eyes well up, but she doesn't cry.

Now, Smith does move to her side of the bar and gathers Christa in his arms. She slumps against his chest, and he holds her tight, trying to make her feel protected, to remind her she can count on him.

"I want him to go away, Smith."

"I know," he says, voice raspy and low. He rests his chin on the top of her head, clasping her shoulder in one hand. He figures she can hear his heart beating against her ear and hopes it doesn't give away his fear. He shuts his eyes and fantasizes about running away with his cousins, just for a moment. Taking them and the dog in his truck and disappearing, leaving Buck and John Henry and this town and the rodeo in the dust. He doesn't know where they would go and doesn't care. He could live in the middle of nowhere with them, cut off from the rest of civilization, and do just fine. He wouldn't have to hide or remember—Christa and Cooper wouldn't have to be afraid.

"You know I won't let anything happen to you, right?" he says to Christa, speaking softly. "Give me the gun if you don't want it. I'll carry it. I'll do something about him."

She pulls back, their arms still around each other, and gazes at him. "You can't follow me everywhere."

"Why not?" He gives her a little smile. "I'll close this place up for a couple weeks and you hire me as a bodyguard."

She smiles back. "Do I have to pay you?"

"Yeah, in beer."

Christa snorts.

"And hugs. Or you could make me a couple pies, and we'll call it even."

They smile at each other, and he feels better about her looking less sad, the intensity gone from her eyes.

"I've been meaning to make you a lemon pie," Christa says and hugs him close again.

"I've been meaning to eat one," Smith replies. "Looks like my luck's finally changing."

*

She waits for him in the parking lot, watching the stadium entrance from behind the wheel of her truck. She's parked a good distance away but close enough to see the faces of whoever walks out. The sounds of the announcer, the buzzer, and the crowd reach her loud and clear from inside the stadium, even with her windows rolled up. She checks her watch: 8:47. The rodeo's always over by nine.

Cooper's eyes fall to her gun lying on the passenger side of the bench seat. It's a Smith & Wesson .44 Special revolver, the 629 Deluxe model, fully loaded with six rounds in the chamber. She has other guns, but this one is her favorite. She keeps the stainless-steel frame polished to a shine and well oiled. The grip is a textured wood, rich reddish-brown in color. Smith calls it her cowboy gun.

She hears the announcer run through the names of the night's winners, then thank the crowd for coming out. She has no idea how many times she's listened to rodeo closing announcements, clapping after Smith's name and smiling at him as he stood in the arena with the other winners. She might as well be an ex-rodeo rider herself, with how deeply the sounds and smells and sights of the life are carved into her psyche.

She watches as people emerge from the stadium, dispersing throughout the parking lot and driving away in

Ford and Chevy pickup trucks and the odd SUV. The riders come out from around the back where the animals are led through, all of them in their cowboy hats and chaps. She waits to see him, hoping he came in his own vehicle without any passengers. When she sees him step out of the shadows, something cold slithers into her belly, something primitive.

She wants to kill him and wear his blood on her face like a lioness.

She tracks him across the parking lot, sees him get into his truck alone and start it up. She turns the key in her own ignition and hangs back long enough to give him a head start.

She follows him at a distance. It starts to rain as he leads her east on Yellowstone Avenue. He turns off the road a few minutes away from the rodeo grounds, onto the lot of the Big Bear Motel. The white light of the retro sign on the side of the road appears hazy at the edges, through the rain.

He parks his truck right outside one of the rooms, and she parks hers in the middle of the lot, a few paces away. She watches him get out of the truck and hop under the overhang roof covering the doorsteps. She grabs her gun off the passenger seat and gets out of her own cab.

"Hey!" she barks, raising her voice above the rain. "Hey!"

Buck stops and turns around. "You talking to me?"

"Yeah, I'm talking to you, asshole." Cooper stops a couple yards away from him, still in the parking lot, getting rained on. She points her gun at him.

His whole body tenses, and he raises his hands in front of him, looking spooked. "Woah, hey, I don't want any trouble."

"You stay the fuck away from Christa. You stay away, or I'll make you the sorriest son of a bitch in the world. Are we clear?"

"Christa? How do you know Christa?"

"None of your Goddamn business." Rain snakes along the carved edges of Cooper's face like water over stone. Her eyes are dark and hateful, her voice full of venom. "You're going to leave her alone. You're never going to send her anything again. You're not going to go looking for her, you're not going to talk about her, you're going to forget she exists. Or I swear to God, I'll kill you."

"Who are you? Did she send you here? Did she tell you to do this?"

"You understand what I just said? Because I'm not going to tell you again."

Buck watches Cooper as if she is a creature he's never seen or heard of before, both intimidating and grotesque. He's not as afraid of her as he might be if she were a man. But he's more afraid of her than he would be if she were a woman like Christa: long-haired, feminine, dainty. She can see his eyes, even with the water streaming through her own, and she knows exactly what he's feeling. She can see how he's torn between fearing the gun and not fearing a woman, sees how disarmed he is by the image of Cooper: her shape in the night, the gun shining in the white light, her eyes smoldering like coals in the jagged anger of her face, her short hair soaked and plastered to her skull. She stands on the wet, black pavement with her feet spread wide, like a bull cornering a fallen rider with horns ready to gouge out his heart.

But something surfaces in Buck, an arrogance, and he sloughs off his survival instinct like snakeskin, straightening up and lowering his hands. He smirks but stays where he is, his back against the door of his room.

"You better kill me," he says, the uneasiness gone from his voice. "Because if I want her, I'm gonna have her. There's nothing you can do to stop me, 'cept pull that trigger."

Cooper almost does, her finger curled around the metal, hands squeezing the pistol grip. She snarls, wolfish, cold with rage.

"Go ahead," Buck tells her.

It's quiet on the motel property, the only sound the rain beating the ground and the cars and the roof of the building. The road is empty behind her, pitch dark. They're alone in the lot. They might as well be alone in the middle of wilderness, deep into Smith's land. She could kill Buck and drive away. She might just get away with it.

The gun is heavy and slick in her hands. The muscles in her arms start to burn and tire.

He's looking at her with a gleam in his eyes, not quite smiling.

Cooper lowers the gun, turns, and stalks back to her truck. She gets behind the wheel, her clothes soaked through and sopping, puts the gun down on the seat again and starts the engine. She squeals out of the parking lot, glancing in the rearview mirror to make sure Buck isn't grinning.

He is.

*

John Henry's alone in Smith's camp, reading next to the firepit when Jordan shows up. He doesn't see her truck coming until she's close enough that he can hear the engine and the tires rolling on the ground. Before her face comes into view, a rush of nervousness overwhelms him, and he thinks of his gun left inside the camper. Once he sees his visitor is a woman, he relaxes. She hops out of the truck and smiles at him, and he gets on his feet, closing the book.

"You must be John Henry," she says. "I'm Jordan Lange, a friend of Smith's."

They shake hands.

"What can I do for you?" he replies.

"Smith asked me to stop by and talk to you."

John Henry feels a mix of amusement, affection, and embarrassment at Smith thinking he needs to be checked on and wonders why the man didn't call him, considering he's running errands alone.

"I could use a walk," says Jordan, already facing westward. "What do you think?"

"Sure. You want anything to drink first?"

"No, I'm good."

He leaves his book behind on the seat of his chair, and they start walking side by side away from the campsite, keeping a slow pace.

"Smith told me what happened to you the other night. At the bar."

John Henry glances at her and purses his lips, his head down.

"Don't be too mad at him," she continues. "He was worried about you and wanted my advice on how to help."

"Well, as you can see, I'm not hurt."

"Yes, you are. The hurt isn't physical, but it still matters. It's still serious."

He doesn't know what to say to that. Two nights ago, when he arrived here after the incident at the roadside bar, John Henry slept fitfully in Smith's bed, comforted only by Smith holding him close. He hasn't left the land since then, calmed in the isolation of Smith's camp, wanting to stay out of everyone else's sight. Smith hasn't left him until this morning, calling out of his bar shift yesterday and explaining to his cousins his need to keep John Henry company. The kindness and concern took John Henry by surprise, and he's been grateful for it. Smith never once told him he was making a big deal out of what happened with the white men.

John Henry and Jordan walk in silence for a minute or two, not looking at each other.

"Anything like it ever happen before?" Jordan asks.

"Not really. I've had some confrontations, but not like that. Not with guns involved. They were the worst part."

"I can imagine."

"And the thing is I have a gun of my own. Don't go anywhere without it, especially when I'm on the road. But I was by myself and there were five of them. With half of them firing, it didn't matter that I could've shot back. They could've killed me if they wanted. I knew that."

After a moment, John Henry says, "Do you know what it's like to be really afraid?"

"Yes," says Jordan. "Going through life as a woman, a Shoshone woman, I don't think I'll know the last of fear until I'm dead."

John Henry gives her a slight nod of respectful acknowledgment, then glances at his boots again and back up at the sky. "Those guys only saw I was Black. They didn't even know about—" He stops when he realizes he doesn't know what Smith told Jordan about him, if she knows John Henry is Smith's lover.

Jordan studies him, and something in her dark eyes indicates she understands, whether Smith told her the truth or not. "Where's your home?"

"Missouri."

"Is it easier for you there than it is in the West?"

"I think so. Not because the white people are so different, just because there are more Black people there. I don't stick out everywhere I go."

"I know what you mean. It's the difference between reservation land and white land."

"You live on a reservation?"

"I used to. Not for a long time. Life is easier out here—that's the sad truth. My people live in great poverty on Wind River. Conditions most white people wouldn't believe exist in this country. There's a lot of suffering on the rez. Violence, drugs, alcohol. I had to choose between a life surrounded by my tribe and my mother's family, and a life where I can have a career and feel hope for my own future. I shouldn't have to choose... None of us should."

The sky covers them in a blanket of gray, sunlight muted in the late morning. It's beginning to warm up, but the day will stay mild. John Henry and Jordan are both dressed in long sleeves and jeans though it's August now. Her boots give her a little extra height, but so do his, and he silently acknowledges her willingness to be alone with a strange man in the middle of nowhere. He doesn't see a weapon on her though he wouldn't be surprised if she's got one concealed.

John Henry almost doesn't want to know the answer, but he decides to ask the question anyway. "How do you and Smith know each other?"

Jordan smiles. "We met when he was still in the rodeo. He came into town to ride, one summer. After he bought this land and started living here, we became... friends."

He hears what she's too polite to say, but somehow, it doesn't hurt him. He likes Jordan. He can tell she's a good person—like his girlfriend Sula. He wonders how long it's been since she was Smith's lover. Months or years?

"You going back into Cody eventually?" Jordan asks.

"I don't know. I've been doing my best to stay out of it all along. I don't want people to talk about me and Smith."

"Why would they? All they would think is you're an old rodeo buddy of his. Which is true."

"It's a small town. I'm probably the only Black person in this whole county. People would talk. They probably did after I went to see him at his bar."

Jordan looks at him as if still waiting to hear the reason John Henry should stay out of Cody.

"The less people talk about Smith, the better," John Henry says.

"They talked about him all the time, his first few years here. If he were more social, they would talk about him less, I think."

The corner of John Henry's lips curl in a sad, reflexive smile. "He wasn't always the man he is now."

Jordan makes eye contact with him. "I know."

They stop and scan their surroundings, the open plain flat and endless in every direction, the wind blowing past them westward bound. The landscape resurrects different ghosts for each of them: other stretches of desolate land miles away; too many moments of loneliness to parse out; the feeling of running away without a destination; and the past they've both lived, right here, in the arms and the sight of a man they can't shake.

"You could stay," Jordan tells John Henry.

He looks at her like the possibility didn't exist until she spoke it.

"You could stay here," she says. "On this land or in Cody. He would protect you if you did."

John Henry never allowed himself to imagine living here, not even before he met Sula, when he circled Wyoming on rodeo events like a bird that can't abandon its stolen nest. It was too dangerous to let himself fantasize about finding Smith and moving here to find out what might be.

"He's just a man," John Henry says to Jordan. "He can't protect me from the whole world forever. He can't even protect himself."

Jordan clasps John Henry's forearm with surprising strength. She looks right at him. "Don't let your enemies rob you of your birthright. If you live your whole life controlled by fear, they win."

"My birthright?"

She nods. "Freedom. The freedom to follow your heart. To choose your home. The freedom to roam this country and be wherever you want to be."

He stares at her, amazed by and skeptical of her courage. "I don't think you understand what it feels like. Being something so many people want to destroy."

"Of course I understand," she replies, her voice breathy and quiet, her face full of emotion. "Look at me."

He does, sees her black hair, light brown skin, her Indigenous features, her womanhood, and recognizes his mistake.

"Standing your ground while others run doesn't make you less afraid than they are," she says.

"No," he says, quiet. "I guess it doesn't. But being brave could get you killed quicker than running."

"We're all dying, John Henry. What value does a long life hold if it's spent unhappy? Imprisoned in your own secrets, your own fear?"

She's still holding on to his arm, her eyes full of feeling, and he's not even sure what she's pleading him for.

"I have a woman back home," John Henry tells her. "A woman I love."

Jordan drops her hand but doesn't seem offended. "Then you have to decide which life will make you happier and give you peace."

She turns back toward Smith's camp and starts the long return walk, her pace slow enough to allow John Henry to catch up. Her long, sleek hair swings to the cadence of her steps. He watches her before following, thinking if Smith wanted a wife, there couldn't possibly be a better woman for him in this whole state than Jordan.

When they reach the campsite again, the tension of their conversation has disappeared, left behind on the plain. They stop and face each other between the firepit and Jordan's truck.

"You know, being brave," she says, "living with fear—it gets easier the more you do it. It's never easy. Not exactly. But it's not always as hard as it feels to you right now."

He nods. "You're probably right."

She offers her hand, and he takes it to shake. She holds his in both of hers and looks at him with those penetrating eyes. "Don't think of the past. Think of today. Think of the future. That's all we have."

"Thank you for coming out here," John Henry tells her, the words heartfelt. "I appreciate it."

Jordan smiles. "Take care of yourself, John Henry."

"You too."

He watches her drive away, standing in the midst of Smith's camp as the pickup truck kicks up dust on the trail leading to the paved road. She turns left and heads east for Cody.

*

The trailer door's open when Smith gets home on Monday morning after breakfast with John Henry, who's on his way north to Montana. Cooper's sitting on the bench seat opposite the door, drinking a beer from the six-pack she brought with her. Smith leans through the doorway, standing on the fold-out steps with his hands braced against the doorframe. She looks at him, and he looks at her.

"Hey," he says.

"Hey," she replies.

"You waiting for me?"

"I needed somewhere to think. Alone."

"I can go if you want."

"No," says Cooper. "Stay."

He steps into the trailer, standing up straight with his hands on his hips. The top of his hat brushes the ceiling. "Guess I need a beer if we're drinking."

He heads into the little kitchen and pulls a bottle of his usual out of the fridge, pops the cap off with the bottle opener that always lies on the kitchen counter. He takes a sip, watching Cooper from the middle of the kitchen while she stares out the open doorway with a somber expression. The dog watches Smith from the dining booth, lying in one of the seats.

"Why don't we go outside," Smith says. "It's pretty nice out."

Cooper glances at him, then picks her beer up from the floor and leaves the trailer. Smith follows her with the dog behind him.

They sit in the beach chairs Smith keeps around the firepit, looking out at the land stretching on forever and the sky wide and clear above it. The air smells like rain and wet earth. They're quiet for a while, comfortable in silence together as two people can only be after spending plenty of time sharing it. Smith figures she has something on her mind, and when she's ready, she'll start telling him about it. Until then, he's happy just being with her.

It used to be when they were kids, she would wait for him to talk. She always knew when something was wrong, when he was nursing some kind of upset, and she learned how to be patient with him, how to stop asking him to explain and wait out his silence until he couldn't help but tell her everything. Once he got his license and his daddy's old truck, they would go driving—just the two of them, flying down the flat highways cutting through Natrona County, the windows rolled down and the radio off. Quiet. Quiet until Smith started talking at some point during the ride back or once they were parked in front of his house again or at the convenience store that never rejected the fake IDs the high school kids used to buy beer. Cooper was always the one person he could talk to about anything. And he told her everything. Even when she was fourteen and fifteen to his sixteen and seventeen.

"I'm trying to figure out how selfish I am," Cooper says, staring at the mountains on the horizon line. "How much of my need to protect Christa from that asshole is rational, and how much of it is jealousy."

Smith turns his head to her. "What do you mean by jealousy?"

She stalls, taking a drink. "I mean, I don't want her to leave me. I don't want her to fall in love with some guy and leave me." Cooper pauses. "And maybe if I didn't feel that way, I wouldn't see Buck as some kind of predator. Maybe I'd be telling Christa to give him a chance."

Smith doesn't answer for a long time, mulling over the information. As Cooper waits for his response, they drink and observe the land.

"Christa's been spooked by him from the start," Smith says. "And that's got nothing to do with you."

"I know. How she feels about him has nothing to do with what I'm talking about."

Smith pauses again. "You've never tried stopping her from dating."

"Yeah, and I wouldn't. I can't tell her what to do. But I want to. I want to ask her to stay single, to stay with me."

Cooper's voice is soft and pained, and the intimacy of this moment—his cousin's complete vulnerability and the trust she puts in him—is so fragile, he's afraid of saying the wrong thing.

"Have you felt this way about every guy who's shown an interest in her?"

"No."

"Then, maybe you should trust your instincts."

"Even if my instincts are right and this guy is a son of a bitch, I'm still hoping Christa doesn't fall in love with anyone. I'm still putting myself over her happiness. And that makes me the worst thing I could be—a bad sister."

"Hey." Smith's tone demands Cooper's attention. "You're not a bad sister. You're the best sibling I've ever heard of. The best cousin too."

She gives him a smile, but her eyes are glassy and pink.

"Most people don't give a damn about their family when they grow up. They move on and get married and start families of their own, and they don't bother with anyone else. Christa's lucky to have you, Coop. I think she knows that. I'm lucky."

She gazes at him, face full of emotion, lips pressed together.

Smith reaches over and takes her hand in his.

She averts her gaze, into the sky. He presses into the calluses on her palms and her fingers with his own, her skin tough from working on cars but not as tough as his.

"What do I do?" She sounds small and shudders at the end of the question, a single tear rolling down her cheek.

Smith surveys the land again, his fingers laced with hers. "Tell her the truth. Give her a chance to work something out with you."

"I can't. I can't tell her the truth. She could get mad at me. She could think I don't want her to be happy."

He listens to the pain and sadness in Cooper's voice but doesn't turn to her. "You've been with her since she was born, Coop. You really believe she would misunderstand you that bad?"

Cooper doesn't reply.

Smith pulls on his beer, still holding hands with her, giving her time to talk or cry or get a hold of herself.

When she speaks again, her voice is steady and clear. "I'm afraid of what Buck might do. I talked to him."

Smith turns his head sharply toward Cooper. "When?"

"Last night."

He's still holding Cooper's hand, his arm stretched between their chairs.

She glances at him, with a darkness in her eye. Something he hasn't seen there before.

"He told me he's going to have her if he wants her. And I'll have to kill him to stop him."

"He said that?"

"Yeah."

They peer ahead into the wilderness together, finishing their beers and dropping the empty bottle and can on the ground.

"You shouldn't have gone alone. Does Christa know you did?"

"No. I took my gun."

"Did you threaten him with it?"

"Yes."

Smith scrubs at his eyes with his free hand. "Shit, Cooper. Why didn't you call me?"

"I wasn't thinking about anything except him. And I didn't want you in the middle of it anyway. In case I did kill him."

Smith takes his hand out of hers and gets on his feet. "Christa's not just your sister, Cooper. She's my cousin. And so are you. If you don't want me in the middle of all that concerns you, I suggest you pack up the house and leave town."

Cooper eyes him, slouching in her chair. She doesn't answer.

He starts to pace in front of her, back and forth, combing his fingers through his hair.

"He followed her, Smith. A few nights ago, they were both at the grocery store, and he followed her halfway home. She was ready to go up to Powell and spend the rest of the month there until he's gone. I didn't know what else to do."

"You sure he was following her? Did he notice her at the store?"

"Christa wasn't sure if he noticed her or if he knew her car belonged to her, but after last night, I'm pretty damn sure he knew, and he followed her on purpose."

"Why?"

"Because he's staying at the Big Bear, which means he should've gone west after leaving the store. He had no other reason to go east with Christa as far as Twenty-sixth Street. He was following her."

"What if he knows people in town and he was going to see them?"

"Come on, Smith."

"He didn't follow her home. He went somewhere else before she got home, didn't he?"

"Yeah, but how does that change anything? If he didn't want to confront her, it makes sense he left her alone before she stopped."

"I'm trying to consider the possibility he's not a stalker, even if he is an asshole."

"Why?"

"Because if he's not a stalker, you don't have a reason to shoot him, Cooper. And I'd like it if you didn't, all right?"

Cooper gives Smith a hard look, rising to her feet with her hands balled at her sides. "I'm going to shoot him if I have to, Smith. Not even you can stop me."

He stands still and stares at her, into the cold wilderness of her eyes, and he shivers. She'll kill Buck if he comes for Christa, throw away her whole life to do it, and it makes him want to find Buck right now and run him out of town.

"Don't go after him," Smith says, his voice soft and

quiet. "If he leaves her alone, you leave him alone."

She doesn't answer, gazing into Smith's eyes. It's only when she turns to find her chair and sit back down that he notices the gun tucked into the front of her waistband, the steel glinting at him even without any sun to catch. She pulls another beer out of her six-pack and cracks it open, her knees spread wide and her elbows set on them. He stays put, running both his hands through his hair and deflating in the broken tension of their standoff. He appraises her, then goes back to his chair.

He realizes he only brought one of his own beers outside and glances back at the open trailer door. He holds out his hand to Cooper, and she gives him one of her beers. It's cool but not as cold as beer ought to be. He's going to drink it anyway.

"You could bring her here," Smith says after a while "You could both stay here until he's gone."

Cooper shoots him a skeptical look. "Where? In the trailer? Are the three of us going to share the double bed?"

"You two could have the bed. I'd sleep outside, in the truck or on the ground."

Cooper shakes her head.

They watch the storm clouds breaking up, leaving behind a pale, washed-out sky. For the first time since he bought this land, he sees the three of them—Cooper, Christa, and himself—waking up on it in a house.

*

It's Friday night after rodeo hours, and some of the guys have come out to Bud's Bar to start the weekend right. Buck and four of the riders he's been hanging out with over the summer have a table on the side of the dive opposite the pool table. They order several pitchers of beer, and a few of them start smoking. They review their night at the rodeo, then play a couple rounds of cards with the deck Jake carries. They've got some women in their company who have been following them since June. The women are from somewhere else in the county, but they come out to Cody most weekends just to see the rodeo men they're screwing.

Bud's Bar is a roadside stop along the North Fork Highway, west of town. A dark dive for rough men and fast women who stay until the sun comes up, it's a place that doesn't call the cops when fights break out and pretends not to know Park County's drug dealers meet their junkies in the back lot on a regular basis. The air is always charged with the tension of unruly men one drink or mistake away from starting something. The dive reeks of cigarette smoke, cheap beer, cheap whiskey, and male musk. September through May, Bud's is a biker, trucker, drifter haunt with the odd cowboy thrown in, but for the summer, it opens up to the rodeo riders and the women who want them. The regulars make room for them, trading stories and providing the ornery drunks with the brawls they're hankering for.

Sometime after midnight, Buck gets up from the group table and tells his friends he's going to order a drink. He goes over and stands at the bar, buzzed and preoccupied. He asks for a whiskey, and the bartender pours him one. He sips on it, debating with himself about talking to the bartender. The bartender, a man in his fifties with a graying cowboy mustache, doesn't pay Buck any attention as he stands with his back to the wall and lights up a cigarette.

Buck leans toward him, one elbow on the bar top, and gives him a secretive look. "You know a woman in town by the name of Christa?"

The bartender thinks for a second. "I know of a Christa Boone."

"That's her."

"And? What do you want to know?"

"Tell me about her."

"I've never met her. I've only seen her around town."

"How'd you know who she is then?"

"Everybody in Cody knows who she is. She's Smith Rose's cousin."

Buck straightens up, surprised. "Smith Rose, three-time NFR all-around world champion?"

"That's the only Smith we got, last I knew."

"He lives here? In Cody?"

"Yeah. You didn't know that? I figured the local Nite Rodeo guys brag about him to the out-of-towners every year."

Buck pauses, shifting his focus off the bartender's face. Smith Rose retired before Buck's rodeo career started picking up steam, and he hasn't thought about him much since. He followed Smith's career the last three years of it, only because he followed pro rodeo as a kid in his early twenties still stuck in the amateur circuit. He watched Smith compete live a couple times but never got any closer, never met him or anyone who knew him well. When Smith retired at twenty-seven, it made no sense to him. Now Buck himself is twenty-eight, past his rodeo prime, and Smith's early retirement makes even less sense than it did before. Buck never had Smith's kind of talent—not many men in the rodeo do—and if he did, he would milk every last dollar out of it.

"I been here all summer, and I haven't seen him,"

Buck says to the bartender.

"Smith keeps to himself. He's got a place outside of town somewhere. In Cody, he usually doesn't go far from his bar."

"He's got a bar?"

"The Bad Moon Saloon, on Sheridan. It's on the east end of the street, just before the turn off."

Buck hasn't been there, but he must've driven past it at least once.

"He's been here a couple times this year," the bartender says. "Comes alone and drinks. My regulars know to leave him alone. I think that's why he stops by once in a while. He's not a big talker, or maybe he's private. Never imagined that when I used to watch him on TV."

Buck picks up his drink for the first time since he started the conversation. He doesn't know what to make of Christa being Smith's cousin. It could be a complication. It could be leverage. He's going to have to think about it before he makes his next move.

He puts his drink down, returns his attention to the bartender. "You know if Christa Boone has a friend, a woman with short hair?"

"Yeah," the bartender says. "That's Cooper. Her sister."

It occurs to Buck that the night in the motel parking lot wasn't the first time he saw Cooper. She was at the party where he met Christa. She was the one who took Christa away.

"What do you know about her?"

The bartender shakes his head. "Nothing. I think she's a mechanic."

In the dark, she looked like a man for a second, then

something unreal, the gun no more than a glimmer, like a piece of moon or bared teeth. He didn't get a good look at her face, only saw the shape of her. Her voice was strong and lower than most women's. She never sounded afraid, not once. But he doesn't think she can bring herself to shoot him or anybody else even if she wants to. Women don't have it in them. She might pull the trigger if he backed her into a corner, but she'd feel guilty about it after.

Buck wonders if Christa has a gun.

"You know if she goes to Smith's saloon a lot?"

"Who? Christa?"

Buck nods.

"Yeah," the bartender says. "Pretty sure she and her sister are there sometimes. But I couldn't tell you how often. I haven't been to Bad Moon in a while."

Buck finishes his drink and goes back to the table. Only two of the guys are there—Dale and Ryan. Dale has a woman in his lap. Ryan has one leaning against him, in a chair right next to his. Buck returns to his seat and reaches for the beer pitcher, empties it into his glass.

"Buck," says Dale. "Were you telling your life story over there? Goddamn, that is the longest it's taken someone to order a drink in history."

Buck glances at him. "Where's Jake and Evan?"

"Jake's in the can," says Ryan, sitting with his elbows on the table and his whiskey glass in one hand. "Evan's over there, talking to those guys."

Buck peers over his shoulder and spots Evan near the back of the room with some local men.

"What the hell are you so down in the mouth for?" Dale says to him, holding onto the blonde in his lap.

Buck glances at him. "Mind your business," he says

and drinks some of his beer.

In a couple weeks, the Cody Nite Rodeo will end with the summer, and he'll go home to Amarillo, Texas. He's running out of time.

*

Christa parks her car down the street from Wind River Tattoo and walks over, the Ruger tucked into the back of her jeans. It's quiet outside, the western sky streaked red, pink, and orange and a soft darkness settling over the town. She doesn't see anyone else out on the sidewalks, just a handful of vehicles lining both sides of the street and the electric signs shining above their business doors.

The Open light in the tattoo parlor's front window is turned off, but the door is unlocked. Christa goes inside and sees Jordan sitting behind the counter where she keeps the cash register, using her computer.

"We're closed," Jordan calls out. When she looks up and sees Christa, surprise flashes across her face.

"I know," Christa says, approaching her. "But I didn't come for a tat."

"You're the last person I would've expected to see in here," says Jordan. "How are you?"

"I've been better. That's why I came. I wanted to get your advice."

"My advice?"

Christa nods. "Your brother's a cop, right?"

Jordan pauses. "My half-brother is a sheriff's deputy with the county. What's going on?"

Christa hesitates before explaining. "There's this guy. He's in the rodeo, not from around here. I think he's been stalking me."

"You've got to be kidding," Jordan says, frowning.

"Since when?"

"Not that long. I met him at a party last month, but nothing happened. I didn't even give him my real name. But he found out who I am and— I think he's been following me, and I'm worried he won't leave me alone."

"And you want to know if you should report him."

Christa nods.

"But he hasn't done anything illegal, has he?"

"No," Christa says. "He hasn't."

Jordan bites her bottom lip.

"I was thinking about a restraining order," Christa tells her.

"Yeah. You could do that. I don't know if it'll do any good."

"It'll send him a message, make it clear I don't want anything to do with him."

"True. But restraining orders are easy to ignore, Christa. Bad guys ignore them all the time. And this one's leaving town as soon as the rodeo's over, right?"

"As far as I know."

"That's only a couple weeks away. If you got a restraining order against him, by the time it's served, he won't have much time left here anyway."

"So you think I should wait it out."

Jordan studies her, reading her face. "I'm saying you'll be waiting for him to leave Cody, with or without a restraining order. And because he's leaving soon, something like that may not make a difference."

Christa has her arms crossed against her chest, and she looks away, sees a big illustration hanging on one of the walls and moves toward it. She stands before the image of a Native woman riding a bear, superimposed on a background of outer space. The only details on the woman are her facial features and the lines of her hair, her body a silhouette. She's holding a long spear, and her hair flares out around her as if she's underwater. She and the bear could be a constellation, and Christa wonders if they are, to the Wind River Shoshone.

"I had a friend make that for me," says Jordan. "Cool, huh?"

"Who is she?"

"The Great Mother. Protector of women. Everything came from her. The bear is her form on earth. Her spirit."

"Your people believe in her?"

Jordan pauses, considering the image. "No. But I do."

Christa turns to face her, arms still crossed. "Could you talk to your brother for me? Tell him about Buck and see if the sheriff's department can do something?"

"That's his name? Buck?"

Christa nods.

"You don't know his last name?"

"No. But it should be easy to find in the rodeo listings."

"Okay. I'll talk to my brother."

Christa offers a small, unhappy smile. "Thanks. I appreciate it."

"You're not going to file a restraining order?"

"I guess not."

Christa starts heading for the door.

"Hey, wait," Jordan says.

Christa stops and turns back to her.

Jordan takes something out of a drawer in the counter and brings it to Christa, presses it into her hand. "Take this. It's always given me courage."

Christa inspects the object—a black stone carved into the shape of a bear. It's cool and heavy in her hand, smooth under her thumb when she rubs it. She looks up at Jordan. "Thank you. I'll give it back. Soon."

Jordan smiles and nods.

Christa leaves the shop and walks back to her car, hand closed over the bear.

*

West Yellowstone, Montana is a small town right on the other side of Wyoming's state line. It's a three-hour drive through the national park from Cody, but Smith goes because the Wild West Yellowstone Rodeo is John Henry's last event of the summer. Similar to Cody's Nite Rodeo, Wild West Yellowstone runs all summer but only on weekends. It's not a pro-circuit rodeo, and as far as money goes, it's small time. Smith has attended before as a spectator and a competitor. He figures John Henry entered for the fun of it to finish off the summer season at the latest possible date and on a light note.

Tourists from the tristate area fill the town, most of the motels and hotels packed with them and visiting rodeo riders. Because the town is one mile from Yellowstone National Park's western entrance, plenty of people who travel to visit the park stay in West Yellowstone if they don't want to camp. Out-of-town rodeo riders book rooms months in advance to beat the summer park goers.

Smith doesn't go to the rodeo when he gets into town. The one he went to in Montana last month was hard enough. He drives around looking for somewhere to stop and ends up waiting for John Henry in a coffee shop. He's the only customer who stays, a few people coming and going during the two hours he's there. He sits at a table by the window, drinking his coffee and watching the street.

After a while, he opens his sketchbook—a brown leather softcover book filled with horses and bulls and rodeo men, his dog and his trailer, Cooper and Christa—and adds the finishing touches to a drawing of John Henry. There are only two, the first a sketch of John Henry standing naked on the plain the day they had sex on Smith's land. The sketch shows John Henry from behind, his face hidden as he talks to one of the horses in the distance. In the second drawing, the one Smith finishes now, John Henry, decked out in his rodeo attire of fringed chaps and a cowboy hat, is lighting a cigarette.

Smith always liked art as a kid. He completed stacks of coloring books and burned through boxes of crayons faster than his parents could stand. Before he learned how to shoot, how to ride a horse, before he got interested in the rodeo, Smith learned how to draw, and he did it every chance he got until he started high school. He was the only boy who took art as his elective each year, but otherwise, he hid his drawings from public view because the other guys would've harassed him for being an artist. Starting a band with your buddies outside of school was acceptable, but only fags took drama, art, or choir at school. Cool guys were supposed to get on one of the athletic teams, ideally football or basketball, and choose electives like woodworking, welding, or auto.

Smith did his best to hide his art class enrollment, never talked about it to any of his friends, and when he won a blue ribbon in the state art show his junior year, he convinced the girl who read the morning announcements to omit his name from the list of Natrona County High winners.

Before Smith discovered rodeo, he secretly considered going to college for art, which his parents would've thought was a waste of money. They never gave him a hard time for drawing when he was growing up, but he knows they would not have been proud of their son the artist the way they're proud of their son the rodeo champion.

Cooper has always been a fan of Smith's drawings, no less than she was a fan of him as a rodeo star. He used to send her drawings in the mail when he was on the road. He'd mail her postcards with doodles crowding the words, sometimes with just a drawing and no message. He's pretty sure she still has them all in a shoebox somewhere.

When he's done looking at the finished drawing of John Henry, Smith closes the book and sets it aside on the table. He checks his watch, then gazes out the window again. After a few minutes, he pulls his wallet out of his pocket and finds the small, worn photo he keeps tucked behind his driver's license. It was taken eight years ago at his favorite hometown bar, right after he won his second all-around champion title at the PRCA National Finals. He's in between Cooper and Christa with a jubilant smile on his face. Christa, who was eighteen and right out of her first year of college, is bright-eyed and glowing with her head pressed against his. Cooper, aged twenty-two, is on Smith's other side, kissing his cheek and beaming at him with pure love. They're all wasted.

He smiles at the picture, running his thumb over the bottom. He looks at it whenever he wants to remember feeling on top of the world. He's looked at it a lot in these last five years, living in Park County. The memory of such complete joy might crush him under the weight of his present unhappiness, but he also uses the photograph to remind himself that while the rodeo is in his past, Cooper and Christa aren't. Their love, their connection, their unity is alive—and deeper now than it was back then, growing stronger as time passes and changes them. He will always have his cousins. He never has to give them up. And since he retired from the rodeo, just about every moment of feeling good again, of appreciating his life, of liking who he is, has been wrapped up in them.

Pretty soon, John Henry is going to leave, go home to his future wife and take his friendship with him. Smith doesn't envy John Henry's life though the other man seems far happier. John Henry may have the rodeo for a few more years, and he may have a girlfriend who wants to spend the rest of her life with him. But Smith has the acceptance and support of the two people he loves most in the world: his cousins. He may have to hide his attraction to men from everybody else, but he doesn't have to hide it from them. He never did.

Near the rodeo's official end time, Smith leaves the coffee shop and drives west out of town to the rodeo grounds ten minutes away along the 20. He waits for John Henry standing against the back of his truck as the parking lot empties out. He tries not to search for him too much amongst the faces of strangers, most of whom are white. When he does spot him, Smith looks away as if he isn't waiting.

John Henry smiles when he sees Smith but doesn't hurry over to him. He's got a bag of his gear slung over one shoulder, all traces of being a rodeo competitor gone from his person. He's wearing his cowboy hat, jeans with a belt, and a thin, long-sleeve T-shirt. It's strange to see him without a button-up shirt on. Smith tries to remember seeing him in a T-shirt before but can't.

"Did you watch?" John Henry says when he reaches Smith.

"No," Smith replies. "Did you win?"

"Placed second in saddle bronc, third in bulls. They got some good riders coming out here. I wasn't expecting that."

Smith looks away, thumbs hooked into his hip pockets, then back at John Henry. "You hungry?"

"Yeah."

"Why don't we drop your stuff off at your motel and take one truck from there?"

"All right. Follow me."

They leave John Henry's truck at the motel and go to a pizzeria a few blocks away. Despite the Wild West theme, the food is pretty good. They wash it down with cold beer. By the time they step back outside, daylight has faded into bluish-lavender, the sun nowhere in sight but darkness still a few hours away.

They go for a walk, side by side with their hands in their pockets, quiet for several blocks. The silence, which feels big here the same way it does on Smith's land, breaks only with the sound of cars passing by on the road every few minutes.

They stop at a bar and stay there until nightfall, drinking whiskey. It's a dark dive with electric neon signs mounted on the walls and no windows. Just the kind of place where Smith would pick up male strangers for sex when he traveled for the rodeo. He doesn't drink as much as John Henry, anticipating the short drive from the pizzeria to the motel, but he does drink enough to laugh at the funny things John Henry says, enough to smile silly and feel a pang of sadness as he realizes this is likely the last time they'll have a drink together.

As they walk back to Smith's truck parked at the pizzeria, Smith makes sure John Henry doesn't stumble into the street or weave too much on the sidewalk. He drives them to the Moose Creek Inn still buzzed, keeping his eye on the speedometer the whole way to make sure he never breaks the speed limit. There are even fewer vehicles on the road than there were earlier.

The motel grounds are picturesque, with well-kept trees and shrubs and flowerpots suspended in front of the rooms. There's no one in sight as Smith pulls into the parking lot, the only sound the chirping of crickets.

John Henry staggers on his way to his room, boots scraping against the pavement, and Smith catches him, dragging him upright. John Henry flings his arm around Smith, wobbling on weak knees, and gazes at him with a stupid grin on his face in the light.

"You're drunk," Smith tells him, smiling a little. "I don't know if you can get it up like this."

John Henry presses his hips into Smith's and says, "Trust me. It won't be a problem."

Their faces are close enough that Smith feels the heat of John Henry's breath and smells the alcohol. Before he can stop it, John Henry's kissing him, the kind of hot, openmouthed kiss that shuts down Smith's brain and leaves him with nothing but his body. They lean against the door, holding on to each other, and make out like they have the whole motel to themselves.

Smith breaks away from John Henry and scans their surroundings. He doesn't see anybody outside or across the street. The road's empty, and the motel grounds are quiet. "You got your key?" he says to John Henry, his mouth red.

"Yeah," John Henry says, digging into all his pockets until he finds the room key. He manages to unlock the door and flips on the light as he steps inside.

Smith follows him and locks the door behind them.

*

Buck Haley sits in his truck on the edge of the parking lot, watching them, cringing in disbelief and disgust. He followed Smith from Cody on a hunch, not knowing exactly what he was going to do when he caught up to the other man. Maybe he'd try talking to Smith, play the nice guy and get him on his side about Christa, or maybe he'd do something else. Smith is in Buck's way, and he'll have to be dealt with before Buck can have Christa. Watching the ex-rodeo star sucking face with a Black man outside a motel room door, no doubt about to have sex with him, it becomes clear to Buck this is something he can use. He doesn't have to convince Smith he's a nice guy worthy of a date with Christa. He can blackmail him into convincing her.

*

This time, they meet on purpose. Leeann's already there when Cooper shows up at the diner, sitting in a window booth and facing the entrance. Their eyes meet as Cooper stops just inside the door before walking down the aisle. She slides into the seat opposite of Leeann.

Leeann quirks one corner of her mouth and peeks out the window. "You might want to rethink your choice of meeting place. People see us alone together like this, they might start getting ideas."

Cooper gives her a look. "They already got ideas about me."

"Yeah, but not about us."

The waitress, Josephine, comes by with a water pitcher and pours Cooper a glass. She hands Cooper a menu and says, "You want anything else to drink?"

"No, thanks," Cooper replies. "I just need a minute."

"Take your time."

The waitress leaves the two women alone again.

Cooper unwraps her straw, sticks it in her water glass, and drinks. She skims the menu as Leeann stares out the window, each of them glancing at the other at different times.

"So what did you want to talk about?" Leeann says.

Cooper pauses, then says, "You ever love someone so much, you were willing to kill for her?"

Leeann looks at her. "Probably. But I was never given a reason to know that I would."

"I guess it's one of those things—you don't know you can until you have to."

Leeann's quiet for a beat, watching Cooper without alarm or concern. "Who is he?"

"His name's Buck. Buck Haley."

"Is this about Christa, or Smith?"

"Christa."

They fall silent. Josephine returns to take their order. She collects their menus, leaving the table clear between them except for the water glasses. Once they're alone again, Leeann waits for Cooper to explain.

"He's a rodeo man. He met her at a party last month. She doesn't want anything to do with him. He doesn't seem to care."

"If he's only here for the rodeo, he'll be gone soon, won't he?"

"Yeah. But what's stopping him from trying something with her before he goes?"

"Nothing, I guess."

Cooper nods and averts her eyes. "Nothing. Nothing except me."

Leeann pauses, sipping on her water. "Have you seen him?"

"Yeah. Did my best to scare him away."

"But you don't think it worked?"

"No. The bastard doesn't take me seriously."

"He should."

The two women share a look over the table, loaded but discrete.

"Yeah, he should."

"So what are you going to do?"

"What should I do?"

"I can't tell you that, Cooper."

"So you're not going to tell me to leave it alone."

Leeann looks at Cooper like she's something she's never seen before. "No. I'm not going to tell you to leave it alone."

"Why not?"

"Because I know you can't."

Josephine brings them their food, and they start to eat in silence.

"But you need to think about your family," Leeann says after several minutes, glancing up from her plate. "The consequences of your actions don't just come down on you but on them too."

Cooper looks at her and drinks some water. After a pause, she says, "There's something else I wanted to ask you."

"Yeah?"

"How do you do it?"

Leeann blinks at her.

"How do you come out in a town like this and stick around after?"

"Are you coming out to me right now?"

"No. But I know someone who's in the closet."

"Who?"

"I can't tell you."

Leeann pauses to eat, glancing back and forth from her plate to Cooper. She chews, swallows, then drinks from her water glass. "I figured out I loved women when I was in high school. I couldn't tell anyone. My parents are religious types. It was a small town, even smaller than this one. Nobody was gay in Sundance as far as I knew. I had to let a boy take me to senior prom so my parents could get a picture. As soon as I graduated, I packed my bags and got the hell out of there, thinking it would be easier in a big city. I went to college in Bozeman. But even there, it never felt safe. I came out when I got involved with my first girlfriend because I didn't want to sneak around with her. It wasn't bad, I guess, but it wasn't comfortable. It was the '90s, but out here, people have always been able to stay behind if they want to."

Leeann pauses, looking past Cooper for a beat and taking another drink of water. Cooper eats the last of her food and waits for her to go on.

"You know, they killed Matthew Shepard my senior year," Leeann says. "I went home for Christmas, and people in town were still talking about it, two months after it happened.

"My parents didn't know I was a lesbian. I didn't tell them 'til I was damn near thirty. Every time I went home while I was in school, it was clear to me I could never live there again. I couldn't be out in a small town like that, near my parents. I didn't think I'd end up here. Cody's a lot bigger than Sundance, but it's still a small town. It took more than a decade of living in Missoula and Cheyenne before I had to admit to myself I liked small towns better."

Cooper nods because she feels the same way. She and Christa grew up in Casper where the population was in the forty thousands, but even as a child, she was happiest in the wilderness, alone with her family. As soon as she got her driver's license and her truck, she spent as many weekends as she could in neighboring small towns and following Smith around the state to watch him compete. When Smith retired from the rodeo and chose to settle in Park County, she saw it as an opportunity to finally leave cities behind and join him at the same time. It didn't occur to her back then that living in a small town meant judgment for her and the closet for Smith.

"At some point, you get tired of hiding," Leeann says, setting her fork and knife down on her empty plate. "And too old to lie to yourself about who you are and what you want. You realize pretending to be something else and worrying about what people think is no way to live. It's soul crushing. You can either quit or get cancer. So I quit."

Cooper wanted to talk to Leeann about living in Cody as an out lesbian because she's been thinking about her cousin and the mystery of his early retirement from the rodeo and why he's been unhappy since he moved to Park County. She spent the last five years believing Smith regrets retiring and misses the rodeo but won't go back for reasons that have nothing to do with his age or how long he's been out of the sport. After Smith told her and Christa about fooling around with John Henry, Cooper started thinking maybe her cousin's unhappiness has less to do with missing the rodeo than it does with hiding his bisexuality. He hid it in the rodeo, too, but he was never in one place with the same people long enough to work hard at it. And there were other riders who had sex with men, the ones he hooked up with, so he knew he wasn't the only one. Cooper hasn't heard of any openly gay or bisexual men in Cody. Leeann's the only out lesbian, and Cooper thought maybe she was the only one, period, until

Lou asked her on a date.

"Is it as bad as you thought it would be?" Cooper asks. "Everyone knowing?"

"No."

They share a quiet moment, the dusty sunlight shining through all the wide windows lining the diner on three sides, classic country music filling the background softly. Cooper's focus travels outside to her truck and Leeann's parked in front of the diner, then past them at the sky and the highway and the thin ridge of mountains on the distant horizon. The diner isn't downtown where most of the businesses are. It stands alone on a remote stretch of the US 14A, right before the highway leaves Cody proper, and shoots north through open green plots. In the wintertime when snow blankets the mountains and the land is brown and bare, facing the landscape from inside the diner feels like being the last person alive in a dead world.

"How is she?" Leeann asks. "Your sister."

Cooper looks at her. "She's been better."

"You know, if you ever need a safe place to stay, my door's open."

"Thanks. But we don't want to bring our trouble down on someone else."

Leeann doesn't argue.

Josephine, the waitress, picks up their plates and leaves them two separate checks.

"You know Lou Pace?" says Cooper, picking a few bills out of her wallet and putting them on the table.

Leeann shakes her head.

"You should meet her."

"Oh, yeah? Why's that?"

"I think you'd get along," Cooper replies.

*

Christa sits on their front porch, one foot up on the seat of the rocking chair, knee bent in front of her. She has the Ruger .38 on her thigh, her hands on the chair's armrests. She's staring at the stone black bear where it stands on the handrail. She glances at her sister as Cooper, sitting next to her on the short stool, hands her one of the glasses of iced tea she brought with her. They look out at their street for a minute. The sky is dim in these last few hours of daylight, but the sun hasn't begun to set.

"I was thinking maybe I should go to the cops," Christa says, her voice calm and quiet.

"Tell them about Buck, you mean?"

"Yeah. At first, I thought about a restraining order. But it wouldn't make much sense now."

"You're probably right."

"But maybe—maybe the sheriff's deputies in town could watch over me. Keep an eye on him."

"You really think they would do that?"

"It's worth asking. They could appreciate having something to do besides writing traffic tickets."

Cooper smiles a little.

Christa drinks some of her tea, then says, "Jordan Lange's half-brother is a deputy with the county. I asked her to talk to him for me."

"You did? When?"

"A couple days ago."

"Does Smith know about that?"

"No. Not yet."

Cooper stays quiet for a while.

"I talked to the son of a bitch," she says.

Christa gives her sister a sharp look. "To Buck?"

"Yeah. I tried to scare him off."

"When?"

"Two weeks ago."

"And you didn't tell me? Why?"

"I thought maybe you'd get mad. And I didn't really want to tell you how it went."

"So what happened?"

Cooper shakes her head. "Nothing. Just a standoff." She pauses. "He said he wasn't going to give up."

Cooper looks at Christa, who's watching her with eyes full of darkness. Neither of them pays any attention to the gun, but its presence is like a living thing standing behind them. The weight of it on Christa's thigh is heavier now than before.

"Don't do that," Christa says to Cooper, her voice low. "Don't put yourself in harm's way for me and keep it a secret."

"I'm sorry," Cooper replies, matching her sister's volume and tone. "But I had to do something."

Christa lingers on Cooper's face, then turns to the street again. She doesn't speak for a minute. "He'll be gone soon. We just have to wait."

Cooper doesn't answer, drinking her tea instead. They sit for a while, listening to the birds and the thin hush of the wind.

"You know, when I picture my ideal future, it's like this," Cooper says.

Christa looks at her. "This?"

Cooper nods. "You and me, sitting on our porch."

Christa thinks about it. "So we're still living in this house when you're fifty?"

"It's not necessarily this house. But it's ours. That's what matters."

"Is the house in Cody?"

"I don't know. It doesn't have to be."

Christa goes quiet, sensing Cooper's vulnerability. They've never talked about the future much, certainly not the distant future. They don't have any plans or promises. Christa knows her sister better than anyone. She knows Cooper has never been interested in romance, that she's never going to get married or have children. She knows Cooper takes family seriously. She knows it made Cooper uneasy when Christa dated in college though Christa never had a serious boyfriend. When Smith was fooling around with Jordan Lange off and on, a few years ago, Cooper asked Christa once if she thought Smith was going to make Jordan his girlfriend—and Christa could tell her sister wanted reassurance he wouldn't. Cooper has never discouraged Christa or Smith from dating, but it's obvious to Christa that whenever the possibility comes up, Cooper's relieved when they pass on it.

Sitting here on the porch, gazing out at their quiet street and the red geraniums in their hanging pots, Christa realizes Cooper is asking her to stay. Asking her not to leave for a boyfriend or a husband. Asking her to promise that home will always be the two of them together. Christa can suddenly sense her sister's fear: fear of being alone, left behind, replaced. It has a presence like the revolver forgotten in her lap, at once harmless and lethal, silent but heavy.

Christa moved to Cody four years ago because she couldn't think of a good reason not to. She was twenty-two, fresh out of college with a dance degree and no idea what to do with her life. Cooper had always been with her, had moved to Laramie to be with her while she was in school. Christa wasn't attached to her college town, and she didn't want to go back to Casper where she and Cooper and Smith had grown up. Cooper wanted to move to Cody to be with Smith, but she didn't want to go without Christa. Christa could've gone to Cheyenne instead, where most of her college friends headed because it's the biggest city in Wyoming. She could've tried her luck in another state, in Seattle or Portland or San Francisco. But she couldn't say no to Cooper. She didn't want to go anywhere without her, and she didn't want to keep Cooper from Smith.

When she was younger, Christa fantasized about falling in love with a man and getting married, no different than most of the girls she knew. Nobody ever said there was an alternative. Her friends in grade school and high school would've thought she was weird if she didn't have a crush on a boy or talk about her future fantasy husband. In college, she went on assuming one day she'd meet the right guy and marry him, and at the time, it felt important to her.

But now, she's not sure how much she wants romance or marriage or if she wants it at all. Buck Haley has her feeling more wary of men than anything. And when she assesses her life as a single woman living with her sister, Christa decides she's been pretty happy. She tries to imagine walking away from this house and Cooper to go live with a boyfriend, tries to imagine a life where she hardly sees Cooper and Smith at all, and she can't do it.

Christa closes her eyes. She can't see or hear her sister, and they aren't touching. But she can feel her there, close enough to grab onto. She has no memory of life without this feeling, without Cooper's presence. Even when they're physically apart, Christa can feel her—like an extension of her own soul.

"You okay?" Cooper asks.

Christa opens her eyes. She looks at her sister and understands something for the first time. "Let's go inside."

The screen door bangs against the jamb behind them as they head into the kitchen to put their glasses in the sink. Christa sets the gun down on the counter, and without warning, she turns and pulls Cooper into a hug. A fierce, warm, tender hug. Cooper wraps her arms around Christa, and they hold each other for a long time, Christa's eyes shut and her grip strong. Cooper smells like pine and leather and motor oil, and beneath that, Christa can still make out the scent of her skin that hasn't changed since they were two little girls in the same playpen.

"I love you," she says.

Cooper tightens her hug. "I love you too."

Christa pulls back enough to see her sister's face. Cooper's expression is fragile and raw, her eyes glassy but her jaw set. They still have their arms around each other, and neither one lets go as they look at each other.

Christa smiles and says, "I'm not going to leave you. I don't know how my life will go or who I'll meet—but I know I want us to be together. You're the first friend I ever had. The first person I ever loved. I trust you more than anyone. I need you."

Cooper bows her head as if she wants to hide her face, but doesn't pull away from Christa.

"Cooper," Christa says, her voice soft.

Cooper raises her eyes to peer back at her.

"Don't be afraid," Christa tells her. "I'm not going to leave you. Not for a man, not for anything."

A single tear escapes the corner of Cooper's eye, streaking down the side of her cheek. She doesn't speak, doesn't let go of Christa, doesn't smile.

"You'll never be alone," Christa says before pulling Cooper back against her. She strokes her sister's back with one hand, waiting to feel the tension leave Cooper's body. "Trust me."

*

Buck's parked across the street from the Bad Moon Saloon, in the shadows between streetlights, sipping on his flask of Jack Daniels and watching the door. It's late now, about closing time, and Cody seems deserted except for the odd vehicle passing through downtown. There's nobody out walking along the darkened shop fronts, no voices or laughter or music to hear. Only the wind rushing through silence and the traffic lights changing in empty intersections. The stars and the waxing moon cast a bright, milky light over the sleeping town, the sky clear and endless. The clock's pushing midnight—he can barely see the hands on his watch in the darkness—and the Boone sisters should be in bed at home, work shifts waiting for them in the morning. But instead, they're still on Big Horn Avenue, like a pair of dogs who won't leave their master even when they're told to get.

Buck recognizes Cooper's pickup truck from the night in his motel parking lot. It sits in front of the business to the right of the saloon. The only other vehicle near the bar is a truck that must belong to Smith. The sisters came together. He wonders if Christa ever shows up to Bad Moon alone.

He tastes the sharpness of the whiskey on his tongue, welcoming the bite. It keeps him awake, now he's hours past his usual bedtime. He's drunk but not so much he can't make it back to the motel. He was drunk when he left it on impulse, thinking about Christa. He doesn't know where she and the sister live—and showing up there would be riskier anyway—so he followed the main road through town, remembering Bad Moon was somewhere on it but not remembering where exactly. Just his luck the neon sign was still shining, electric blue and silver.

He watches the sign's light go out, the hands on his watch slapped together at the twelve. A minute later, the door opens, and the three figures file out, their faces hidden in the dark of the unlit street. He recognizes Smith Rose's silhouette, tall man in a cowboy hat, trailing behind the sisters on their way to Cooper's truck. They stand on the sidewalk for several seconds, probably saying goodbyes they could've exchanged inside, and the animal part of Buck gets the urge to stalk over there right now, shoot all three of them without any witnesses and leave the bodies where they drop. To hell with Christa—if she won't give him a chance, if the other two won't let her, he should make her pay, make them all pay. Cooper has a gun, Smith probably does, too, but if Buck starts shooting without warning before he even reaches their side of the street, they'll be too shocked to pull their weapons out in time probably.

Buck's chance disappears, and the urge to wipe out the cousins along with it. Christa comes around the front of Cooper's truck to get into the passenger side, and he sees her, bare white legs glowing in the starlight, thick hair hanging loose over her shoulders. A different urge stirs in the pit of his belly, and he can taste it too, mingling with the whiskey in his mouth, almost metallic. Like blood.

Cooper starts her engine as Smith hops into his truck. Cooper's headlights slice through the darkness, focused on the rear end of her cousin's pickup, and the brightness of them makes Buck flinch in his seat, afraid they'll notice him. Cooper pulls out into the street and heads east. Smith drives west, stopping for the red light at the nearest intersection before disappearing in the same direction Buck came from.

Buck starts his own engine and debates with himself which option to take. He could catch up to the Boone sisters if he peels out of here fast and follow them all the way home or however far they get before noticing him. What he would do once he comes face to face with them, he's not sure. He could get out of his seat, cross the road, and do some damage at the Bad Moon Saloon, leave the cousins a message. He could follow Smith to wherever the ex-hotshot lives and take him out of the equation. Or he could go back to the Big Bear Motel and sleep off the Jack, sober up tomorrow and think on this situation again.

He screws the cap on his flask and tosses it into the empty passenger seat next to him. He turns his truck around and starts driving west, away from the Boone sisters and back toward his bed. He doesn't see Smith's taillights ahead of him. The older cowboy must be long gone.

*

They meet on the side of the road, just south of the Buffalo Bill Reservoir, the only two vehicles in sight. It's sunny and cool after 10 a.m. on a Sunday. Jordan's sleek, black hair shines in the light as soon as she gets out of her truck. She gives Cooper a genuine smile as they approach each other, and the two women shake hands.

"How are you?" Cooper says.

"Pretty good. You?"

Cooper gives her a shifty look. "I've been better. But I didn't ask you here so I could talk about me."

She leads Jordan to the back end of her truck, opens the bed, and hops up into it. She pulls Jordan up, and they sit at the edge, legs dangling over the side. Cooper reaches into the mini cooler she packed for a cold beer and offers one to Jordan.

"It's not even noon yet," Jordan says with a slight chuckle.

Cooper gives her bottled water instead.

They sit there without talking for a while, which is surprisingly easy given how little they know each other. Cooper nurses her beer, squinting in the sunshine as they both survey the reservoir in the near distance. The sky arches above them in big Wyoming blue, a color that always made Cooper feel a mixed sense of hope and aloneness. For a split second, a memory flashes through her mind: Lying on a blanket in her backyard when she was a girl, looking at the sky. Dreaming, maybe, of the future.

"Why did you and Smith break up?" she says.

"Wow, I wasn't expecting that question," Jordan replies. "Um—I don't even know if you can call it a breakup. We weren't exactly in a serious, exclusive relationship at the time."

"Neither one of you was involved with anyone else, so. I'd call that a breakup."

Jordan thinks about the question before responding. "I think I wanted more from him, but I could sense he was happy with the way things were. So I decided to end our affair."

"Did you explain why?"

"Not really. If you mean, did I tell him I wanted a serious boyfriend and eventually a husband."

"So what did you tell him?"

Jordan shrugs. "That I thought we made better friends than lovers."

Cooper pauses, holding her beer between her thighs. "He was sad when you broke it off. He missed you, when you started coming around less."

"I was sad too," says Jordan. "I wanted to be a better friend to him these last few years but—it was hard to do, especially once I got married. I always liked Smith a whole lot more than I did my ex-husband."

Cooper grins, and Jordan laughs.

"So the bisexual thing never bothered you?" Cooper asks.

Jordan shakes her head. "No. Not really. All I would've asked for was monogamy if we'd gotten serious long term. I think he could do monogamy if he wanted."

"You have to know how much he trusted you, to tell you that," Cooper says. "As far as I know, you're the only person he's ever told besides me and my sister. It was a big deal."

"I know. I know it was. I wish he could be more open about that part of him. But I understand why he isn't."

The two women lapse into silence again, drinking from their respective bottles.

"Do you think my cousin would be happier if he had a spouse?" Cooper asks.

"I don't know," says Jordan, searching the landscape. "I don't think he's looking or hoping for one—but maybe he needs one and doesn't know it."

"Or he's afraid. Afraid of what happens if he chooses a man."

"Yeah. That too."

Cooper chews on Jordan's words and takes another drink.

"I don't think Smith knows what he wants," Jordan says. "I'm not trying to say a lover or a spouse would solve all of his problems. I know from experience that isn't true. But maybe what he needs is something he doesn't know to want yet."

"Smith has never been a conventional man in the relationship department," says Cooper. "I figure that's part of the problem."

A moment of quiet passes between them.

"I don't know him as well as you do," Jordan says. "You can answer your own questions about him better than I can."

"I've always wondered what you thought of me and Christa, and how we fit into Smith's life. If you were cool with us while you were seeing him."

Jordan doesn't respond at first, eyes roaming over the water and the sky and the mountains. "It's funny. I wondered the same thing about you."

Cooper drains her beer and keeps her eyes trained ahead. "I always had a good feeling about you. Even if I had a bad feeling about the possibility of you and Smith running away together."

Jordan smiles. "Run away together? We would've stayed right here."

"I wasn't being literal."

Jordan's quiet as if waiting for Cooper to explain. When she doesn't, Jordan moves on. "He always made it so clear, how much he loved you and your sister. Mostly, I just thought it was sweet. And special. I haven't met many white people who have that kind of bond with family."

"I know we're not typical. Sometimes, I wonder if it scares outsiders away."

"It didn't scare me away. But I'm Shoshone. I grew up on the rez. I have a different sense of family and tribe than most white people do."

Cooper bobs her head in a nod, looking at the other woman and away again.

"I don't think it has to be one or the other," Jordan continues. "A spouse or a very close bond with others. Family or friends. I think we would all do better with both. I know plenty of people disagree with me; they live differently and do just fine, but—your cousin is not one of those people. Maybe that's one reason we got along so well."

Cooper smiles. "I don't know why he ever let you go, Jordan."

"I left him, remember?"

"Yeah, well—if you ever want to give him a second chance, you have my support."

"I appreciate that," Jordan says.

Cooper checks her watch and grabs a bottled water for herself from the cooler. "Have you figured it out yet?"

"What?"

"How to be happy."

Jordan smiles. "I'm feeling better these days than I have in a while. It's amazing what a good divorce can do."

They both laugh.

"You seem well," Cooper says. "You really do."

"I guess I am."

"What's your secret?"

Jordan shakes her head. "No secret. Trust your gut and try to go after what you really want, not what other people think you should want."

All Cooper can think is: that's what Smith has always needed to hear.

*

Smith's drinking alone at The Buffalo Crossing in Powell on a Saturday night, ignoring the looks women shoot him. Three empty shot glasses linger on the bar in front of him, and he nurses a frosty bottle of Bud, listening to Shooter Jennings singing softly on the speakers and letting his eyes drift to the big-screen TV once in a while. John Henry's finished with his summer rodeo season, but he booked a room at a hotel in Powell for an indeterminate number of days, so Smith drove up from Cody to see him. He doesn't know why he's stalling—he's been in town for almost an hour—but he's not ready to quit drinking alone yet.

Smith glances at the end of the bar to his left and recognizes Lou Pace sitting there like she might squirm right out of her skin. A man Smith hasn't seen before is sitting next to her, running his mouth, no doubt wanting to take Lou home with him or at least into the backseat of his car. Doesn't Lou know better than to go to any bar other than Bad Moon by herself? A young, pretty woman like her can't drink in peace anywhere without somebody to ward off the jackasses.

Smith polishes off his beer and sets the bottle down on the bar resolutely, gets up from his stool, and makes his way to where Lou and her unwanted admirer sit. He steps right up to the man, feeling buzzed and appearing sober, and says, "Hey, buddy."

The man stops yacking to Lou and turns his head to glance up at Smith. "Do I know you?"

"No, but you met my cousin there."

"This is your cousin?" the man says, pointing back at Lou with his thumb.

Smith nods, crossing his arms against his chest. "Yes, sir. And she clearly doesn't want to be entertaining you. So do me a favor and find another seat."

The man cracks a toothy grin. "How do you know what she wants, huh? Did you read her mind from across the room?"

Smith stares at him, stony-faced, hoping this doesn't turn into a fight. "I know you ain't her type, and she's too polite to tell you to fuck off. You're not leaving here with her. And I'm not going back to my seat until you move. So save us all the trouble of a big scene and just go away."

The man scoffs and stands up, forcing Smith to take a couple steps back to make room for him. The man is shorter than Smith, stockier and older. They face off for several tense seconds, but when Smith shows no sign of backing down, the other man finally purses his lips and slinks off, bumping into Smith on purpose as he goes. Smith watches him leave the bar, then turns his attention to Lou.

She smiles at him, relief plain on her face. "Thank you. I had no idea how I was going to get out of that one."

"Always have an escape plan," Smith replies, then sits on the stool the unwanted stranger warmed up. "Why are you drinking in Powell alone instead of Cody?"

"I could ask you the same thing."

"Sometimes, I need to get away."

"Yeah," Lou says. "Me too."

Smith can tell there's something on Lou's mind, something she came here to avoid—maybe her own John Henry. He can't remember ever seeing Lou around Cody with a boyfriend or hearing about one, but he doesn't pay much attention to town gossip, the way most of the locals do.

"I hope you're okay to drive yourself home," Smith tells her.

"Oh, I'm fine. I've only had one drink. But if I really needed to stay in Powell overnight, there's a hotel down the street I've used before."

John Henry's hotel.

Smith digs into his shirt pocket for the pack of cigarettes he tucked there for later and pulls his Zippo out of his jeans. He offers the pack to Lou, who considers it for a second before picking out a cigarette. Smith lights one up for himself first, then lights hers. He seeks out the bartender who's hanging out at the opposite end of the bar, and the bartender gives him a nod of approval.

"You ever been in love?" Smith asks.

Lou turns toward him, taken aback by the question.

"Sorry," he says without looking at her, puffing on his cigarette. "It's none of my business. The subject's on my mind, is all."

Lou doesn't answer at first, then says, "Yeah. More than once."

She sounds sad.

"I don't know if I have," says Smith. "I just know I've loved people. And it's never been enough—what I can give them."

Lou lets the confession settle between them before speaking again, and Smith wonders if she's going to match his candor or let him pour out his personal troubles in a one-sided conversation.

"Are you lonely?" she asks.

Smith smiles and taps the ash off his cigarette into the empty glass the male stranger left behind. "If I say yes, you'll feel sorry for me. If I say no, you won't believe me."

"It's an honest question. Give an honest answer."

Smith peers at her and finds only earnestness in her face. "Yeah, I guess I am. But not the way you probably think."

Lou slides her eyes away from him, at her glass as she traces the rim with her finger. The glass is empty, but there's a beer bottle still in front of her that might not be. She doesn't touch the beer for now, just takes the cigarette from her lips with her other hand and holds it between her thumb and forefinger. "I don't know you, Mr. Rose. But I've heard nothing but good things about you ever since you moved to Cody, and I want you to know if you're struggling with a matter of the heart and need someone to listen, I can do that and keep it a secret."

Smith smiles. "My father is Mr. Rose. Call me Smith."

Lou nods, still staring at her glass.

"Thank you," Smith tells her.

She meets his gaze, and there's something about her, something in her eyes or her face that gives Smith the feeling she's one of his people somehow. He doesn't even know what people that is. Bisexuals, maybe. But it could be broader than sexuality: The secret-keepers, the liars, the fearful of the small-town West. The outcasts of America, some of whom wear respectability like a disguise, a costume they can never take off because they're afraid of death and everything worse.

"I'd like to make you the same offer," Smith says to Lou. "You need to make a confession; I don't mind being a priest for an hour or two."

Lou smiles at him, then picks up her beer bottle. "I'm not Catholic," she replies and drains the last of her beer. She puffs on her dwindling cigarette, letting out the smoke with a big sigh.

"All I'm saying is, I don't judge the way other people live, the way they love, what they want. I can't—because I'm a man who would be judged."

She makes eye contact with Smith again, and they share a silent understanding, the recognition which passes between certain types of strangers in public places. He takes a drag on his cig, and so does she.

He looks sidelong at the other end of the bar and says, "I want things I'm not supposed to want, according to the people who don't want those things. And if you ask me—it's not fair they expect me to go through life pretending I'm like them."

"I agree," Lou says, her voice soft. "I'm in the same boat as you."

"That's too bad. You don't seem like the type who deserves it."

She scoffs. "You think you deserve this problem of yours?"

"No. I guess nobody does."

They listen to the music filling the bar and watching people come and go through the front door on the other side of the room. A lot of middle-aged people at least ten years older than Smith and Lou, married white couples, some of them old enough to be their parents. The kind of people who would tell their grown children to keep something like homosexuality to themselves, who would look sideways at two men or two women holding hands in public. They're not like the gang of young men who attacked John Henry, at least not sober and in public, but they're the reason those young men exist.

"What do you want, Lou Pace? What would make you happy?"

A shy expression comes over her face, and she gives her cigarette one last smoke before putting it out in her empty glass. "A wife." She glances at him right away to gauge his reaction, and he watches her with gentle eyes, a little drunk and pleased with her answer. "I want a wife who loves me as much as I love her."

"Well. I would drink to that, but I'm all out of booze."

She smiles, rosy in the cheeks now, and Smith can see her with a flower wreath in her hair, getting married under Wyoming's blue sky.

"What do you want, then?" she asks.

Smith leans on the bar top with his elbow and holds his cigarette stub in his fingers. "That's a good question."

She looks at him, waiting for the answer.

"I don't know," he tells her after thinking on it. "I think I just want to be free."

They leave the bar together, and Smith walks Lou to her car where she parked it down the street. He stands on the sidewalk and watches her drive away into the night, then turns and heads for John Henry's hotel.

*

Christa sees John Henry walking down Bent Street in the late afternoon, hands in his pockets and head ducked as if he could hide his skin from view. The sun hangs low in the sky like a fat, ripe peach, casting a golden-yellow glow over the town of Powell and the mountains sprawled behind it to the north. The light gleams in the chrome of old trucks lining the streets, in the hubcaps and bicycle frames, reminding her she's too familiar with the beauty of this place to recognize it every time she visits. She stops outside the flower shop and watches John Henry across the street, moving like he's got somewhere important to be or someone he's running from. But there's no rodeo in Powell, no rodeo anywhere within fifty miles except the one in Cody coming to an end in a few days.

He disappears into the Horseshoe Hotel, and she hesitates, her curiosity getting the best of her. She crosses the street, heading straight for the hotel entrance with the bouquet she bought gripped in her left hand.

The clerk at the front desk greets her, but she doesn't stop, just returns the greeting on her way up the stairs. It's a two-story boutique hotel that looks like it might've been opened in the 1800s and updated sometime in the late twentieth century. The salmon-pink wallpaper with floral print, the dark wood staircase railing polished to a high shine, and the lace curtains drawn over the windows make her feel like she's on a movie set for an old Western film. She climbs the stairs to the second floor and doesn't see anyone in the corridor.

She doesn't know what else to do but call him. "John. John Henry? Would you come out, please? I'm here to see you. John?"

The door to room nine opens, and he comes out in his cowboy boots and his shiny belt buckle, his shirt unbuttoned at his throat. He stares at her as if he doesn't remember her.

"Hey," she says, not sure what happens next.

"Hey," says John Henry.

Christa wonders if there are any other guests here and if they can hear the conversation from inside their rooms.

"I saw you outside," Christa explains. "I thought I should talk to you."

John Henry blinks at her. "Come in," he says and disappears back into his room.

Christa pauses, then follows him and shuts the door behind her.

He sits on the foot of the bed, which seems barely slept in. The room is undisturbed, the only sign of him a bag on the chair in the corner.

"You're Smith's cousin," he says.

Christa nods. "And you're his old rodeo buddy."

John Henry lowers his gaze to the right, his hand resting on the bed next to his thigh.

"Why are you here?" she asks.

He looks back up at her. "Why are you here?"

"Well, technically, I work here. At the college. I don't have any classes in session now, but I know people in town. Sometimes I come up here for a change of scenery."

He glances at the bouquet in her hand. "Who are the flowers for?"

"A friend of Smith's. My way of saying thank you."

"For what?"

Christa smiles a sad, fragile smile. "Trying to make me feel better about my troubles."

John Henry doesn't press her for details, and she appreciates it. He sits there quietly, watching her.

"You still haven't answered my question," she says. "Why are you here, in Powell?"

John Henry doesn't speak, his expression difficult to read. He gets up and goes to the window, rests his hands on his hips the way Smith so often does. She waits for him to answer, the silence stretching between them as delicate as spider thread. He breathes like he's about to tell a dangerous truth.

"Your cousin is a hard man to leave," he says without turning around to show her his face.

The corners of Christa's mouth twitch. "I know."

John Henry stands quiet, leaning in the window, and from where she stands behind him, he looks as lonesome as Smith ever has. The kind of man who's alone even in a room full of friends, alone in bed next to his lover, alone like he's the only human being who ever was or ever will be. Men like John Henry and Smith are all the same—not realizing their isolation is self-imposed. Wrestling with it as if the universe forced it on their shoulders, a heavy yoke.

"Tell me something," Christa says, the same little girl she always was. Trying to be kind in a mean world she doesn't understand. "Do you love him?"

John Henry doesn't answer, keeping his back to her. They share the silence for a long time, the question a charge in the air. Just when she starts to consider walking out, he slowly turns to face her, staying close to the window and keeping the distance between them. He doesn't say a word, but she sees it plain on his face, in his dark eyes. Love he's never known what to do with. Love that scares him. Love robbed of its joy and made a burden.

"Well," Christa starts, her voice thick with emotion. "I love him too."

John Henry doesn't speak, looking bewildered and afraid, and her heart wells up in her chest with compassion. She wishes she could help him. She wishes she knew how to bring back the old Smith, who smiled for no reason other than he was alive. She wishes she could give them both a better world.

But she can't do any of those things. And she doesn't know the right answer to the question of Smith and John Henry, any more than she knows how to live in a world full of men like Buck. She knows what it means to feel unsafe and powerless. She understands why John Henry hides in this room, why he doesn't leap into the unknown with the reckless abandon of a man in love with a woman.

Christa considers Jordan's bouquet of sunflowers, baby's breath, and dark purple irises. She chose the sunflowers because when she was a girl, her mother used to say a sunflower was the earth's way of smiling. She pulls one out of the bouquet and crosses the room to give it to John Henry.

He takes the flower and doesn't ask what it's for, his spell of turmoil broken for a minute.

She smiles at him, trying to convey reassurance. "Whatever you do," she tells him. "Do it out of love."

She turns and walks out, her eyes stinging with emotion that takes her by surprise.

Outside, the air smells clean, and the sun still hangs on to the edges of town. She pauses on the sidewalk in front of the hotel and takes in the street and the sky and the mountains silhouetted in the distance. Feeling her smallness.

*

Buck finds the front door to the Boone house unlocked and lets himself in after only a second's pause. Without any vehicles parked outside, odds are good the place is empty, which is exactly what he was hoping for when he set out with the address. The unlocked door is more a stroke of luck. He would expect most people in this town to trust their neighbors and fellow Cody residents, the way people in small towns all over America tend to trust their own, but he would not have been surprised to find the Boone sisters taking basic precautions on Buck's account.

The house is better furnished and decorated than a mechanic and a dance teacher can afford. Smith Rose and his rodeo prize money must be responsible for that. Buck heard the man still lives in a trailer on his parcel of land after all this time, and Buck wonders how much time Smith spends sleeping in this house, his cousins' keeper. Maybe more often now if he knows about Christa's admirer.

Not too many framed photographs in the house, but the ones up are all of the sisters and Smith, with a conspicuous absence of rodeo pictures. He stands in the living room for a long time, staring at a photograph of Christa that must be a few years old. She's younger, wearing a brown Western hat and sleeveless dress, looking over one white shoulder with a bright smile on her face.

Buck takes his time touring the whole house, running his fingers along tabletops and walls without moving anything. He pauses in the kitchen to imagine fucking her from behind, pressing her up against the counter next to the sink. He sits on the living room sofa and notices his silhouetted reflection in the black screen of the TV. He gets up and investigates the guest room, knowing that must be where Smith lays his head when he spends the night and wondering if Smith has ever brought another man into that bed when his cousins aren't home.

Buck knows Cooper's room the moment he sees it, knows it can't be Christa's, and he resists the impulse to trash it. He notices the framed picture on the night table—Cooper, Christa, and Smith all together—and leaves it flipped facedown. He sees the rifle mounted on the wall and smirks, draws his own pistol out of the holster on his hip and aims at Cooper's pillow. The dyke bitch needs to be put in her place, and the only place for her is a hole in the ground.

Buck sheaths his weapon and moves on to the last bedroom, the master suite, full of Christa's flowers and pastel colors. He takes a deep breath just inside the door, trying to smell her in the air, then scans the room. He snoops into all the drawers, checking for a gun. He runs his hands over the bed as he fantasizes about taking her on it. He scans the top of her dresser, steps into the walk-in closet and flips through her clothes. He looks at himself in her bathroom mirror and decides he likes the image.

Buck picks a pair of red panties out of Christa's underwear drawer, the only pair he can see without digging through the pile, and finally sits on the foot of the bed to do what he came here to do. He unbuckles his belt, unbuttons and unzips his jeans, and takes his dick out. He starts to rub himself with one hand, holding the red panties up to his face with the other hand. He can't smell Christa in the panties, only the faint scent of laundry detergent, but it doesn't matter. Jacking off in her house, in her bed, with her panties—the forbidden nature of it all—is enough to get him hard.

"You like that?" he says out loud. "Huh? You fucking like that, you slut?"

He sees Christa's face and the naked bodies of women from all the porn he's used in his life, rubbing himself hard and fast. He comes into Christa's red panties, grunting and cursing, feeling a rush of adrenaline that surprises him. After he's done, he sits there for a while, dick and panties in hand, basking.

He walks out of the house with the stained panties in his pocket and a grin on his face.

*

John Henry calls Sula on a pay phone in the morning because he wants to make sure the connection doesn't drop. The wind whistles past him, and the sun shines on his white Stetson as he stands behind the empty Stampede Park Arena in Cody. The phone rings three times before she picks up, and he smiles the second he hears her voice.

"Hey, you!" she says, sounding happier than he's been in weeks. "I almost didn't pick up because I didn't recognize the number. You using somebody's phone?"

"A pay phone," John Henry replies. "Sometimes, the cell signal isn't so good out here."

"A pay phone? They still got those?"

"In some places."

"You in Montana?"

"Wyoming."

"Wyoming? I didn't think you had a competition there."

"I don't," he says. "Not on my schedule, anyway. But I'm here to see an old friend and maybe consider riding in the Cody Nite Rodeo, just for fun."

"Who's your friend? I don't remember you mentioning anybody in Wyoming."

"His name's Smith. I knew him when he was in the circuit. He's been retired a while now. Lives out here, not far from this town Cody, so I thought I'd finally stop by and see him again."

"How's it going so far? Like old times?"

"Yeah," John Henry says, his voice soft. "Just like old times."

"Well, that's good," Sula tells him, sounding genuinely glad for him. "Old friends are the best kind."

He doesn't say anything in response, already brimming with guilt.

"Maybe I'll get to meet him one day," she says. "Get him to tell me stories about your younger self you don't want me to know." She sounds playful when she says it, oblivious to the sinking feeling in John Henry's gut.

"How are you?" he asks, wanting to change the subject. "You at work right now?"

"I'm on my lunch break, so we got some time. I'm fine. It's been pretty average around here since the last time we talked. I've been missing you though. When are you coming home?"

"Pretty soon, I think. No later than a week from now, probably sooner. You know it'll take me a few days to drive back."

"Yeah, I know. You better call me when you're on your way and let me know you're all right."

"Don't I always?"

Sula doesn't respond, and they're quiet together for a few seconds.

"Hey, um—can I ask you something?" John Henry says. "What did you think of me when we first met?"

Sula pauses, caught off guard by the question. "Well, obviously, I thought you were good-looking, or I wouldn't have agreed to a date."

He smiles. They met at a farmer's market on a mild day in April, over crates of bright green cucumbers and red tomatoes. He tried not to stare, but everything from her glowing, dark skin to her big, brown eyes to the shape of her bare shoulders deserved a long look. On that day, she wore her hair in a thick bundle of tiny braids, gathered in a loose, low ponytail. He hadn't seen a woman that gorgeous in a while, and he half expected her to be married. He was afraid to speak to her, so he offered her a bouquet of sunflowers instead, just shoved them right at her without opening his mouth. She laughed at him a little, but he didn't mind.

Sula Reynolds. John Henry's never loved a woman as much as he loves her, never felt as comfortable with a woman as he does with her.

It isn't lost on him her initials are the same as Smith's.

"I thought you were the shyest man I'd met in a while, which was a nice change from all the corny pickup lines and masculine bravado I got from guys before you," Sula says. "The flowers were sweet. I don't know; I guess I had a good feeling about you. You were different."

"You never had any doubts? About me? About us?"

"I don't think so. I mean, I wasn't sure we would end up getting serious when we first started going out. But I've always been slow with men. If you're asking me whether I ever doubted you were worth dating, the answer is no. If I had that kind of doubt, I would've broken it off pretty early on. Why are you asking about this stuff now?"

"We've never talked about it, and I was just thinking lately about us... I want to know everything there is to know about you."

"Well, now you gotta tell me what you thought about me when we met. It's only fair."

"I thought there was probably no way in hell you'd go out with me," he says.

She laughs, and he smiles at the sound.

"She's too pretty, Walker. She can do better than you, and she knows it."

"But you took a chance anyway."

"I had a moment of courage. Sort of."

"Lucky for you and me."

He took her to a honky-tonk bar for their first date, and they ended up slow dancing to an old country song. She smelled like spring. She still does.

John Henry feeds a couple more quarters into the pay phone and checks his watch out of habit. "When did you know you were in love with me?"

"Wow. That's a question."

She's quiet for a little bit, and he wonders if she's trying to remember the moment or if she's hesitating to tell him about it.

"It wasn't long before you told me you loved me for the first time," says Sula. "One morning when you woke up before I did, I found you in my kitchen, making breakfast and feeding the dog some of the bacon you fried up. I could smell the coffee you brewed. You didn't notice I was standing there watching you, so I didn't say anything for a minute. I don't know why it was then I realized. There was nothing romantic or incredible going on. But that's when I knew I really did love you."

"You didn't tell me you did until I told you," John Henry says.

"I never tell a man I love him before he tells me. Not since college."

He can respect that.

"Now you have to tell me when you knew," says Sula.

John Henry doesn't answer right away, thinking back to those days when they were less familiar with each other, when he lived with the exciting hope he'd finally found the lover he could be with for life. "I knew the night you came to watch me ride in person for the first time. In Springfield. Seeing you in the stands, smiling under those lights. And then after, when we looked at the stars together in the bed of my truck. Hit me like lightning."

"You didn't tell me then."

"I had to be sure. And I kinda wanted to enjoy it all on my own for a while before I let the words loose."

All of a sudden, he remembers the attack in the bar parking lot again, the stars even brighter in that night sky than they were in Springfield, twinkling over his truck without any of the same beauty or peace.

"It gets lonely out here, you know. On the road in the West."

"What do you mean?"

He's never said anything about loneliness to her since they met three years ago. It didn't occur to him before he mentioned it how her interpretation of his words might take her to sexual territory. The slight edge in her voice she probably isn't aware of alerts him to her probable fear he's about to confess infidelity.

"Being surrounded by white people all the time," he explains. "Going days, weeks sometimes without seeing another Black person. Not having anyone to talk to about whatever white bullshit comes up."

This is a situation Sula can only imagine as she's never lived in a place without a significant number of Black people. Born and raised in Richmond, Virginia, where half the city is Black, she went to college in New Orleans and law school in Nashville before finding her way to Jefferson City, Missouri, where the two of them live now. Her whole life, most of her friends have been Black. She's never lacked Black coworkers, Black clients, Black community.

"Did something happen?" she asks.

He curls one corner of his mouth into a little smile she can't see. Female intuition is a hell of a thing. "Just some locals around here acting like fools. I handled it. But it's hard not having anybody with me I can talk to about it. Nobody who understands what it's like dealing with this shit."

"I'm sorry. I wish I was there with you."

He smiles with his whole mouth now. "I wish you were too."

"Why didn't you call me as soon as the incident happened?"

"I didn't want you to worry." John Henry knows better than to make a Black woman he loves feel powerless if he can avoid it.

"I worry about you no matter what."

"I know. I don't want to give you extra reason. I wanted to cool off before I said anything to you. Might've made it sound worse than it was if I'd called you right after."

"Did you get hurt?"

"No. I'm fine. Promise."

"Okay. I believe you. But next time anything bad happens to you, I need you to tell me about it as soon as you can. Whatever it is. I need to know what's going on with you, John Henry. That's the only way this long-distance situation can work."

"I get it."

The guilt wells up in him again, bubbling like lava that could destroy the both of them and everything they share if he loses control of it. He doesn't want to hurt Sula. He can live with hurting himself, hurting Smith, hurting anybody and everybody in the world, but not Sula. He's never felt guilt so deep and so painful as the guilt he feels for cheating on her with Smith—and if it was anyone other than Smith, it never would've happened. He's been faithful to Sula since they became a couple—until now. He lied to Smith about it, trying to make it sound like falling back into bed with him was about having sex and not about a love that won't die.

"Sula, I need to know if you really are willing to try the farming life with me," John Henry says. "I know we've talked about it before, but I've never asked you straight up if you mean it when you say you support me doing it. I'm serious about the farm. I've been saving up my whole career to make it happen. And if we get married one day... You wouldn't be an engineer's wife or even a rodeo man's wife. You'd be a farmer's wife unless I fail to get the farm off the ground."

"John Henry," Sula says. "I don't know where all this is coming from, but I do support you. I wouldn't have told you I did if I didn't mean it. I know you got plans for a farm. And I know how hard it can be to make a living out of that. But I'm not going to try to talk you out of it. If you ask me to marry you, I won't say yes thinking you'll stay an engineer the rest of your life. I would only say yes if I felt prepared to help you start your farm."

"I wouldn't ask you to give up your career," John Henry says. "I know the farm is my dream, not yours. You wouldn't have to work on it with me full-time. I could hire people for that. You would just have to be okay with what the farming life means for me, for us. More risk, less money. Harder work, I guess. Maybe less free time. I don't know; I think there would be sacrifices involved that wouldn't come up otherwise. I'm willing to make them myself. I don't want you making them with me if all it's going to do is drive a wedge between us."

Sula is silent on the line, and John Henry waits with a tight chest, held breath, for her response. He didn't even know until just now how desperately he wants her to say she's open to the future he's imagined for them both.

"It means a lot to me that you respect my career," she tells him, and he can hear it in her voice.

"Well, you're too smart to be nothing but a farmer's wife," he says, half-joking and half-serious. "Can't let that law degree go to waste."

"Thanks for the compliment. But you know—maybe one day, I'll feel different about my job and how I want to spend my time. If I have children and a good marriage... Land of my own... There's something tempting about the idea of living a simple, quiet life. Surrounded by family and nature instead of all the noise out here in the city, the drama."

"I know," he says softly. "That's how I've always felt."

They stay on the phone with each other, quiet, letting the possibility take shape in their individual imaginations: the sun setting on fields of green and gold, their children running free outside, their dog lounging on the front porch and chickens clucking in the backyard coop, John Henry's hands smelling like earth, and Sula smiling no matter what direction she looks in because it all belongs to them.

"We should talk about this some more when you come home."

"All right. Sounds good."

"I better hang up. Gotta get back to work."

"Okay. I'll call you again soon, next few days."

"Use your cell phone, so I know it's you."

"I will."

"I love you, John Henry. Take care of yourself."

"Love you too. Have a good rest of your day."

"Bye."

"For now."

She hangs up, and so does he.

John Henry blows out a long breath and rests his hands on his hips. What is he going to do?

The silence of the empty stands and rodeo arena offer him no relief from the tide of guilt washing over him. He leaves the pay phone behind and crosses the desolate parking lot to his truck, the only vehicle present, hops in and starts the engine.

He pulls the truck up to the chain-link fence enclosing the west end of the arena, shifts gears into Park, and sits there a minute, surveying the whole scene and the scoreboard that reads Cody, Wyoming—Rodeo Capital of the World.

*

When Smith shows up at the garage, Cooper's working on the bike with the radio on. The rest of the crew's gone home, and she's alone with the doors wide open. She wipes her hands clean as he comes up to her with his fingers in his hip pockets, and they don't smile. They're close enough, they don't have to put on faces for each other, and neither one of them is in a smiling kind of mood. Smith grimaces, the way he does when he's got something heavy on his mind. Cooper stands in front of him, intending to have this conversation on her feet.

"How's it coming?" he asks.

"It's coming," she replies with a little nod. Lately, she's been using the bike as a distraction and staying late after work more than she ever has before.

"You all right?"

Cooper glances away from him and doesn't answer. "I asked you here because I didn't know where else I could say this without getting interrupted or overheard."

His expression changes just enough to signal he's uneasy. "Sounds serious."

Cooper rests her hands on her hips and looks him dead in the eye. She's been rehearsing this in her mind for hours, and none of the openings ever felt right. She decides to cut right to the quick.

"I love you more than almost anything. Always have. Thinking about living without you hurts so bad, I can't stand it. But I'm tired of seeing you miserable, Smith. And ever since John Henry rolled into town, you've been lighter somehow. I don't know if you're in love with him or what, but—you should give yourself permission to be happy. Go after what you want. Man, woman, doesn't matter. Just don't hold yourself back from settling down with someone if it's what you really want. That's all I have to say."

Her eyes linger on him for a moment, registering his quiet stillness and the sensitive expression on his face. She turns her back on him. She doesn't take more than a few steps away, then stops. The air thickens between them, the radio faded out in the background. Cooper's eyes well up with tears only long enough to scare her, and she sniffs them back, waiting for Smith to leave or speak.

"When'd you go and get noble, Cooper?" Smith says, his voice soft and serious.

She doesn't feel noble. She feels, in this moment, about as alone as she did at sixteen when she watched him dance with some girl on a floor full of couples at her high school homecoming.

Smith comes up behind her, so close the energy crackles between them, charged with a lifetime's worth of emotion, history, and whatever primal connection lies in their blood.

"Why do I get the feeling you have one foot out the door and your mind made up about leaving?" His voice is softer, with an echo of the raw sadness she's felt him carrying for years.

There have been times throughout their relationship where one knew what the other was thinking before the one thinking it did. Maybe this is one of those times. Cooper doesn't have a plan or a packed suitcase—but when he asks her the question, she feels found out.

"I don't know why you think I need you any less than you need me," he tells her. "It ain't ever been true."

"This isn't about me and you," Cooper says, her voice fragile. "It's not about me at all. It's about you getting happy."

"I'm never going to be happy without you." He pauses. "Don't make me chase you, Cooper."

Finally, she hears and feels him move away, his shuffling footsteps on the concrete floor. She turns to watch him go.

"I meant what I said," she tells him.

He stops and peers back at her. "I know. So did I."

She doesn't look away until he pulls his truck into the street and disappears. Once he's gone, she lets out a long breath and turns around again, eyes landing on the Triumph. The motorcycle gleams like her very own mechanical bull.

*

In the cooling dusk, Smith heads out of his camper with the dog and walks west, wearing his oldest and most comfortable pair of boots. He keeps a slow pace, listening to his footsteps breaking up the silence of the plain. The last of daylight hangs onto the horizon, a line of brilliant orange fading out to a pastel hue shrinking under the weight of night. The trees dotting the landscape darken to silhouettes, losing their details, and not a wild thing shows itself, except what man and dog would have to see up close to notice.

Smith sniffs at the air and smells only the clean, earthy scent of the land. Not rain or livestock or car exhaust. He watches the dog follow a scent on the ground, then lose it and stop for a beat, gazing ahead as if she expects the thing to be there waiting for her.

Alone out here, surrounded only by the natural world, he thinks about how he isn't fit to live anywhere else. He can't be in a city or even the small town of Cody all day every day. His soul won't find any peace in the middle of so many people. He wants to live apart from everything but these essentials, where he can escape public scrutiny and all other manner of bullshit. He may not be able to forget himself out here, but he can at least be himself, coexisting with the parts of nature that hold no judgment.

He could never give up this land. He didn't even know he wanted some until he had nothing left and laid eyes on this plot. If he retreated to it five years ago the way a wounded animal hides away to die, he still doesn't regret claiming the land as his. And his cousins rely on it now, too, as their own refuge from society, their own reminder of what they are in the grand scheme of things. He still remembers the first time he showed it to them, the three of them roaming across the acreage until they'd seen it all, like a few wolves searching for a place to survive without any more of a pack.

Smith stops somewhere twenty minutes from his camper and surveys the landscape, hands on his hips. He doesn't look back at where he came from. He focuses on the purple mountains in the distance fading into the night sky and at the dying orange light still lingering along one section of the horizon line. He notices the first few stars winking in the darkening vale above him, and he listens to the quiet of the wilderness never as absolute as it seems.

Later, Smith builds a fire in the makeshift firepit outside his camper and sits in one of the fold-up chairs, lighting a cigarette. The dog sniffs around behind him before settling down, and then the only sound is the flames crackling. The night sky opens above him in a soaring stretch of black and midnight-blue, moonless and dusty with finely stippled stars. By now, the Cody Rodeo has wrapped up for the day, and the only people left in his bar are the alcoholic regulars. He hasn't heard from his cousins or John Henry all evening, and he's chosen not to break the radio silence. He made himself dinner in the kitchen for once—three cans of soup and some biscuits—and ate alone at the table.

He doesn't mind eating alone. Doesn't mind living alone either, though he never had to do it the way he does now before he retired. He can appreciate having the time to think in peace. His rodeo days were mostly spent in hotels and motels with other riders and a host of crew, staying out until his bedtime and often bringing someone back to his hotel room for sex or else not coming back until morning. He didn't have his own space, besides his truck. No home to go back to except his parents' place and eventually his cousins' apartments. It was a life of never-ending noise, activity, motion, and occupying public places. A lot of that, he's glad to be done with.

Smith puffs on his cigarette, staring into the fire. He's got Buddy the plush beagle in his lap, and he rubs one worn ear between his thumb and forefinger. Cooper won the toy for him at the North Texas Fair and Rodeo in Denton when he competed there in the summer of 2004. He took it with him everywhere for the rest of his career, keeping it on his night table in every hotel and motel room he stayed in. Now Buddy lives on the ledge above his bed, next to the framed photograph of Cooper and Christa he snapped their first Christmas in Cody. He was in a deep depression then, reeling from retirement, and the picture is the only happy thing he remembers about that year's holiday season.

He closes his eyes and tries to see himself in a house too big for him, with a woman he's never met. With John Henry—just for a moment. His cousins aren't there. Of course, they wouldn't be, all of their nights alone on the land a thing of the past. Their campouts in this yard behind them.

He opens his eyes again and knows that isn't right. This land, the saloon, the house he hasn't built yet, empty of Cooper and Christa... The idea makes him so lonesome it almost physically hurts in his heart.

He sticks the waning cigarette in his mouth and gets up out of the chair. The dog follows him into the camper.

Smith sits at his kitchen table with his journal and a pen, opens to the next clean page, and writes at the top: If I could have any kind of life I want, what would it be?

He puts out his cigarette in the ashtray on the table and stares at the question.

When he lifts his eyes and sees the photos of himself and his cousins stuck to the side of the refrigerator with magnets, he gets the courage to be honest, without caring about what's realistic.

He starts writing.

*

John Henry walks back into the saloon on a Wednesday night after closing time. Smith's truck is the only vehicle parked outside within walking distance. He's alone inside, sitting with his back to the door and his feet up on one of the tables. He's staring at the mechanical bull. There's a glass of whiskey at his elbow on the table. He doesn't look over his shoulder to see who's coming, and he seems a little surprised when John Henry finally reaches him.

"What are you doing here?"

"I need to talk to you."

Smith blinks and slides his feet off the table, sits upright. "What about?"

John Henry sticks his hands in his pockets. "I've been done with this season's rodeo tour since West Yellowstone. But I'm still here in Wyoming because I haven't been sure what to do next."

"What do you mean?"

John Henry looks at him, really looks at him, the way he looks at someone he might not see again. He drinks in the face of this man he isn't supposed to love, amazed Smith still doesn't get it. He pulls one of the chairs out from Smith's table and sits across from him, leaning forward with his elbows on his knees. He doesn't know where to start or if he can really say what he needs to say, but he's resolved to leave things right between him and Smith.

"I wasn't sure I could leave you again," John Henry says, staring at Smith dead in the eye. "I still don't know if I can."

Smith stares at him like he might've said any crazy thing.

"I want to do the right thing," John Henry continues. "I love Sula. A lot. And she deserves a man who's sure he wants to be with her."

Smith starts to shake his head. "John, what are you—"

John Henry holds up his hand. "Please. Let me finish now or I might not." He lowers his gaze and pauses, trying to find the words. "I quit being friends with you because I was in love with you. I wanted us to be...a couple. And I knew we couldn't be. Not then, not ever. When you retired, I wanted to go see you, make sure you were okay. But I didn't. I knew if I saw you again, I wouldn't be able to walk away. And I wasn't sure you'd even want to see me after how I left things."

John Henry lifts his eyes to Smith again and finds the other man's face tight with emotion, eyes gleaming.

"I thought I'd moved past you. But I started thinking about proposing to Sula and the more I did, the more I thought about you. Even after all this time. I had to come see you. And now—now, I don't know. I still love you. But I can't see the future with you, the way I can with her. Maybe because I'm afraid of it. I don't even know how you feel about me. Never did."

John Henry stops, trembling.

Smith reaches out and takes John Henry's hands in his. "You could've told me the truth back then. I don't know what I would've done, but we could've figured it out together."

John Henry wishes he had told him. He wishes he had come here sooner.

"Don't you think I'm afraid too?" Smith says. "Afraid of people finding out about me? I always was. That's one of the reasons I left the rodeo."

Somehow, John Henry had never suspected that, and hearing it now stings.

"What are you asking me?"

"I don't know," John Henry replies.

Smith looks down at their hands clasped, quiet for a long beat. "I can't tell you how to live your life. I don't even know how to live mine."

John Henry doesn't speak, waiting for Smith to do something or for the universe to send him a sign. He came here thinking he knew what the right decision was, but he won't settle on it until Smith confirms it.

Smith gazes into his eyes again, his lips pressed together in a grim line. "You said you want a family. Marriage, kids, all of that. I can't give you those things. But she can. You can be safe with her—as safe as you can get. But you'd never be safe with me. And I don't want to spend the rest of my life worrying about you."

John Henry gives him a sad, reflexive smile with a hard lump in his throat.

"I don't know your Sula," Smith says. "But I know she can love you the way you need. And I don't know if I can love anyone like that. I don't know what I want the way you do. And you need to be with someone who does."

"Did you ever love me?" John Henry blurts out before he can stop himself. His heart aches in his chest, knowing everything Smith said is the truth. He knew it before he heard it. He just didn't want to accept it.

"I loved you back then," Smith says, his voice soft and quiet, his eyes full of something like regret. "And I love you now. You were my one, true friend in the rodeo. I miss you. I'll always miss you."

John Henry takes his hands out of Smith's, overwhelmed. He stands up and turns his back on Smith, in case he spills a tear or two. He faces the damn mechanical bull, hands on his hips, at a loss for what to do. He does love Sula, and for years, he's nursed the budding dream of a normal life with a woman like her. A little farm in the country, a wife, and children running wild on the land he can pass down to them. But a part of him wants to throw all of that away, move to Wyoming, and grow old with Smith. Even if his parents disown him, even if he has to look over his shoulder everywhere he goes, even if it means he has to quit the rodeo sooner than he planned.

"Fuck this world," he says, shaking his head. His voice is almost a whisper, still loud enough in the deserted saloon for Smith to hear it.

Smith is silent behind him for a long beat. Then he stands. "What do you want? Deep down, you know. You've made your decision. What is it?"

John Henry shuts his eyes, a tear rolling over each cheek. He rubs his face dry with the back of his hands, sniffs, and turns back to Smith. "I'm going home. And I'm going to ask Sula to marry me."

Smith nods. "Yeah," he says. And he doesn't seem heartbroken.

John Henry lets his fate sink in, his emotions receding like the tide. He knew all along how this was going to end. He hoped Smith would change his mind, but he didn't count on it.

Smith gives him a wistful but reassuring smile. "You're going to be all right."

"Are you?"

"Don't you worry about me." Smith shuffles over to the jukebox, one hand on his hip. "I can take care of myself."

He hits a couple buttons on the juke, and a slow song fills the saloon. Patterson Hood's "Back of a Bible." Smith returns to John Henry, saying, "I think you owe me one dance, Walker."

Smith takes his hand and wraps his other arm around John Henry's waist, pulling him close enough that they can smell each other. John Henry lets him, smiling as wide as he wants to because there's no one else to see. Smith sways his upper body, feet moving slow enough for John Henry to fall into step with him, the song starting to pick up and go. He peers at John Henry with warmth and affection, and John Henry can't make eye contact with him and do this dance at the same time. He averts his eyes off Smith's left shoulder instead and allows himself to be led, to be moved, to be held.

The music swells into a long guitar riff of feeling, and Smith steps in even closer, the two of them looking over each other's shoulder, rocking back and forth on their boots. John Henry keeps his hand pressed to Smith's back, his other hand still clasped in Smith's, and surrenders to the whole thing. He shuts his eyes as Smith winds them in a circle and listens to the guitar twang filling the saloon, hoping he can always remember exactly what he's feeling right now.

In another life, he might be the man who runs away to this small Wyoming town, to live with a cowboy in a camper. He might be the man who decides to come out and come home to Smith, who chooses the life of a gay Black man in a rural white community. He might be brave enough to make that gamble, day in and day out. And if he was, he could have enough moments like this to start taking them for granted.

But John Henry knows he has to live in the world outside all the secret places he's been, and he knows what that world has in store for him, even if he returns to Missouri, marries his girlfriend, and raises a couple kids. He's not ready to retire from the rodeo. And he's not fearless enough to volunteer for the consequences of choosing a white husband instead of a Black wife.

He doesn't dwell on any of it now. He just gives Smith his dance. He gives it to himself too.

*

The last weekend of August and the final nights of Cody's rodeo roll around, the tourists checking out of their motels and hotels and trickling out of town. The parties start on Friday afternoon all over the residential neighborhoods and on the ranches and other isolated properties surrounding Cody, the locals celebrating the end of the rodeo and the summer.

Cooper and Christa are holed up at Bad Moon on Saturday night, drinking in their favorite booth while Smith tends the bar.

Buck Haley walks in, and Christa freezes when his eyes land on her, that roadkill look on her face. It takes a moment for Smith to realize who the man is, and when he does, Buck's already approaching the Boone sisters, ignoring Cooper as if she doesn't exist and looming over Christa like a standing bear. He smiles at her, wolfish, obviously pleased he finally has his prey cornered.

"Christa," he says. "I was hoping I'd find you here."

The way Buck hovers over her while she sits is aggressive. Smith can read that move for what it is: an attempt at intimidation. He steps out from behind the bar to keep his cousins in his line of sight.

"Why don't we get a table?" Buck says to Christa. "We can have a drink and talk."

"She doesn't want to talk to you, asshole," says Cooper, glaring at him with fury. "Get the fuck out of here. Now."

Buck's eyes slink onto her with subtle contempt, like he would put her through a wall if only Christa wasn't watching. "You don't speak for her."

Cooper stands up, draws her gun, and points it at Buck's face, the safety switched off. The saloon goes dead quiet except for the country music playing on the jukebox. Buck stares right down the barrel of the S&W and doesn't back away. Cooper is steely-eyed with cold anger.

"Go ahead," Buck says. "Make good on your threat."

"Cooper, don't," says Christa, her voice small and quiet, eyes wide on her sister and the gun.

"Get out," Cooper says to Buck.

"I'm not going anywhere until I buy Christa a drink."

"I want you to leave me alone," Christa says, raising her voice even as it quivers.

Buck slides his gaze off Cooper and onto Christa.

Christa forces herself to stand up, hands on the tabletop as if she needs it to stay on her feet. "I want nothing to do with you. Get out of here. Leave me and my family alone."

Smith finally crosses the room to his cousins, reaches out and lays his hand on Cooper's gun. "Let me handle it, Coop," he says, keeping his voice calm and steady. "It's all right."

He pushes the gun down, and she lets him, staring at Buck in a predatory trance. When the gun is at her side with the safety back on, Smith slides in front of Buck, his back to the sisters. He and Buck are about the same height, and they stand toe to toe, eye to eye, too close for anyone's comfort.

"You need to get the hell out of my bar," Smith says, almost murmuring, too quiet for anyone but Cooper and Christa to hear. "And the hell out of my town. Christa doesn't want anything to do with you. She never has."

Buck looks at him, the air in the saloon thick with tension. He doesn't move.

Smith lowers his voice further, leaning in a little. "If you don't leave her alone, I'll kill you myself."

"I'm not afraid of faggots," Buck says, loud enough for everyone in the saloon to hear.

Smith goes still.

"Did ya'll know that?" Buck says to the room, surveying the locals sitting in the booths, at the tables, and at the bar. "Did ya'll know Smith Rose is a fucking queer? I saw him with my own two eyes, kissing a Black man at a motel in Montana not two weeks ago. And I'm pretty damn sure they didn't get a room to watch TV."

Smith stands with his back to his cousins, silent and glaring at Buck. Nobody in the saloon makes a sound, watching the two men in disbelief.

"Your rodeo star hero is a fucking cocksucker," Buck says, louder now. "Aren't you?" He scowls at Smith a few paces in front of him, his face full of nasty spite.

Smith doesn't answer, heat rising in his face and through his neck.

"Why don't you tell your fans the truth, huh?" Buck continues. "Tell everybody who takes it up the ass—you or that Black fag I saw you with."

Smith punches Buck in the face, and Buck staggers backward, thrown off balance. A chorus of gasps rises like steam off a hot engine. Cooper starts toward her cousin, but Christa stops her with one hand firmly gripping her sister's forearm. For a split second as Buck regains his footing and straightens up, bottom lip glistening with blood, it looks like he's about to attack Smith. But Smith beats him to it, charging Buck, grasping him by the shirt collar and punching him again with his other hand. Buck swipes at him, pushes him away hard, closes the distance again and swings at him.

The two men collide like a pair of stags locking antlers, wrestling to the floor, rolling around as each one struggles to dominate the other. Everybody else in the room watches without moving to interfere, wide-eyed and startled, on edge. There are enough guns in the room for a small battle, but nobody draws on the brawlers, not even Cooper who's still holding her cowboy revolver.

Smith throws Buck back against the bar, the two of them on their feet again, red-faced and breathing hard. They eye each other before Smith lunges at Buck again, and Buck collides with him. Buck shoves Smith into an empty table, and Smith braces himself against it with his hands on the top before turning to snarl at Buck and jump him again. They trade blows, bruising each other's face, Smith driving his fist into Buck's belly, Buck snatching Smith into a headlock and choking him only until Smith elbows him hard in the groin and trips him to the floor.

Smith stands over Buck, his fists balled and throbbing at his sides, chest heaving as he pants. Buck lies flat on his back with one knee bent up, wheezing as he breathes with his mouth open, the blood thick around his nostrils. Nobody speaks a word for half a minute, the only sound in the saloon the two men's heavy breathing. The music has been switched off.

"If you don't get the fuck out of my bar in the next thirty seconds, I'm calling the cops," Smith says, wiping his nose and mouth with the back of his wrist and hand as if he's the one bleeding. "I catch you in this town or near my cousin again, I'll fucking kill you. Understand?"

Buck glowers at him but doesn't reply.

No one in the bar says a word, all of them staring at the two men. A few customers glance at the Boone sisters, maybe to see if Cooper is going to do something with her gun. But Cooper and Christa stay where they are, standing near their booth at a distance from Buck and Smith. Christa's staring at Buck with an expression of disbelief, then raises her eyes to Smith in grateful wonder. Cooper doesn't pay any attention to Buck at all, just watches her cousin. Smith recognizes her fear for him, her powerful urge to protect him, in her eyes.

He stands his ground, ignoring everybody in the saloon except Buck. He's wound up in a way he hasn't been for years, and if Buck doesn't leave in the next minute or two, Smith might start beating on him again. He's pissed off like he didn't know he could be. Maybe it's because of what Buck has done to him and his cousins, or maybe this is anger he's been stockpiling the last several years without knowing it. Maybe both. Buck rolls over and gets on his knees. Smith wants to kick him all the way to the door and out into the street, so he doesn't go get Cooper's gun and shoot Buck himself.

Buck crawls a little ways toward the door before pushing himself up onto his feet. He doesn't look back at Smith but stops to see Christa for the last time, his face ugly with contempt.

"Get out!" Smith yells at him.

Buck staggers out the door and disappears.

Finally, Smith turns and faces everybody in the room, his hands open. He surveys the saloon from left to right, sees the people staring at him, and makes a decision.

"What that asshole said is true. I sleep with men and women. If anybody has a problem with that, feel free to leave and don't come back."

Nobody speaks or moves. Some of them stare at Smith while others trade glances.

Smith waits, and when he doesn't get a reaction, he walks out of the saloon on jelly legs.

Buck is nowhere to be seen, and the street is quiet, empty. Smith takes a deep breath and gazes up at the stars, half expecting Cooper or Christa to come after him. He picks his keys out of his pocket and starts toward his truck, parked in front of the business next door.

He gets behind the wheel, starts the engine, and drives.

*

Monday morning, Smith leans in the doorway of his trailer with a cup of coffee, admiring the land bathed in the weak, early light. His face is sore and tender with bruises, his lip scabbed and sensitive to whatever he drinks. He doesn't have to show up at the saloon until after noon, but he's already thinking about it, uncertain of what he'll find when he gets there. He stayed out of town yesterday, hiding from the gossip that inevitably spread through Cody like wildfire in the wake of Saturday night's fight between him and Buck. By now, most locals know what happened, and they know Smith is bisexual. He's going to have to face them eventually, and contrary to what he had always imagined, he feels like he can do it. Despite his concern they'll make him the town pariah and business at Bad Moon will dry up, Smith is relieved in a way he never anticipated being. For the first time since he moved to Park County five years ago, he doesn't have to pretend to be anything he's not, and he doesn't have to worry about his secret coming to light.

He recognizes John Henry's pickup long before it reaches his campsite, watching it come up the long dirt road that branches off from the highway. He smiles a little as John Henry's face becomes clear behind the windshield, and waits in the trailer doorway until John Henry parks the truck and gets out. He didn't know if John Henry had gone home already, but he'd hoped to see him one last time.

Now, John Henry stands a few paces in front of Smith, gazing at him with his hands akimbo. He seems to be in good spirits. He doesn't know about Buck outing Smith in the saloon or Buck seeing Smith with John Henry in West Yellowstone. Smith is going to keep it that way.

"Morning," John Henry says.

"Morning," says Smith.

"What happened to your face?"

"Some family business."

They pause, taking each other in, feeling small in the wind and silence of the plain.

"There's coffee if you want it," Smith says.

"No, thanks," says John Henry. "Already had some."

They could have sex, but Smith knows they won't. Their night in Powell—when he saved Lou at the bar before meeting John Henry—was the last time. He felt it then, and he doesn't need confirmation now.

"You know, last I checked, Cody is not on the way to Missouri from Powell. In fact, it's out of the way."

"I wasn't going to leave without saying goodbye. I told you."

"Could've just called."

John Henry shakes his head, giving Smith that look again, like the man is hopeless.

"All right, then," says Smith, straightening off the doorjamb and bracing his free hand against the top of it. "Say your goodbyes and go on. You got a long drive ahead of you."

John Henry walks up to him, stops at the bottom of the trailer steps, and waits. Smith hesitates before going down the steps to meet him, standing in John Henry's personal space and clutching his empty coffee mug in his fingers like an excuse for being there.

"It was good seeing you again," John Henry says, his eyes fixed on Smith's.

Smith nods and tries not to break the contact. "Yeah," he says, in a rough whisper.

John Henry steps in and hugs him, warm and close and final, and Smith holds on to him with a sadness rising in his throat, sharp and hot. Smith's eyes water and burn, and it's not because he's in love with John Henry or heartbroken to see him go. It's the loneliness he's been denying the last five years, the closure he finally feels after six years of waiting. It's gratitude—for John Henry setting him free and showing him he can move on.

"Take care of yourself," Smith says, grinding the words out into John Henry's shoulder.

John Henry pulls back out of the hug and grips Smith in both hands, by the biceps. "Do me a favor," he says, dark eyes soulful and voice thick with emotion. "Let yourself be happy."

"You too. Be good to Sula."

John Henry nods, then let's go of Smith and walks backward, away from him. Smith doesn't move, watching as he eventually turns and heads for his truck. John Henry gets behind the wheel, starts the engine, and pauses to look at Smith again before putting the truck into gear and driving away.

Smith stays where he is until the truck reaches the highway and disappears in the distance.

Once he's alone, he lets out a breath he didn't know he was holding, sagging on his feet.

*

When he pulls up to the house, Smith sits in his truck for a moment and studies it, noticing the house's beauty and fine details in a way he hasn't since the Boone sisters first moved in. The blue paint is the color of the Wyoming sky on a clear spring day, the white paint clean as cold milk. The hot-pink geraniums, bright green lawn, and trees that turn yellow and red come autumn, postcard perfect, somebody's simple dream of happily ever after. He's spent a lot of time on the porch, sometimes alone and sometimes with the women. Every year, the weekend after Thanksgiving, he decorates the house with string lights, and Christa puts fake poinsettias in the hanging flowerpots. He's had a few snowball fights with his cousins in the front yard, chased Christa around in the pouring rain there last summer until they were both soaked to the bone and he threw her over his shoulder, her ankles and bare feet covered in mud. He and Cooper walk up and down this street some nights when the weather's good. They never say much, shoulder to shoulder under the stars.

He unlocks the front door and goes inside. He finds Christa in the kitchen, sitting at the table with her computer.

"Hey," she says, glancing at his duffel bag that hangs on his shoulder. "Are you staying the night?"

"I think I'm staying a few nights, if you don't mind."

"Of course we don't mind." She looks at him, and her eyes soften. She stands up and goes to him, touching his arm with gentle fingers. "How are you? I wanted to call you, but Cooper thought you needed space."

"I'm all right. Where's Coop? I need to talk to you both."

Smith looks over his shoulder at his other cousin's footsteps, finds her standing in the kitchen entryway.

"Is everything okay?" Cooper asks, looking uncertain. "You're not leaving town, are you?"

"No. I'm not leaving town."

She passes him and sits at the table as Christa returns to her own seat.

Smith puts his bag on the floor and faces them, standing next to the table with his hands on his hips. "First of all, I'm sorry I didn't call yesterday. I should have. But I needed time to think about the situation."

Cooper and Christa don't speak, listening and watching him.

"John Henry's gone. I'm fine. I'm bringing him up because of what happened at the saloon and because him being here got me thinking about what I want in my life, what I'm going to do with my future. I've been holding back because I didn't know. I didn't know who I was without the rodeo, or who I wanted to be. But I think maybe I've figured it out now."

He looks at his two cousins, at their faces full of guileless hope, faces he has seen change with time and maturity but never enough that he fails to recognize who they've always been. He looks at Christa with her long hair pinned up in a messy bun, wearing her dance tights and leg warmers, no different than his oldest photograph of her at four years old. He looks at Cooper in her T-shirt and jeans, a leather bracelet on her wrist he bought for her years ago with his initials impressed on the inside. He has one that matches, with her initials. These are the women who have loved him the longest and the most, the ones who know him best and give him the greatest sense of peace. These are the women who have known all along what he is and never hesitated to accept him. These are the women who make him laugh, who comfort him, who make him feel the realest kind of love he's ever felt in his thirty-two years. They came out to Cody to be with him, and he has no idea what he would've done without them.

"I'm going to build a house on my land," he says. "And there's going to be a room for each of you in it. I'm not saying you have to give up all this and live with me, but there's going to be a place for you in my house. Always. You decorate those rooms any way you want."

Christa and Cooper smile at him.

"I was thinking maybe I could start looking into part-time work," Smith continues, shifting his weight onto one foot. "I don't need to be at the saloon all the time. Rhett Ellison, who owns the North Star Ranch, he's always wanted me to come out there. Maybe now's the time to take him up on his offer—if he'll still have me."

"He will," says Cooper, her eyes bright with joy in a way Smith hasn't seen for a long time.

Smith looks from her to Christa, who's leaning back against the wall with one foot up on the seat of her chair. Her expression is glad, less raw than her sister's.

"We were afraid you would decide to leave Cody after what happened," she says to him.

"If I did that, I'd have to come out all over again someplace else," he says and smiles. "I ain't leaving."

"Good."

The three of them are quiet for a spell, looking at one another.

Smith hooks his thumbs into his belt loops and gathers his words. "It's time I straighten something out with you. I need to get all this across while my mind's in the right place, so please—let me finish before you say something." He takes a breath. "I think I've been holding myself back from you, ever since I retired. Holding some part of me away. I created distance between us, and I didn't mean to. Holding back was never about you. I don't really know what it was about. I think maybe I just wouldn't let myself be happy, without the rodeo. But I want to be. I want to move on. I want to feel good about my life again. I'm tired of being hung up on what I lost."

Christa smiles first while Cooper stares at their cousin with misty eyes. Neither of them makes a sound.

"You two are the most important people in my life," Smith says. "Everything good I've felt these last five years, I felt with you. Because of you. Ever since you got here, you've been looking after me, keeping me human, making sure I don't get lost. And it's time I give you what I can give you. Cooper—you told me I need to want something again. Before I said goodbye to John Henry, I didn't know what to want, but now I do. I want you and Christa. I want us to be a family. I want to be as close to you as I can."

In silence, Cooper stands up and goes to him, wraps her arms around him, closes her wet eyes as he hugs her back. They stand there, holding each other for a long time. Smith looks at Christa as they do, and she sits at the table beaming at him, her own eyes glassy.

When Cooper finally lets go and steps back from Smith, Christa gets up to hug him, too, and she laughs when he tightens his arms around her, happy and relieved for both of them.

"I love you," Smith says, holding on to her and trying not to think about what he would've done had Buck hurt her.

Christa stands back and looks at Smith with her hands on his shoulders. "I love you too. I'm glad you figured things out."

Smith nods, then moves to face Cooper again, who still does not smile. He raises one hand to her cheek, and they look at each other. "I love you, Coop," he says, his voice quiet and raspy. "You know that?"

She pauses, her dark brown eyes gleaming. "I love you back."

"I know."

He takes her face in both his hands and presses a kiss to her hairline, shutting his eyes and holding his lips there for a beat.

Somebody knocks at the front door. Christa goes to answer it, Smith and Cooper following at a distance. Smith had left the front door open when he arrived, so they can see a man in uniform stands on the other side of the screen door. Christa pushes the screen open, standing between it and the jamb.

"Afternoon, ma'am," the deputy says.

"Hi," says Christa.

"Are you Christa Boone?"

"Yeah."

"I'm Deputy Wallace, with the Park County Sheriff's Department. Jordan's brother. She talked to me about your situation?"

Cooper and Smith step further into the living room, listening to the conversation.

"Oh, it's nice to meet you," Christa says to the deputy, sagging against the doorjamb. "Do you want to come in?"

"No, that's all right. I just came by to let you know Buck Haley left town. I stopped by his motel this morning. He was already packing up, and I spoke to him about the incident at your cousin's saloon. I made it clear that it was in his best interest to go back wherever he came from before Smith had the chance to press charges, and I followed him out of Cody to make sure he took my advice."

Christa doesn't answer at first, peering over her shoulder at Smith and Cooper behind her. Her smile is full of overwhelming relief. Her eyes glisten. She faces the deputy again. "Thank you. You have no idea how grateful I am for your help."

Wallace gives her a small nod and a smile. "You let me know if you have any more trouble. Jordan can give you my number."

"Thank you. I will."

Wallace turns away and starts to leave.

"Deputy," Christa calls, taking a step outside onto the porch.

He stops and looks back at her.

"Tell Jordan I need the bear a little bit longer."

Wallace nods, not asking what she means.

She watches him go, down the porch steps and the path splitting the front lawn, watches him get into his marked car and drive away.

When she goes back inside, Cooper and Smith are standing side by side in the living room, smiling at her.

*

In the first few weeks of autumn, an old pickup truck follows a Triumph motorcycle southbound on the highway, through the golden plains of Wyoming. The sky is an endless blue, and the country sprawls beneath it, glittering mountainsides and miles of forest and open fields. The two-lane blacktop winds around and around, the truck and the motorcycle running it like a pair of wild horses. Somewhere behind them, a lone bison stands in the road, waiting for something to stare down.

Playlist

"That Kind of Lonely" by Patty Griffin

 Cooper's song

"Monument" by Mirah

 Christa's song

"John Henry Split My Heart" by Songs: Ohia

 Smith's theme song

"If It Hadn't Been for Love" by The SteelDrivers

 John Henry's song

"Almost Was Good Enough" by Songs: Ohia

 Smith's brooding song

"You Put the Hurt On Me" by The SteelDrivers

 John Henry and Smith's song

"The Heart That You Own" by Dwight Yoakam

 Cooper and Christa dance together at the house party

"Work Me" by The Black Keys

 Smith and John Henry have reunion sex for the first time

"Keep Your Hands Off Her" by The Black Keys

> Cooper confronts Buck in his motel parking lot

"Someday Soon" by Judy Collins

> The song Smith listens to on the jukebox when Christa visits him at the bar

"Desire" by Ryan Adams

> Smith and John Henry have sex on Smith's land

"A Kiss Before I Go" by Ryan Adams & The Cardinals

> Plays in the dive bar where John Henry's attacked

"Back of a Bible" by Patterson Hood

> Smith and John Henry's dance in the saloon

"Don't Let Me Down" by Dillard & Clark

> John Henry and Smith say good-bye

"Hold on Magnolia" by Songs: Ohia

> Smith returns to Cooper and Christa after his outing

"Ho Hey" by the Lumineers

> Smith, Cooper, and Christa's song when they play around on Smith's land

About the Author

Marie S. Crosswell writes long fiction, short fiction, and poetry. Her novellas *Texas, Hold Your Queens*; *Lone Star on a Cowboy Heart*; *Alchemy*; and *Cold, Cold Water* are available online wherever digital books are sold. Her short fiction has appeared in *Thuglit, Betty Fedora, Plots with Guns, Tough*, and other indie crime fiction publications. She's a graduate of Sarah Lawrence College where she studied creative writing. She lives in the American West.

Website: www.mariescrosswell.com

Also Available from NineStar Press

Connect with NineStar Press

www.ninestarpress.com

www.facebook.com/ninestarpress

www.facebook.com/groups/NineStarNiche

www.twitter.com/ninestarpress

Connor Molina's summer can't get any worse. He's stuck in his college town taking summer classes, and he's got a dead-end lifeguard job he's too old for and a baby gay who's thirsty for all the wrong guys.

Even worse? Tristan, a wild patron, won't leave his section of the pool, splashing him and pulling stupid stunts to get his attention. When Tristan fakes a drowning to get closer to him, Connor's furious, but he quickly realizes that Tristan's reckless nature isn't always infuriating...it's also intriguing.

Can he let his guard down and let Tristan in, or will he be bound by his own rules and drown in the self-doubt this summer could free him from?